BEST EIGHT

Martin Jones

FOREWORD

Science fiction is writing set in the future dramatising new technologies. Okay, but there's a recent science fiction novel by Ian McEwan which is set in the past, the 1980s to be precise, a reimagined 1980s where there are robot companions. So, sci-fi can be set in the past or future, and involves futuristic technology; except sometimes the tech is not futuristic, but rather more Victorian, as in the sub genre known as steam punk. Sometimes there isn't really any tech at all, which gives us another sub genre called speculative fiction, focusing on social change. Often these social changes are portrayed in the future, except where they involve some kind of reimagining of the past, as with Ian McEwan's book, which then gives us something called alternate history. Sometimes the future and the past are muddled up, as in Star Wars, where people fly around in spaceships, even though we are told that everything happened long, long ago. Sometimes the setting is the present, but fantastical elements come in from some more powerful, futuristic place, as in a super hero story. Then of course there are occasions when the setting is a totally different universe to our own, which takes us across an indefinite border into fantasy.

Science fiction seems to be so many things that we might agree with writer Damon Knight who describes this malleable literary designation as "what we point to when we say it". Except that Damon hasn't read my book, written as science fiction, but which an editor at a sci-fi imprint has described as "not science fiction".

So I was aiming at a great big open goal. The goal keeper stood there glassy eyed, looking as though match preparation involved drinking large amounts of alcohol and not sleeping for three nights. It was only necessary to kick the ball past that swaying, stumbling goalie, into the waiting net. I took my run up, went for the kick, tripped over the ball and sent it flying backwards. Picking myself up, I wondered how this had happened. How was it possible to write a science fiction book which misses that enormous, open genre goal? I must have written the only science fiction book in history which is not science fiction. That must be some kind of achievement. Damon Knight could say that science fiction is anything we point to when we say it, except for that book Martin Jones wrote.

According to the editor - who was unwilling to classify my book in his field - the sci-fi crowd are not likely to favour stories about an imagined future for the royal family. That's what this book is about, by the way. It envisages a future world where a single government has adopted a version of what was once the British royal family as a figurehead monarchy. The King makes plans to extend the monarchy to Mars, in an attempt to ease tensions between Mars and Earth. He also tries to use university rowing as a blunt instrument to toughen up his lazy heir.

Whilst science fiction is a lot of things, it is apparently not this. I was asked to consider how many science fiction readers out there are royalist rowing fans. It is true that the sci-fi demographic might not buy into rowing royals, even if the Boat Race has twice the viewing figures of the British Grand Prix, and most people in the UK want to keep their monarchy. But who knows? I am a sci-fi fan, and my story is the one I wanted to read, but couldn't find, set in the future, playing out in traditional locations as people try to cope with the new whilst seeking security in the old. I don't know what the future holds, but I do know about the contradictory ways I react to change, and the way I see people in general reacting to change. That's what drove me to write my royals in the future story.

Whatever kind of story it is, I hope you enjoy it.

CHAPTER 1 (FOLLY BRIDGE RESTAURANT, OXFORD)

Two young men sat on the terrace at Oxford's Folly Bridge Restaurant. They lingered through the afternoon, subdued restlessness fretting inside a langour that was pleasant enough to delay activity indefinitely. Sunlight from sky and river bathed the scene. Folly Bridge brooded on its own arches, shimmering in golden Thames water.

"I am going to unburden myself," said the young man dressed in a sky-blue linen suit. In a figurative sort of way, he took off his jacket and hung it on the curving back of a bistro chair.

"Really?" said his companion, flicking blonde locks away from the collar of a Hackett rugby shirt, which had never seen a rugby pitch. "We've tried this before and it just doesn't become you."

"Yes, I know it's usually good times and snippy remarks with me. But circumstances have driven me to earnest reflection. Today, Alistair, I need you to take me seriously. You are my oldest friend and I must talk. All the stress has backed up in my soul like an emotional constipation. It must out, and you are going to be my groom of the stool, if you will."

"Groom of the stool? I draw a line at becoming one of those toilet servants. Anyway, was that ever actually a real thing?"

"It most certainly was. In fact, the Groom of the Close Stool, to give the proper title, was always a powerful and sought after role. Deep matters of policy would be discussed behind the toilet door. We are just restoring the tradition. You know how much the Palace likes tradition."

Alistair was studying Edward.

"Are you alright?"

"I'm not alright, and now this conversation is on a fittingly serious and meaningful level, I will tell you that I do not want to be king."

Alistair did not appear surprised by this announcement.

"I understand, Edward. You feel frustrated. But listen to me; your situation is not so different to mine, or to anyone else's. Are any of us actually free to choose our career?"

Edward gazed into his drink, as though objections to Alistair's words were swimming like fish in the glass.

"I would just point out that you can do whatever you like. The world is your great big oyster, or clam, mussel, scallop, or whatever shellfish you choose."

"I am allergic to some of those items you mention. So think about it; I'm not going to be a fishmonger, what with the allergies. We can also forget figure skating, opera singing, flamenco dancing, mining, professional poker playing, anything military, anything to do with physics and maths - anything in fact which has to do with numbers or science in general. We can also forget all roles requiring a high level of hand and eye coordination. Do you see? The world is not quite such a wide and open set of possibilities for me now, is it? After organising your social life for years, events management is really all I'm fit for."

Edward held his drink to his cheek, looking askance at Alistair.

"That sounded very rehearsed. Has someone briefed you?"

"No. I have just briefed myself. This isn't the first occasion you've said you don't want to be king, is it? You spent most of your time at school declaring your desire to renounce the throne."

"But I mean it this time. I meant it every time, to be honest with you. That's the sad thing. But there's hard work following through on something like that. Can't you think of a way, Alistair? It would just be some kind of comfortable exile somewhere, with a reduced household. Let me remind you of my dream…"

"Edward, I don't need to hear about your house by the sea again."

"Ah yes, but I have been working on the details. It would be a place that I could call my own, so that I'm not just a tenant in a big palace."

"So where is it going to be this time? Nellcote Mansion in Villefranche Sur Mer? Tony Curtis's old house in Pacific Palisades? Golden Eye in Jamaica?"

"No. The final choice is Whitstable."

"Whitstable? That little town in Kent?"

"An old-time film star called Peter Cushing lived there. I would live in his house, decorated in white and blue, with carefully sourced accent pieces smoothed by local surf. It's near that nice fish restaurant, the one we visited by accident after I opened the Northern Hemisphere Space Anchorage, and the venue planned for lunch had a violent kitchen fire. And as for staff I'm sure it's possible to get by with just a butler and a chef."

"Just a butler and a chef? Edward, you have no idea how to live in the real world. Where will you get the money for your reduced household? That's one question you have never been able to answer every other time you have indulged in this little daydream."

"I knew you would ask that, and a plan is now in place. The answer is writing. It's something you can do anywhere and doesn't require any training or set up costs."

"Writing is it now? That might not be as easy as it looks."

"Yes, that's possibly true, but there are frightfully able and self-effacing editor people, who, unbeknownst to the reading public, shape and mould the raw material. Royal insight will be my contribution. It won't be necessary to do any actual writing. I would chat to my editorial fellows, and a little while later, as if by magic, a bestselling book would appear."

The real and reflected arches of Folly Bridge went on another motionless turn around their endless, elliptical orbits.

"It's this King of Mars thing. That's what's really behind this wobble."

"Come along, Alistair, we don't have to take that seriously, do we? The whole notion is utter madness."

The conversation petered out as the boys looked to the river where two eight-seat racing shells pulled their way towards Folly Bridge. The crews were an alternating combination of stressful hunching and explosive release. All that effort expended, only to produce a bow wave that looked like the last, tired squirt of water lingering at the mouth of a hosepipe when you turn off the tap.

"Here they come," mocked Edward. "That fellow Oscar Wilde, who went to my college - apparently he hated all outdoors sports, except for dominoes played at pavement tables outside Parisian cafes. I am of the same mind."

"Well at least you can choose to avoid rowing, eh, Edward?"

"At least I have that. But listen, this extending the monarchy to Mars idea, what have you heard?"

"I've heard that the King is not to be dissuaded. In fact...."

At this point Alistair leant across the table toward Edward. This gesture seemed redundant as a method to ensure privacy. Large men and athletic looking women in grey suits monopolised the tables directly around the two boys. None of them appeared to be here for a pleasant afternoon tea. They did not look relaxed. In fact, they gave the impression of rowers in the hunched stage of their relentless rowing rhythm. The explosive, stretching stage would probably involve martial arts and firearms.

"I have heard," continued Alistair, "that the King is going to make an announcement during his speech at the Mars House."

Edward sighed with a measure of self-dramatisation.

"Maybe this is a blessing in disguise. There's a very good chance that Grandpap's speech will be a humiliation. With any luck, the reaction will be so negative, involving such a lot of media satire and sniggering, and maybe psychiatric health speculation in the more high-minded outlets, that this announcement will put the whole crazy idea to bed once and for all. Then I can relax and try to come to terms with being heir to just one planetary throne."

An urgent shout now interrupted Edward's conjectures, an exclamation that the afternoon's mildness made both shocking, and difficult to take seriously.

"Weapon!"

"No, no, please, not now."

The grey-suited bodyguards fell upon Edward. They ignored Alistair of course, who with arms folded, pushed his chair back with his feet, giving space for the protection team to charge towards the royal person and bundle him off the terrace. Alistair followed, carrying the blue jacket that Edward had hung over the back of his chair. He looked like the boy nominated to hold coats while the bigger boys fight. A scrum-like struggle culminated with guards throwing their charge into a waiting vehicle. Alistair, hands in pockets, stepped in after Edward.

Semi-reclined and leather cosseted, Edward looked down at his now crumpled pale blue linen.

"I assume this was a drill?"

There was no answer to this question from in-car guards, who kept their professional eyes on the world outside.

"Leave them alone," muttered Alistair. "And if you ask me, these little practice runs become more frequent when you moan. You think that's a coincidence? Personally, I don't."

There was a squawk of radio chatter from the forward compartment.

"Situation is secure, Your Highness," said the driver to the windscreen in front of her. "We are standing down, and will return you to college."

"Jolly good." Edward turned towards his friend. "What shall

we do when we get back? Head down to the bar?"

Alistair had an inward look, which suggested he was concentrating on something other than Edward.

"Am I boring you?"

"No, I'm just listening to the news."

"On one of those implant things?"

"The King has arrived at Kew. He's making his way to the Mars Dome."

"Those implants are distasteful."

"Well look at your phone then."

Edward took a small cylinder from the pocket of his jacket, which with a swish he made into an object the size of an old paperback novella.

"So quaint," said Alistair.

Edward was concentrating on the screen.

"Well, if the King has completely lost his mind, we will soon know."

CHAPTER 2 (KEW GARDENS)

In his mind, King John addressed the same speech to himself that he would soon give to others. He worked on his own characteristic delivery, which took its cues from old BBC radio broadcasts. Subtle inflections combined Chamberlain announcing peace in our time, Churchill vowing resistance on the beaches, and Humphrey Littleton presenting *I'm Sorry I Haven't a Clue.*

He became aware of Lord Montagu walking beside him.

"Strange lot - Martians I mean," muttered Montagu in the King's ear.

"Martians are people," replied the King, with Churchill and Chamberlain sounding about equal, while Littleton jollied things along. "Where they live is but a detail. A good coronation will win them over. Just wait until they see the State Coach."

"Yes, Your Majesty. The officials are moaning of course. Practical difficulties with the horses, they say. Bad travellers. Never been transported through space. They keep bringing up those little problems we had getting Sandringham Lad to Ascot last year."

"Sandringham Lad is a racehorse, highly strung, spirited. We are talking about the State Coach here, pulled by reliable Windsor Greys."

King John's royal progress moved through an avenue of cheering people, along Lichfield Road, through Kew Gardens'

Victoria Gate and into shadow cast by the Mars House. This great flame coloured dome sat just beyond Decimus Burton's Temperate House, reduced by comparison to a toy building you might find decorating one of the King's ambitious train sets. Afternoon sunlight dazzled on a dusky dome canopy as King John walked through an entrance arch seemingly sliced through a mother lode of hollow topaz. Orange crystal walls carried visiting eyes upwards towards a recreated, yellow Martian sky. This cyclorama sky introduced Mars to Earth. Look up, it said. Even if you looked down, because for example, you were an elderly royal with neck pain, you still found yourself gazing skyward, via a circular reflecting pool of still water. The Statue of Martian Liberty thrust a glowing globe of cardinal red up towards butterscotch clouds. Titian robes rose in soft pleats over Martian Liberty's toes. By some trickery involving a transparent plinth, these limousine-sized digits appeared to hover a few meters above the water surface, as if already floating off to other worlds.

King John made his way around Liberty's suspended image, pulled a fleece cloak over his shoulders, and strode through a second cave-like portal onto the Martian Plain. Since the Mars House aimed to represent an entire planet, a few visual tricks came into play. There were large rocks in the foreground, with smaller ones further away. Downstage boulders displayed dramatic texture and colour, while those upstage were more muted, with fewer surface details. King John felt obliged to assist in creating a sense of space by regulating his pace to the processional. It was impolite to rush at this ritualistic journey from Earth to Mars. Besides, with old legs already tiring, cultural sensitivity provided a useful disguise for fatigue. A slow pace gave time to take in the twisting arroyo through which a river flowed, advertising the fact that there really was water on Mars. The rocky riverbank carried a dusting of a turmeric-yellow fungus, more reminiscent of the minerals it lived upon, rather than the organic life it aspired to be.

Beyond this Martian river scene, dune fields stretched away across sharp, wind-sculpted sand ridges and meadows of platinum-blonde marram grass. Clumps of bulbous cold-cacti hunkered in the slack between dunes. King John's eyes moved outwards to curving dome walls, where image engineers from nearby Shepperton had created an impression of a far-off, flushed horizon, becoming lilac with distance.

"It's a bit like the Emperor Fountain at Chatsworth," said the Duke of Devonshire who had now joined the tight huddle in the immediate vicinity of the King.

"Lovely to look at, but expensive to run. They'll probably turn it off later."

A smear of amethyst cloud hung above a journey reaching its end, at a shallow, circular mound, an echo of moots where leaders of ancient Britain once gathered.

"Be upstanding for His Majesty, the King."

An audience rose from a semi-circle of seats, only for King John to gesture for everyone to sit down again. Now his voice veered towards Churchill, commanding the room, which in this case represented a planet.

"We are here today at Kew Gardens, a research centre which has for centuries developed plants for the benefit of humanity on Earth, now playing the same vital role for Mars. It is in this historic location that I ask you now to consider the assistance that the monarchy can offer a new planetary society."

King John's words petered out as he struggled to access his medically enhanced memory, which was fragile and, he suspected, vulnerable to external manipulation.

"The year 973," continued the King, finding words just at the moment when his pause was crossing the border from thoughtful to awkward. "Ever since the Romans left early in the fifth century, England had been a chaotic mass of fighting provinces. Then 973 brought the coronation of Edgar the

Peaceable. Once crowned with due pomp, England's regional kings rowed Edgar from his palace at Chester along the River Dee to the Church of St John. Competing leaders became Edgar's rowing crew. This is a lesson from history. There has to be a leadership that brings us all together. Only the monarchy can provide this, drawing upon an ancient power that goes beyond political division. I implore you to support our vision for an extension of the monarchy to Mars. Mars may lie out across the endlessness of space, but this noble planet is not the first frontier that humanity has explored. We have always explored, and we have always faced the unknown by packing the experience of what has gone before in our luggage. I'm standing in front of you now, hoping you will welcome the support that the monarchy will bestow upon you, the support of the past for the future."

King John paused for cheers that did not come. There was an embarrassed shuffling sound, like Martian marram grass blown about by winds gusting down from the Planum Boreum. Blankets of genetically modified Alpine greenery seemed to shrivel in discomfit against their rocky habitats. The King was grateful that good old Montagu tried to start some applause, clapping with his elbows out. Nevertheless, this lonely attempt at respect had the unintended appearance of low grade heckling.

The King continued as if hoped-for acclaim had been loud and heartfelt.

"Plans for a Martian coronation are in place, and only require goodwill and cooperation to come to fruition. We know that some of you might be uncomfortable with this aspiration, but we humbly ask for time in which to convince you. Royalty is all about time. Mars has only just begun its long journey, and for those years, centuries and millennia to come you will need a monarch. We will link our worlds, benefitting both, and look outwards to other places where the State Coach might then go."

Once more, King John waited for appreciation. Lord

Montagu renewed his struggles to provide some, a few of his robed colleagues trying to help. Devonshire then made an intervention that should have been the preserve of a Master of Ceremonies:

"Ladies and gentlemen, the King!"

This brought the crowd to its feet, for a more sustained ovation, of a purely courteous nature.

As delegates milled around following King John's speech, the small group that had been standing with their monarch on the moot, formed a cocoon of shared generational sympathy, like a dwindling group of expatriates finding each other in a foreign land.

"Tough crowd, Your Majesty."

"Don't worry, Montagu. We're in this for the long haul."

CHAPTER 3
(GOODWOOD)

Passing years had begun to leach memories away rather than add to their store.

"You might have a sense of confusion initially," warned the doctor. "Just try to remember where you are."

"I had trouble with my speech at Kew."

"Don't think about that. Just focus on the here and now. We'll see how you go."

King John knew he was at Goodwood, in the Music Room of the Kennels clubhouse. He meditated on long blocks of colour created by classic triband spines of Penguin books lining floor to ceiling shelves in this light-filled room. Picking out a few titles - *Ariel* and *A Farewell to Arms* - offered distraction from what the doctor was doing. There was a scratching on the left side of his head, accompanying measured words about the hippocampus. The King did not care for this dispassionate, medical tone. A sense of emotion was one way of identifying a memory, as opposed to a rebooted memory file. Who knew what they were putting in there. If information presented itself in isolation from emotion, then it could not be trusted.

The King shut his eyes and tried to feel. He saw a line of motionless soldiers bearing witness to a flag of segmented colour jolting down a white pole in the middle of a parade ground. Gold buttons on red jackets glittered through a haze of partial recollection. The only sound was the two opening notes of the Last Post, replacing all of life's customary noise with their sad, penetrating perfection. Some data file was busy with information describing those two notes as a perfect fifth. King John ignored this bunkum and gave all his attention to a knot of emotion filling a single beat middle C followed by a two beat G hanging over into the following bar. Notes sat on an image of a stave in his mind, crotchets and minims morphing into birds perched on old-fashioned telegraph wires, running through space between composer and listener. As the King listened, the gloved hands of two soldiers folded the variegated flag in movements of abrupt ceremonial.

He then recalled words of such absurdity that they must have been real. No one would have been audacious enough to create them in a fake memory.

"Your Majesty," said a man whose facial features all drooped in grave symmetry, away from grey hair towards a dark-green, House of Commons tie. "We cannot fight the inevitable. We have to move with the times. I must resign and you have to be King of Earth."

King John laughed, thinking this must be a joke. It had to be a prank organised by Lord Montagu. Recalling that moment, when he realised the PM spoke in earnest, made the King wonder whether a good memory was such a great thing after all.

The images then changed. There was an accident, dimly perceived. A white-faced official said he had bad news about the King's only son. Images tinged with frustration recalled a reckless young man who hung onto his irresponsibility even when he had two baby boys of his own.

At this moment, King John dreaded memories and yearned to forget everything.

"Enough," he shouted.

The doctor took his leave.

King John rested after his treatment, lost and found in his stirred pot of remembrances. He had recalled so many endings, which only hardened his resolve to explode polite assumptions that he would live forever. His hands patted at a blanket on his knees, as though confirming a renewed existence back in the present moment. He stood up, determined to see through the meeting he had planned for this weekend.

"Boles! Bacon!"

Boles and Bacon were a reassuring background hum of things running well, invisible yet ever available. The King's refreshed memory reminded him how lucky he was in these men, who following the consolidation of Palace staff, combined the roles of private secretary, equerry and butler.

"I feel better."

"That is gratifying, Your Majesty. Lord March is waiting outside to take you to the circuit."

King John walked unaided out to the courtyard, a miniature Horse Guard's Parade, the sort of place that in days gone by might have given rise to paranoid suspicions in the owner of the real Horse Guards Parade. This lovely space was currently focusing itself on a grenadier-red E-Type Jaguar, all curving bonnet with a cabin clinging on in the visual slipstream at the back. Against this automotive sculpture leant a figure closely tailored in Van Dyke, Prince of Wales check. He wore bookish eyeglasses that somehow conveyed an optimistic outlook, bruised by life, now requiring help with seeing the world in its former vibrancy. He looked like everyone's idea of an aristocrat, his world and its glamour packaged for all.

"Glasses?" said King John, looking at March's horn-rimmed eyewear. "Is there nothing you won't do in the name of authenticity?"

"Just for a weekend we escape modernity, Your Majesty. That is the joy of our Goodwood Revival. And I must say your tailors have done well this year."

"Thank you, March. It's Hardy Amies. Right, time to get on. We have much to discuss."

The short journey took only a few minutes. It seemed such a waste that the Jaguar should be locked up at Goodwood, like a wildcat in a zoo. This was a car for cruising the Route Napoleon, from Grenoble to Cannes. It was not a courtesy vehicle to carry old men with mobility problems from the Kennels to Goodwood Circuit. It took longer to walk from the car to a private room at the Jackie Stewart Pavilion, overlooking Goodwood's action.

Wonderful racing cars were flashing down the straight. Streamlined styling reached from the nose back to the driver. Behind the driver, style gave way to brute utility, consisting of valves, pipes and noise. King John stood beside March, looking out at the same reincarnated energy that scientists might have found in reviving lost Tyrannosaurus DNA.

Boles announced the entrance of two new guests who had hurried up from the paddock below.

"The Duke of Devonshire and Lord Montagu, Your Majesty."

Devonshire appeared to walk in from a time when serious science was an absorbing hobby. He wore dark, formal garb suggestive of an early twentieth century psychoanalyst, or perhaps a scientist required to dress formally, when he didn't know how to do so. Beside Devonshire swaggered Montagu sporting a gunmetal, windowpane Anderson and Shepherd three-piece. The archaic eyewear favoured by Montagu comprised a pair of highly reflective aviator shades.

King John and his nobles engaged in small talk about racing cars while Boles and Bacon arranged tea. Once again, the King appreciated the exactitude of his staff, which he sensed like the beat of a grandfather clock. Boles was setting a strainer on a delicate saucer. Following two and a half minutes of steeping, golden liquid would percolate through that tightly knit, purifying weave. On a separate tray, Bacon arranged artfully recreated cans of a now defunct soft drink once associated with motor racing. Geometric blocks of blue and silver moved in uneasy yin and yang, the trouble focusing itself on two bulls about to clash horns against a yellow background of a representative sun. Everything seemed to be continuing as it had done for many years. The Revival was part of the royal routine.

With introductions and small talk completed, King John

reached forward and stilled the moving hands of Boles working through his tea ritual.

"I know it's the Revival and you want to enjoy yourselves, but I have come to Goodwood to formally appeal for your help in saving the past, in the interests of the future. I know that fool of a doctor says I'm getting better every day, but where's the evidence? It would be prudent to prepare for the time when I stop ticking over. I want no referral to my strength matching that of various draught animals. I won't have it. We must face this problem and prepare for it."

"Golly," said March, taking his glasses off and putting them on again.

"We must deal in realities. Your duty now is to help me make proper arrangements."

The sound of racing cars was the Doppler effect of an expanding universe - matter, light, noise, everything, approaching, existing for an intense moment, and then disappearing into endless Ferrari red shift.

"I think the government has everything in hand," said Devonshire.

"No, no. I'm not talking about their early morning funeral rehearsals. I'm talking about preparing the boys for a future that includes both Earth and Mars."

"Preparing the boys for the future?" said Lord Montagu. "As I've said before, the only thing we can do with Edward is to send him along to Harley Street and get him a discreet personality intervention. There are chaps there who will turn that boy into Henry V if we pay them well enough. We could do the same for James, though he might not need quite so much work."

"No, Montagu. I believe in the old ways. We have to do things properly. This is what I propose."

The King took from his suit pocket a photograph and placed it on the white linen tablecloth, next to a three-tier plate of fancies.

"It's a photograph," said the King. "I had it done up specially. Nothing modern at the Revival after all."

With reverent fingertips, Devonshire picked up the shiny,

rectangular image.

"Fascinating. Did they use a negative with an enlarger?"

"I don't know, Devonshire. I just asked for something that looked authentic."

"Fascinating," repeated Devonshire.

The image showed a young King John in a blue rowing vest, Boles and Bacon at his side, stripped of their years and formality, standing together as only team mates do.

"I want Edward in Oxford's Blue Boat," growled the King.

Thus followed a shambolic performance by three amateur actors not knowing which emotion they were supposed to portray. March chortled, as though he had just witnessed an example of a robust royal sense of humour.

"I was prepared for my life by rowing in the University Boat Race, and I want the same for my grandson."

The Footlights Royal Command Performance shifted its emphasis. March's expression changed to that of a rowing cognoscente apprising a damn good oarsman. Montagu smiled a satisfied smile, perhaps appreciating the fact that a young man moulded by rowing would suffer a lot more than a young man visiting a personality specialist. Devonshire was the least impressive actor, which the King had been expecting. The Duke was the man most likely to confine himself to the facts and provide some actual advice.

"Really, sir? As I understand it, the prince has little experience of rowing."

"I know, Devonshire. Nevertheless, I want him in the boat, and I want you three to work out a way of getting him in there."

"Tricky, Your Majesty," said Devonshire.

"Oh I don't know," objected March. "With the right training and a positive attitude."

"There is no requirement to spare my feelings. We all know the boy has nothing to offer, and that Oxford won't put him in the crew just because I am king. Outside this room I am but a constitutional monarch."

There followed a silence, full of the sound of motor racing, but a silence nevertheless.

"The prince comes with a news blackout, does he not, Your Majesty?" asked Devonshire, a thoughtful finger tapping an upper lip.

"Yes, while he is at university. The idea is it will help the idiot boy concentrate on his studies."

The wax and wane of a number of engines all peaked together, a freak wave rearing out of the surrounding ocean of racket.

"Maybe we can do something with that," continued Devonshire once the moment had passed. "Maybe Edward could provide cover for something a bit near the knuckle."

"Find a way, Devonshire," replied the King. "I can see you have something in mind. And we mustn't forget about James. We can't have an heir without a spare. Get him ready too. Find a way of putting him into the Cambridge Blue Boat. The media will love the match up if nothing else. I just hope we have enough time."

Boles directed a gilded stream of liquid from the blue and silver can of yin and yang into a pre-chilled glass, as though they had all the time in the world.

CHAPTER 4 (ROOMS AT MAGDALEN COLLEGE)

Matthew Nice stared down at Jerry Dramhaggle. It was all very well for people in positions of lesser responsibility to see the world in simple terms. All Jerry had to do was sit in the back of the boat and cox the crew. When you are Oxford Rowing Club President, things are more complicated.

Matthew had to keep his temper and get this man onside. He gestured that Jerry should follow him to the window. There, from high and low viewpoints, they looked through heavily leaded windows out at a college party, which had spilt from Magdalen's pristine lawns onto the river. Young men in dishevelled dinner jackets, girls in ball gowns and a tangle of awkwardly angled oars, presented to the eye of Matthew Nice a flotilla of oversized prehistoric pond skaters. One of these endangered creatures resolved itself on closer inspection into two men, one rowing, the other standing in the bow quaffing champagne, swaying from side to side. The fellow paddling was doing his best to prevent a crapulent capsize.

Matthew pointed towards the unsteady boat crewed by the champagne-drinking hearty, who now, more by luck than judgment, was lying in a puddle of bilge water, toasting Oxford's sky.

"This is not a joking matter, Dramhaggle. The Vice Chancellor told me personally that we have to put Prince Edward in the boat. She has briefed the coaching staff."

Jerry stared up at the taller man, before looking back towards the river where carefree sinking now seemed a real possibility.

"What are they thinking?"

"It's politics, wider considerations. We have a lot of those on Earth. The government thinks it will develop Edward for his future as king."

"Since when did we become some kind of boot camp for lazy royals? You're not telling me the Vice Chancellor is going along with this. She's an old Balliol woman. She won't want to lose the Boat Race."

"There's more, Dramhaggle. She gave me a brandy and said that in return for taking Edward we could have Caroline McMercy. The government wants people to get used to human enhancement. They think it's the only way Earth can keep up with places like Mars, where it's all the go."

"But medical enhancement is against the code."

"Ah, my little Martian friend, that's where it all links back with Edward. He comes with a news blackout around him while he is at university. That will help keep the press away from Caroline. The Vice Chancellor said that royalty has long pulled a polite veil over aspects of life that don't bear close examination. That's what she said."

Matthew took a moment. The room they stood in did its work. He could almost feel past college dignitaries in formal gowns staring down from grand pictures on dark panelled walls. They knew everything and said nothing. The window he had been gazing through, with its thick stone casings and small leaded panes, appeared circumspect in how much of the world it allowed an observer to see.

"Good God," said Dramhaggle. "What kind of Blue Boat is this going to be, with a lazy prince who can't row and a girl who is half cyborg?"

Matthew Nice turned away from the window.

"I suppose it's a question of degree. Nearly all of us are medically enhanced to a certain extent. Who knows where it will end. Maybe we'll end up as blobs of digital data. But I suppose Edward will help us all turn a blind eye, until we get used to it."

"You realise we might face mutiny because of Edward, and disqualification because of Caroline?"

"Come along now, Jerry. You know rowing. It's best eight, not eight best."

Matthew glanced at Magdalen's immortals, quiet and unchallenged in their portraits. They had watched generations pass by, each with its Blue Boat. He knew they would want to uphold tradition, the tradition that Earth was the centre around which all things revolved, and Oxford was the finest university in this or any other world.

"I sometimes wonder," said Dramhaggle, "why I came to Oxford. There are perfectly good music departments in perfectly decent universities on Mars."

CHAPTER 5
(WHITEHALL)

Within the protected precincts of Whitehall, James could walk without his close protection officer by his side. Enjoying a brief sense of freedom, he felt that odd dislocation that this walk had provoked within him over the last few weeks. James's current work experience had placed him in an office in one of London's old government buildings, overlooking Horse Guards Parade and St James's Park. Civil servants once ran the United Kingdom from places like this. Those days had gone of course, but the edifices remained, carefully preserved, some of them continuing to serve the wider management functions of the present day. Walking through Whitehall, where modern transport could not trespass, James found it possible to believe he was in the London of Churchill, Attlee or Thatcher.

Former departments of government continued to carry their old names. James's footsteps were clipped and sharp as he passed the Foreign Office in Charles Street, which remained the Foreign Office, even though technically speaking nowhere on Earth was foreign anymore. In the Foreign Office Main Building, you could find an area redubbed the Home Office, a quaint curiosity when there was no home to be an office of. Crossing beneath Admiralty Arch, James walked through the portals of a building, which once administered a far-called navy of a vanished country. Reaching his desk, he took off his coat and looked out over St James's Park, reflecting on the fact that people still yearned for somewhere to be foreign. He thought it revealing that Whitehall had maintained or recreated old departmental names. Maybe that was why there was so much trouble with Mars. Mars could be foreign, making Earth home.

James's gaze rambled to a portrait of his grandfather looking down at him. James didn't like these official royal images. He preferred landscapes, and had made his own amateur efforts with traditional watercolours. At school, art was his favourite subject. He liked taking tints used in a sky and picking up those same shades in leaves on the trees. This afternoon St James's Park replicated this simple trick, a red and orange sky echoing across leaf canopies, beginning to turn in anticipation of cold to come. It wasn't possible to start painting of course, but there was a sense of calm in just looking at a view with the thought of painting. He might only have been an amateur, but even a dabbler in art looked more deeply, taking in detail, which might seem irrelevant in normal life.

Prince James was looking out of the window when Francis Nurhaci, the military secretary came in. He didn't knock. In Whitehall, James found himself defined by his lowly professional status, and not by his position as a royal.

"Ah, Mr Nurhaci," said James in surprise, wishing he had been busy at his desk and not staring out over the park.

Nurhaci smiled an economical smile.

"May I speak with you on an urgent matter?" asked Nurhaci, with the lip movements of a ventriloquist.

"Yes, of course, minister."

"Please come through. We will be more comfortable in my office."

James followed Nurhaci through a door connecting the humble outer office, to a busier middle office, and finally through to the grand domain of the military secretary himself. Between two antique-green leather Chesterfield armchairs, an ornate table was set with a pot of tea and two cups. Nurhaci poured Darjeeling into chinaware depicting a mountain scene in blue and white. James sat in response to a ministerial nod and accepted his tea. Holding a waterlily-like cup by a handle that was too small to be comfortable, he looked at a powerful man who had aged like a fine piece of mahogany furniture. Time appeared to have polished him rather than ground him down.

"How's it going here in Whitehall?" asked Nurhaci with an adept friendliness. "Looking after you, are we?"

"Of course, Mr Nurhaci."

More desultory chitchat followed, a type of social interaction in which James was accomplished, communicating nothing except the pleasant desire to communicate.

Nurhaci sat up a little straighter, if that were possible.

"Sir, I would like to discuss your brother."

The atmosphere changed. Nurhaci rarely addressed James as sir. This was an indication that the subject he wanted to talk about came under royal jurisdiction.

"If this is about my brother's fitness for the throne then I have nothing of worth to say. He is the heir. He might seem unsuitable, but in many ways that is irrelevant. He does not have to be elected after all."

"True, Your Highness." Nurhaci faltered. "Not that my remark should construe any negative view of the monarchy in general."

"Of course not," reassured James.

Now that they were deliberating on royal matters, power in the room had shifted somewhat.

"I do not wish to speak of Prince Edward's suitability for the throne. Nevertheless, Edward is to be the subject of our conversation. The Palace has asked me to talk to you about him."

"The Palace?"

"Yes. As we understand it, your brother is a certainty for Oxford's Blue Boat, and will be competing in the next Boat Race against Cambridge."

"Oh? I didn't know that Edward rowed."

"He doesn't. I hope you don't mind if I speak frankly, Your Highness. Perhaps I could ask for your complete discretion in what I am about to tell you."

"You have it, Mr Nurhaci. If there is one thing I have been trained to be, it is discreet."

"The King has reassured me on that point. In which case I am at liberty to inform you that your brother has been recruited for reasons other than his rowing prowess. Apart from the possibility that rowing will stiffen his character, there is a plan to employ media restrictions associated with your brother in a necessary deception designed to keep the press away from a medically enhanced member of the Oxford crew. Your grandfather has instructed me to ask you to join the Cambridge boat, to provide cover for a similar athlete which they have available."

Faced with a bewildering situation, James decided to try simple explanations first.

"You know my grandfather has a medical condition which involves periods of mental confusion?"

The shine faded on Nurhaci's mahogany face. James, with the eye of an artist, realised this was because the minister had dropped his head, away from the light of the window.

"Be that as it may, I must discuss this with you. The King requests that you cut short your period of work experience and attend Cambridge earlier than planned, a request which accords with our own interests. Unfortunately, following last year's elections, a number of Democratic Conservatives were returned. They forced through the bio-enhancement review. Apparently, we are meddling with Mother Nature when we should leave her alone. I am one of many in government who do not agree, and wish to see bio-enhancement pushed forward. In the long term, it is really the only way that we will adapt people to varying environments across the solar system. Earth cannot afford to fall behind in this. We want enhanced athletes to continue competing, even if for the moment we have to engage in a little deception. Therefore, we would like you to join the Cambridge crew. The enhanced athlete you will be covering for is one George Tyndale, a former solider, a young officer injured in an explosion. He was given a new military grade arm, ordered from this very department. Unfortunately, due to present political factors, Tyndale and a number of other soldiers like him have been removed from the army. Under the terms of early discharge award legislation, George Tyndale was given a grant to study at university - which is why he's at Cambridge."

"Tyndale," mused James. "That name rings a bell."

"You have probably dealt with some of his procurement documents. I believe he had some repairs on his arm recently."

Nurhaci paused.

"And on a personal note, sir, as a former Cambridge man, I do not like to see the other side having an unfair advantage. The King understands the value of an evenly matched contest, which is why he wants you to shield our enhanced athlete."

James studied one of the most senior members of government, who it seemed was just as worried about the Boat Race as he was about the future of humanity.

"I believe, as a prince, I am obliged to take advice from members of government?"

"That is correct, sir. However, I have to point out that some of my colleagues would advise you differently in this matter."

In theory, a career as a royal was easy. You just did what the government told you to do. In reality, government rarely agreed on anything, which sometimes made it hard to know who he should be listening to. James recalled his grandfather holding forth about an incident in 1923, when George V had to decide on the replacement for a sick prime minister because politicians couldn't decide for themselves.

James's internal debate did not continue for long. He felt that Nurhaci was his immediate boss. If anyone represented government for James then it might as well be him. The plan was to go to Cambridge anyway, so what was the harm in going a little early?

"Well, I do of course wish to do my duty, Mr Nurhaci. But I can't row, at least not well enough for the Blue Boat."

"That does not matter. In fact, it will probably be an advantage. You just have to go through the motions."

James stood up. Nurhaci appeared surprised that a young man would presume to take it upon himself to wander about in his office. James saw this. Now, acting as a prince, he was playing a different role. Rather than arrogance, it was simple reality. He looked out at the view over Horse Guard's Parade, the same view he had been admiring from his own humble office.

"Just go through the motions, you say? That is something I do well. Have you ever noticed the clock over the archway at the entrance to Horse Guards?"

"The clock?"

"You've seen a little mark next to the number 2?"

"I don't think I have."

"Two o'clock was the time that Charles I had his head chopped off in Whitehall in 1649. We royals have been going through the motions ever since."

Nurhaci now had a look of what might pass as sympathy on his face.

"When do I start at Cambridge?"

"Next week. All necessary arrangements have been made.

You have rooms at King's College. I think you will be very comfortable."

CHAPTER 6 (OLD KITCHEN BAR TERRACE, MAGDALEN COLLEGE)

Matthew Nice was sitting at a table on the terrace of the Old Kitchen Bar, just below Magdalen Bridge.   Graceful arches marched across the Cherwell's green water at a purposeful angle, as if supporting a Brunel railway viaduct, rather than a road bridge in Oxford. During those first nervous minutes of their meeting, Matthew had plenty of time to study this architecture, which stood over the King's right shoulder. Matthew had no idea how to hold himself, whether to go for stiffly formal, or a more relaxed posture. The King appeared to know exactly how to sit, adopting an informality that was never casual. He had an inner confidence, which somehow made whatever he did the right thing to do.

Apart from the King and his guest, the terrace was deserted. Matthew knew their isolation was illusory and within moments, if the need arose, protection officers would surround them, producing powerful, hidden weapons that somehow during concealment did not interfere with the knap of discreetly armoured Gieves and Hawkes jackets.

The silence continued. Protocol dictated that it wasn't proper to start a conversation with one's monarch. As time passed, it seemed equally improper to sit and say nothing.

King John seemed to know what he was doing. Matthew sensed this was all part of the softening up process.

"So," said the King at last. "You are President of the Boat Club?"

"Yes, Your Majesty."

"Tell me, do you think rowers should be selected on merit?"

Matthew tried to slow his breathing.

"Any crew will look for the strongest individuals, sir. But often the need to select the best eight overrides the need to select the eight best."

King John looked thoughtful in a rather Shakespearian kind of way.

"And you and I feel that the best eight should include the most hopeless oarsman in the entire university?"

"As I understand it, there are special circumstances...."

"I am a monarch, Nice. A monarch is someone you have to accept on faith. Merit is all very well but it is unstable, my boy. People have conflicting ideas about it. Merit has fashions that come and go. There are rows, arguments, power struggles. Sometimes different people seem to be of equal merit and it is impossible to choose between them. In the midst of that complete mess, what do you think is required?"

"A... king, sir?"

"That's right, boy, a king - or a queen. Let's not forget the ladies. King or queen, we royals do not doff our hats to merit. Edward has to go in the Blue Boat. He must accept that he cannot be a carefree boy forever. He has to face up to his role in life, and he will do that in the Blue Boat. You follow me, Nice?"

"Yes, Your Majesty."

"So, will you help? Will you put my grandson in the boat?"

"We will, Your Majesty."

"He has no talent, and precious little push. So I want you to do your best with him."

"Yes, sir."

"And of course in return you get to include the young lady I have been hearing so much about."

"Caroline McMercy. Now she is phenomenal."

There was a shared smile of enthusiasm, a passion for advantage in rowing shining through formality.

"I'm medically enhanced you know. That's why I am still alive. Do you think that should disqualify me from the throne?"

"Of course not, sir. Sometimes, I do look around at Oxford..." Matthew tightened his lips as they tried to form the right words. "I do worry about the future and how things are going. But we can't hide from it. Mars isn't hiding from it."

"No they are not. We can't either. We have to face the future. No doubt there will be difficulties, but the monarchy will give a sense of reassurance as always."

"Yes, sir."

"We're going to make a man of him, Nice. My grandson is heir to the throne, the last royal throne in the world. We also need to prepare him for thrones on other worlds. And we want him ready, don't we?"

"Yes, Your Majesty, of course we do."

Matthew watched the King lift his face to the morning sunshine and raise his cup to his lips.

"Good man."

CHAPTER 7 (IFFLEY ROAD STADIUM, OXFORD)

Prince Edward was at Oxford University's sports complex at Iffley Road, in an events room of shadowy dimensions skewed by half-darkness, pounding music, and neural upset caused by an unclassifiable drink. He found his sense of balance further impaired by a pair of handcuffs anchoring his left ankle to the right ankle of a girl he had only just met. This unhappy couple staggered through a crowd that burned with an energy generated when the pull needed to bring new people in, fuses with the push that comes from hatred of outsiders.

"Tell me," said Edward to the girl, "are all rowing get-togethers as charming as this one?"

"No, they're on their best behavior to welcome newbies like us."

"I never wanted to be a rower, that's the irony. I only did rowing at school to get out of rugger."

"Just shut up and find Dramhaggle."

Lurching through the throng, the handcuffed pair found their quarry, lording it with men and women who, looming over him, could have tossed him one handed into the training tank.

"I say, Dramhaggle," said Edward. "I have been obliged to

drink rather a lot of some manner of dark purple mixture."

"Cider, blackcurrant juice and shaving foam I would say," chipped in the girl.

"Ah, shaving foam, that's what it is. Couldn't quite place it. Well anyway, I need the toilet. I appeal to your better nature to release this young lady before that happens. The one thing I know about her is that she is from an all-girl college."

"Your appeal has been noted and denied."

"Oh come along, Dramhaggle."

"He's not going to let us go," sighed the girl. "Don't you have bodyguards or something?"

"My grandfather believes in building up my personal grit. It was just like this at school. Unless my oppressors armed themselves with rocket launchers, I was on my own. And there's another thing; my bodyguards used to be rowers and are just as cross with me as this lot."

"Your Highness!"

A worried face fringed by floppy blonde hair appeared at intervals above a mass of throbbing heads, arranged by strobe lights into lines of black, grey and smoky white.

"Is he your bodyguard?"

"Sadly no. That's just Alistair. I was at school with him. Don't worry, Alistair," called out Edward above the cheering and singing. "It's like this when we're all bods together. It seems I will have to pass water, and quite possibly vomit, whilst attached to a young lady I hardly know."

"I do have a name. It's Caroline."

"Ah delighted. And during the crisis to come, Caroline, you can rely on me to sing *Jerusalem* at high volume."

Alistair managed to force his way through to the prince's side.

"Hold on, Your Highness, help is coming."

Help appeared to consist of Matthew Nice who ambled towards them, raising his glass left and right to revelry that did not include him.

"Come on, that's enough. Let him go."

Jerry Dramhaggle looked up at the club president.

"We all had to go through it. And there were other things we had to go through, like years of training and getting up early on freezing cold mornings."

"Let him go," Matthew repeated.

Matthew's weary order attracted the attention of a man with the face of a Scandinavian, thunder-making-hammer wielding, god. Soft, white eyebrows grew like pale moss on a rocky, arctic outcrop of supraorbital bone. Just for a moment the prince thought the chain of command at an ancient sports club was in danger of breaking down. However, a modulation of Dramhaggle's head was enough to restrain the man god. He confined himself to verbal violence.

"We cannot have this pitiful excuse for a man in the boat."

"He is being considered for a reason, Maanberg."

"Crazy," continued the pale giant. "This is Iffley Road, where Roger Bannister broke the four minute mile. You bring this man in here to dishonor discipline and excellence. What game are you playing?"

"It's a game called rowing," said Matthew. "We need both of these people in the boat."

"I don't have to be in your bloody boat," said Caroline.

"Yes you do. Now getting this sorted out will be the work of a moment. Jerry, where's the key?"

Dramhaggle beckoned over a fellow who had the usual rower appearance. Relentless training, combined with similar backgrounds and education tended to iron out race, creed, or interplanetary provenance. This particular example of rower species had the pale mien of characters who once figured in popular novels, resisting an urge to suck blood, and trying to make themselves acceptable to normal schools. Young Dracula smoothed his shiny, black hair, reached in his pocket and pulled out a device within which an image of handcuffs orbited in space, the words "enter code" flashing above them. He held this just out of reach of his president.

"So we think he has suffered enough?"

Matthew reached for the key, only for the teasing to continue.

"Tarquin, stop it," chided Matthew without much conviction. This game had the potential to go on for a while.

"Oh let me do it."

Caroline's frustration had manifested itself in a slight Scottish accent. Edward found himself hauled with surprising ease towards a pair of empty chairs. Dumped in one of them, Caroline sat beside him, and then reached down and took the ankle binding chain in her hands. The chain whipped into a state of tension, as though an unpredictable tide had swung a freighter at its mooring.

"A brave effort old thing, but I fear..."

Edward's words caught in his throat as a white stain began to spread through the silver alloy. There was no deformation, just this ominous colour change. With a snap the chain failed, its shattered links falling to the floor like shards of broken ice.

"How did you do that? And why didn't you do that before?"

"The boys are right. You are annoying, wandering in here and taking a place in the Blue Boat."

"Lovely," declared Matthew. "Now that we're acquainted, we can get on. Edward is going to be training with us. We need him to keep things quiet about Caroline here. Best eight rather than eight best. People have suffered for that before, and they will again. Grow up and accept it."

Just when Matthew appeared to be putting a lid on the situation, the lines of black, grey and white heads all turned to present their profiles to Edward, and their attention to a scuffle over by the doors.

"Ah," said Matthew. "I believe that's Northcote and his chums."

"Who's Northcote?" asked Edward, poking at the shattered chain links with his toes, wondering where his shoes and socks had gone.

"Stroke in last year's boat, a man of action rather than words."

Maanberg laughed like an opera singer filling the house with the kind of laughter that precedes a tragedy. Tarquin smoothed his hair in satisfaction, before remarking:

"Good luck talking that lot down, Nice. They'll tear your prince to pieces."

"Yes, they seem to have had a few drinks. We'll have to make them see sense later. For now, let's get Edward out of here. Tarquin, hold them back for as long as you can; Maanberg help him; Dramhaggle, with me."

Edward only had time to shout 'bonsoir' to Caroline before Matthew, Alistair and Jerry Dramhaggle bundled their fugitive into a corridor. This narrow space acted to concentrate the drama, like a shell spinning against the rifling in a gun barrel. By the time Edward emerged into the open expanse of a floodlit running oval, he was struggling to wear his chainmail of nonchalance. Alistair was at his side.

"Run, Your Highness."

"I am running."

They careered around the curve of a maroon, eight-lane track, only to see a group of determined looking men cutting across the infield.

"Isn't that cheating?" puffed Edward.

Matthew pointed to an access point in the stands ahead of them.

"Through there."

Edward galloped into the athlete's tunnel, down more corridors, across silent basketball courts, and around the still waters of a rowing tank, glittering like some tropical lagoon resting on a Caribbean evening. A bewildering sequence of these sport themed byways eventually deposited him back in the street-lit darkness of Iffley Road. Matthew shouted his final commands.

"I will draw them away. Alistair, Dramhaggle, get him back to college."

"That didn't go very well," wailed Edward, as he ran barefoot with his unofficial bodyguards back over Magdalen Bridge. "Can't they find some other way to make a man of me?"

"This is what the King wants," objected Alistair.

"Well never mind about my development as a man. Please assist with my rather more pressing need to find a toilet."

CHAPTER 8
(KING'S COLLEGE, CAMBRIDGE)

Prince James, like every other visitor to Cambridge, found himself entering a different reality as he walked down King's Parade. James was expecting to find the most substantive and rooted of places, like a formation of sedimentary rock laid down over eons. He imagined dreaming spires as authentic as the buttes of Monument Valley. Instead, he felt as though he had walked out onto a stage. He might sing an aria beside a fountain, or engage in some comic business involving drink and the proctor's hat. Ahead of him, set designers had excelled themselves with the soaring, gothic dream of King's College Chapel. Beside the chapel ran an ornate screen wall, a sequence of lancet arches providing sunny glimpses of a hidden grass court beyond. There was a splash of red next to the college gate, like a careless flick of scarlet paint on the mottled sepia of old stone. Getting closer, this stroke of accidental pigment turned out to be a fluted, Victorian letterbox. It was easy to imagine posting an old-fashioned letter; a love letter perhaps, that would lead to a scene of romance.

James couldn't help wondering if he was a proficient enough actor to take a role in this theatre. He glanced towards Boles who walked beside him. James felt inadequate, a feeling to which he had long grown accustomed.

"I shouldn't be here," he muttered. "I'm not all that clever."

"Don't talk like that," said Boles. "It's not about whether you are clever or not. You are royal. That is enough."

"Really, Boles? It would have been nice to get here on merit."

"Merit? You know what your grandfather says about that. A source of confusion and instability."

"Yes, that's what he says. But, Boles, how will I manage with the studying?"

"Don't worry about it. There'll be some world literature, Shakespeare perhaps. As is the case for most students, whatever you study is beside the point. The fact that you are here is enough, that and taking a seat in the Blue Boat. And I don't want any whining about your rowing ability either. You were quite good at Eton. Just relax, be your usual pleasant self, and everything will be fine."

"I wish I could be as confident as you, Boles."

Boles laid a hand on James's shoulder.

"Buck up."

A few minutes later James stood outside his rooms. According to an unctuous Provost, the writer E.M. Forster had once used them. In a white door with four panels, the prince turned a smooth, black doorknob, which enjoyed an informal relationship with a slack internal lock mechanism. Walking through the expansive doorway, light poured in through an ecclesiastical window to the left, spilling over a small study desk. A low backed sofa faced towards a fireplace, which had not seen fire in centuries. A grandfather clock stood against a corner, looking out across the room's diagonal, as though pondering some kind of obscure geometry.

Once the Provost had taken his leave, James turned, taking in details. He noticed a monochrome photo portrait, of a man with a pointed nose, slightly protruding lower lip, severely sculpted hair parted on the left, and a downturn on the outer aspect of the eyes. This was a man with worries, about matters of Empire or English cricket. Beneath the image was an inscription: "We must be willing to let go of the life we have planned, so as to have the life that is waiting for us." James guessed the fellow in the picture was E.M. Forster, and those words must be from his writings.

The grandfather clock ticked off a few more seconds in its centuries of life. Sounds of commotion came through the white door.

"You can't just go barging in there, miss."

"If he can come barging into my crew, I can go barging into his room."

"Will you please wait, young lady."

The door opened, revealing Boles, looking flustered.

"A Miss Blackwood would like to speak with you, sir. She was the cox for the Cambridge Blue Boat last year. She appears emotional. Shall I have her arrested?"

"No, Boles, I'll speak to her."

"Are you sure, sir? I can have her in front of a judge within the hour."

"I will see her, Boles. I can't hide away forever."

Boles opened his mouth to object, but then thought better of it. He nodded and stood to one side allowing a small woman with a sensible, serviceable red bob of a haircut, to stride forward.

"That will be all, Boles."

Nodding his assent Boles closed the door.

"Miss Blackwood, so nice to meet you."

"I wish I could say the same about you."

James could see that this wasn't the moment for a

handshake. Apart from the obvious hostility, he recognised a slight Martian accent, which had resisted assimilation into the indeterminate student cadence that reigned supreme on campuses everywhere. He knew that Martians didn't like handshakes, not since that nasty, pustular virus which ripped through their early settlement domes. James had a natural eye and ear for social conventions.

Now that she was in the room, it appeared Miss Blackwood didn't know what to say. A royal smile and unfailing courtesy was having its usual effect. James watched as she tried to hang onto the fury that had fuelled the altercation at his door.

"Can I get you a drink at all? I was thinking of having one. I've just arrived you see. Feeling rather in a muddle. I think a quiet drink would steady the nerves. Do join me."

"No, I'm fine, thank you."

James gestured towards the seating area arranged around the long dormant fireplace.

"Please sit down. We will be able to talk more easily."

James could see that Miss Blackwood was now disconcerted. He knew what he was doing, and sat down on the sofa. His inquisitor sat on a straight-backed chair, in an attitude that suggested she would soon be getting up again.

"I'm sorry to come bursting in here, but I have been told you'll be in the Blue Boat, and, well... you see I take my rowing seriously, and I wanted to discuss it."

"Of course you did. Your frustration is quite understandable, and I can see why you would want to talk about it. May I ask your first name?"

"Marina. I am Marina Blackwood."

"I hope you don't mind if I call you Marina? And can I ask where you are from?"

James knew where she was from. It was quite clear from her

accent. Nonetheless, it was polite to ask.

"Mars."

"Yes, of course."

James was soon chatting with a woman who only a few moments before had felt so angry and wronged that she wanted to attack the prince. She was now addressing him as if she were an exasperated older sister. Usually people would only ever get to the acquaintance stage in their dealings with him, and venture no further. That was why the life of a prince was often so lonely.

"Mars will definitely overtake Earth, and soon," argued Marina.

"Of course you might well be right."

"We don't have all the silly tradition of Earth. We don't have all that weight of the past holding us back."

"Yes, I can certainly see how that might be an advantage, though in some circumstances it is reassuring to have a feeling that you are part of something that has gone before and will continue. After all, on Mars you have been careful to preserve your heritage. There's the museum at Bradbury Landing, for example."

Marina hesitated.

"Well, yes I do agree that there are some on Mars who wish to create history as quickly as possible. Mars is an odd place."

Marina stiffened in her seat, as though trying to find a little of her old anger.

"I am told you have to be trained for the Blue Boat. I am not happy about it."

"Neither am I, Marina. Still, one has one's duty. Just tell me what you need me to do. I don't want to get in the way."

"You know why you are in the boat? They have explained

that to you?"

"Yes, Marina. I am to provide a useful press restriction to protect a medically enhanced member of your crew, and, I have now learned, to help keep secret some changes to the buoyancy of your boat."

"They told you about the buoyancy thing too? And are you happy with that? A team over at the Cavendish Laboratory seems to have defeated Archimedes. What they've done could be revolutionary, but they're hiding it for the Boat Race. Do you feel that covering up all that is part of your duty?"

"Apparently it is."

"And do you always give in and do what you're told, even when it's patently wrong? Don't you ever think for yourself?"

"I do think for myself, and most of the time I come to the conclusion that it is not my job to do the thinking. If I was to think, I might think that the best way to test new buoyancy technology is to try it on a small boat before you try it on a big one. As for your rower with medical enhancement, I might wonder about the prejudice that people with medical enhancement often suffer. I might question if that is wholly correct."

Marina stood up, possessed of a nervous energy that did not allow her to sit for long. James out of courtesy stood up too. He thought his visitor was about to leave, before seeing a cloud of second thoughts cross her face. Marina sat down again, and James did the same.

"Look, I know what Oxford is up to. And I know that unless we take certain measures we haven't got a chance."

Marina made an exclamation of frustration. She seemed to be bracing for the inevitable, coming to some kind of accommodation with herself.

"Meeting you hasn't been quite what I expected. Maybe you will be useful."

"Thank you."

The meeting seemed to be ending on a relatively positive note. James was pleased with himself.

"I just must say," he said as they walked to the door, "Martian skill in rowing is a testament to your planet's ingenuity, particularly as you are so short of water."

James's innocuous and complimentary comment demolished any hint of reconciliation. The prince had known that Martians didn't like handshakes, but feeling oddly relaxed in Marina's company, he had forgotten how sensitive they could be about the subject of water.

"Short of water? These stereotypes are frankly insulting. We took up rowing precisely to show the solar system that we do have water on Mars, and plenty of it."

"Yes, of course. I'm sorry."

"You live this cloistered life where nothing ever changes. Out on Mars we can row for days down the rivers of the Mariner Valley, which might not rival the Thames yet, but are only going to get bigger."

"Quite. I'm terribly sorry. I was expressing myself in a clumsy, insensitive manner. I am so glad we have had this meeting. I do hope we will become friends."

"I have to go."

"Of course."

"Don't be late for training."

"I won't. I'll see you soon, Marina."

Marina turned and left, shutting the door behind her, rattling the loose doorknob. James stood in silence. E.M. Forster looked down at him, as though he had seen it all before.

CHAPTER 9 (OXFORD BOATHOUSE)

Matthew stood back and observed the scene playing out in his favourite place in Oxford. It wasn't just a place; it was also a moment he had enjoyed long before he came to the university, this moment of dawn beside a river. The stillness of morning, Oxford's wood and glass boathouse, polished water running between banks of architectural straightness; all of this appeared to be the work of the same designer. A new day introduced itself, with a tranquility offering reassurance to worries about the rush of history turning flesh and blood people into cyborgs or blobs of data. The river did not appear to flow. It stood like a bar of dusky gold on an eternal September morning.

Matthew drew his attention away from this perfect scene, and tried to concentrate on two bleary looking young men in dark blue tracksuits. They quailed before Jerry Dramhaggle, keen and wide-awake, standing in front of them. A gust of wind perturbed the river's surface, also ruffling Jerry's short black hair.

"I don't like this any more than you do. I have been told to put you in a boat and start some training."

"But dash it all, it's 6 in the a.m.," moaned Edward. "Why can't we do this after lunch?"

"After lunch? What do you think this is, a bit of a stroll to walk off some fine dining?"

"It's just that I'm not an early riser. It's to do with biorhythms. Not entirely my fault."

"I don't want to hear about your biorhythms."

Jerry said the word biorhythms in a manner suggestive of visits to the bathroom.

"How much rowing did you do at Stonemeldrum?"

"Some, but I just did rowing to get out of playing rugger. I'm not very good. Just ask Alistair here."

"Come on, old man," said Alistair, flicking away a blonde fringe, which kept blowing in his eyes. "Royal command and all that. They'll stop your allowance if we don't get on with it."

Matthew Nice now approached the unhappy group. The King had ordered this. Supposedly, the King had no real power and was merely an old man in fancy dress who came along to liven up various classy functions. Matthew knew better. He was a clever boy who realised that authority had not so much been in the King, as in his own desire that somewhere in creation there should be an authority to which all things could be referred. This overwhelming longing had transferred itself over to an old man who knew how to receive it. While Matthew realised this, and even disapproved of his own feelings, it made no difference. Matthew Nice had two of the greatest encouragements to self-regard at his disposal - youth and an Oxford education. Yet the King had reduced him to a head-bowed subject.

Matthew watched on as Edward's introduction to Oxford rowing continued.

"You'll be working today with Tarquin Van Cello," said Jerry to his two charges.

The tall Martian who had held handcuff keys out of reach on the night of the Rowing Club Ball, straightened up from his work, adjusting rigging on a two-man boat.

"And you don't mind the small detail that I am useless at

rowing?" asked Edward.

Tarquin tapped Edward on the shoulder with his spanner.

"Sometimes there's more to winning than just having strong arms. Don't underestimate yourself. People don't get to be royal without a certain spirit."

"Yes, but that spirit was shown by people like Henry V. It's long since been leached away by bridge openings and foundation stone laying."

Alistair looked uncomfortable at this royal mournfulness, but Tarquin laughed. Matthew watched this interaction carefully. He had selected Tarquin as Edward's mentor because, key antics aside, he showed no hostility to the prince. Tarquin was new money, and new Martian money at that. New money is often most respectful of old privilege.

Edward gazed towards the river. Matthew watched him wave to the girl he had shared an ankle with on that unpleasant evening at Iffley Road.

"Ahoy there. Thanks for releasing me from my bonds the other night."

Caroline nodded a reply in time with her mighty stroke, driving along a single seater.

"My God, that girl can row," mused Edward. "Even I can see that."

CHAPTER 10 (RIVER CAM, CAMBRIDGE)

James strained to keep his rhythm in the third seat of a four-man training boat, tearing along the Cam. Ahead of him sat Marina, urging her crew onwards. James knew that at any moment she would be ordering a smooth tuck-down. He remembered his slipway pep talk. These boats had hulls honed with such advanced low drag technology, that a trained crew could reach speeds at which it was impossible to keep up with the flow of water rushing past. Once beyond this threshold, the trick was to tuck oars and hunch down low to reduce drag and increase stability.

"James, that's enough for you. Three more strokes and then bow pair into tuck position. Three, two, one, tuck now."

James grimaced in frustration, furious with himself that he could not keep up with the others. Nevertheless he did as he was told, folding his oar close to the gunwale, and crouching down into the space in front of him. To balance the boat, the man behind James was also required to tuck down, something that did not happen without a number of Anglo Saxon expletives. Meanwhile the two stern oarsmen picked up their pace to a furious rate.

"Come on, pull and through, pull and through. Four more strokes to tuck position."

A scream, a chromatic wail of pain, sliced the morning air.

The broad back in front of James fell forward. A geyser of water shot up from a flailing oar, skewing the boat off course, into the path of the second boat coming up behind.

"Check it, check it," yelled Marina.

James took a few seconds to remember that this was the command to stop the boat. Soaked by plumes of water coming off his crewmates' blades, he jammed his own blade in the water, its handle tearing out of his fingers as he did so. Once the boat had slowed, James forced his bruised fingers to grip the oar again and help row back to the boathouse.

It took three people to lift the injured oarsman out of his seat and carry him to a treatment couch.

The club physiotherapist hurried in and looked down at his patient.

"Get Walden," he said to an onlooker. "And somebody bring me the cybernetic first aid kit."

James stood with Marina and the rest of her crew, clustered around the casualty.

A rushed medical examination began.

"Tyndale, isn't it?" The young man managed a tightening of the face in reply. "Okay, I'm going to take a look at you now, and then we'll decide if you need to go to hospital."

The first aid kit arrived. Inside were bandages, wound dressings, surgical tape, a selection of tiny processor chips, a small screwdriver, and a cybernetics diagnostic computer. After checking the arm, and asking some questions, the therapist started to feel around the base of Tyndale's back. His hands stopped moving on the approach of a man of lean frame, pointed facial features and a head gleaming in its metallic lack of hair.

"How is he?"

James took a step back as the shiny-headed one barged past him.

"You might be an experienced coach with normal athletes," said the therapist, indicating that in the interests of discretion, they should move away from Tyndale, "but you know nothing about enhanced people. I told you this would happen. You've pushed him too hard."

"Come on, we can patch him up and get him on his way. He's ex-army, tough as they come."

Tyndale was alternating whimpers of pain, with cries of agony if he tried to move.

"He was in the Coldstream Guards; spent most of his time conducting the band at ceremonial occasions. Misfiring pyrotechnics at a military tattoo caused his injury. But it wouldn't matter if he was the toughest solider in the army, I cannot just patch him up. You have to realise that enhanced individuals require careful handling."

"You said that man was state of the art."

"His arm is state of the art. He has one medically enhanced arm that brings as many problems as benefits. It's simple. You can attach a biomechanical arm capable of tearing a tree out of the ground, but the stresses of doing so would cripple the human body the arm is attached to. Normal muscles are not as strong as the enhanced limb. If you push too hard, you have a horrendous injury. I think Tyndale has ripped a muscle in his lumbar spine, and there may be disc damage. His entire back has gone into spasm, and given the position of the rupture and possible nerve compression, he may have lost the ability to pass urine without the help of a catheter. And you are telling me to patch him up and get him on his way?"

Walden retreated a step from this outburst. The comment about the catheter seemed to have rattled him.

"Right, that does sound serious," Walden conceded, motioning with a discreet finger to the lips movement for the therapist to calm down and lower his voice.

"We will get him back to Harley Street for further assessment."

"Do what you need to do. But get him fixed. Without him we cannot compete with Oxford."

Marina now pushed past James as she marched up to Walden.

"What's happened?" she demanded.

"Tyndale is badly injured," said the therapist before Walden could answer. "The power of his arm has caused significant trauma in his back. I keep saying cybernetics is not holistic enough."

Walden paced back to the treatment table and looked down at Tyndale. Without an ounce of unnecessary fat on his angular face, James thought that Walden embodied a machine much more convincingly than the injured man he surveyed. The coach turned to Marina.

"So, how did the boat feel before the accident? Were you fast?"

"Our speed was incredible. I couldn't believe what I was seeing on the read outs."

"What, even with…"

James sensed a slight nod towards himself.

"Yes, even with that."

"Excellent."

Walden's eyes were like twin lenses on a sophisticated camera. He seemed unaware of moaning from the treatment couch. James, despite his desire to keep out of the way, could stand it no longer.

"Please can you try and do something for him. He's asking for painkillers."

"Is anyone going to help me?" groaned Tyndale.

James felt troubled at the risky behavior he was covering up. With his guard distracted by ongoing drama, James then did something he had never done before. He slipped away, walking down the river path, past college boathouses, to the footbridge near Cutter Ferry Lane, before making his way over Midsummer Common back to the theatre stage of central Cambridge. Only a line of Hackney Pods on Victoria Avenue reminded him that he was living in the modern age.

Deflated and tired, he winced as his bruised hand made contact with E.M. Forster's loose, black door handle. Back in his room, which had become his haven, he looked out across a courtyard lawn, striped like painted canvas. Those horizontal light and dark green bands rooted the eye on a flat, solid surface, leading its gaze over to vertically sweeping chapel architecture beyond. James enjoyed the overall effect, of anchoring an observer within a space, and then throwing that observer skywards.

Unfurling sore fingers with difficulty, James put his hand on a sketchpad, twisting it around like a compass to accord with the lines of the lawn. He sat down and selected a sketching pencil. Holding it between middle finger and index finger to avoid excessive pain, he worked on an outline drawing of the scene, illuminated in late afternoon sunlight. He was just losing himself in his work, when there was a knock at the door. The doorknob exerted itself once more, revealing Boles looking somber. He came in, glancing around in approval at a neatly kept room. James expected a lecture about being away from his guard, but there was no mention of it. Perhaps Boles sympathised with the King's desire not to mollycoddle the boys as they readied themselves for what was to come.

Boles looked at James's unfinished sketch.

"Very nice, Your Highness."

"Thank you, Boles. This is a beautiful place. It's like living in fairyland."

"Well, sir, enjoy it while you can. Tomorrow I have to take you to the underworld."

"Sorry, Boles?"

"Be ready by nine. It's a bit of a journey from here."

"The underworld? A bit of a journey?"

"Be ready by nine. His Majesty wants you two boys to have an experience of the reality of kingship, and the people you will have to deal with."

CHAPTER 11
(LAMBETH PALACE)

Arriving at Lambeth Palace, a door opened in the long Thames facing wall. Bacon stepped through, Edward following behind so furtively, that an archiepiscopal attendant almost closed the door in his face, not realising he was there.

"I don't see why I needed to come along, Bacon," grumbled Edward. "You would be better at handling this."

"You need to be here. And remember, I want you to join in with the conversation."

Bacon stopped beside a strange thicket standing against a buttressed brick wall. This mass of twisting branches appeared to be a tree so ancient that over centuries it had created its own small forest in which to grow. Bacon pointed at the carboniferous, twisting cat's cradle of snaking boughs.

"This fig tree was grown from cuttings planted by a cardinal in the 1500s. The path of royalty on which you tread is just as tortuous. You have to be prepared."

Bacon led the way to a private suite, buried deep in a hidden quadrangle. Entering a room, which smelt of history with a top note of sweat, Edward saw the Archbishop sitting in a chair next to an open fire, dressed in purple sportswear. Bacon had already explained the elderly prelate's penchant for squash games, which he would use to show off his unacknowledged medical enhancement by thrashing shots around the heads of aged local bishops.

The Archbishop did not get up as Bacon and Edward came in, but gestured to arm chairs opposite him.

Following the usual formalities of greeting, Bacon passed on an apology that due to illness the King wouldn't be able to attend this meeting himself today.

"Ah yes, the King, a sad business. I hope he feels better soon. I hear he wants to be King of Mars. Is this a symptom of his illness?"

The Archbishop uttered these words with as much emphasis as possible on sounding caring and compassionate.

In the background, the same attendant who had opened the Thames wall door, pretended to dust some books. The Archbishop made a fluttering motion with his hand. Then he and his visitors were alone.

"King John is still your monarch," observed Bacon. "I shouldn't have to remind you of that."

"He's not very well though," contributed Edward.

"He's fine," shot back Bacon.

The Archbishop sighed and continued to develop his expression of compassion, leaning forward, one hand embracing the other in a symbolic act of helpfulness.

"Look, Bacon, you don't have to pretend with me. I have known the King just as long as you have. One of my first official tasks ninety years ago was the coronation. Since then I have presided over the christenings, weddings and funerals of the royal family. The King has had more than his share of cruel luck during that time. It's bound to have taken its toll."

The Archbishop's face directed its forced compassion towards Bacon, who appeared unimpressed with this display.

"The King remains a wise man. He hopes to play a role in heading off hostilities between Earth and Mars."

"Quite. We should all live in hope."

"And what does that mean?"

"My son, Mars is a planet with many difficulties. We should give the Martian people space to resolve their problems in their own way. Don't you agree, Edward?"

The prince sensed his head shrinking into his shoulders.

"Well, I mean, it's tricky…."

"What His Highness is trying to say," interrupted Bacon, "is that we are running out of time. The King thinks we should intervene now before it is too late."

"Bacon, I acknowledge the wonderful work you have done for the monarchy over the years, but you really need to start seeing things more dispassionately."

"We are here to tell you what the King wants. When the time comes you will be required to help the royal family with its aspirations in regard to Mars."

The Archbishop sat back. His hands broke their caring grasp and settled like two birds of prey on the arms of his chair.

"King John cannot be King of Mars, and I will not crown him. There are many reasons for this. The main problem, as far as I am concerned, is that the Church of Mars will object that I am straying into their jurisdiction. Mars is a powder keg, Bacon. Think about the sort of people who went there in the early days of settlement: old-fashioned nationalists embittered at the disappearance of their nations; freedom lovers who wanted to sing songs and wear their hair long; and those who wanted the liberty to live strict, fundamentalist lives of one kind or another. Now you have all of those libertarians, religious fundamentalists, and displaced nationalists trying to live together on one planet. It's like a chilly version of what the United States used to be. The only thing that unites Martians is the fact that they all seem to hate Earth."

"That's why the King has a plan."

"But the King is not himself, Bacon."

"You have to admit..." started Edward, only to swallow his words as Bacon threw a furious glare at him. This seemed a tad unfair when Bacon had coached him beforehand to contribute. Edward decided he would just give the impression of listening and leave it at that.

"The King is fine," declared Bacon. "He just has off days. Come, Archbishop, it is at times like this that we are required to have faith."

"Faith?" The Archbishop's demeanour changed. "What are you suggesting?"

"I believe in my King. What do you believe in?"

"You are getting into things that are over your head. The King is a man. You cannot have faith in a man. You are talking about things that are the province of the Church."

"When you crowned the King you did so with holy oil, or don't you remember? You said that God had chosen him."

"Yes, but that was a figure of speech. Those were words of convention used in a traditional coronation service. That's all they were."

"How much more of what you say is just a figure of speech then? All of it?"

"You listen to me. The King is barking mad. My doctor has told me so. I can't crown a crazy person King of Mars. I can't crown anyone King of Mars, because those people do not want a king."

"The King is not mad. He merely has days when his focus is unclear. And as for what people on Mars want, since when has monarchy had anything to do with what people want? People's wants - frequently selfish, often irrational, usually ill informed, always changing; we don't deal with that. We don't deal in democracy. You've been around monarchy long enough to know that."

"Edward, you must be aware that the loyalty shown here by Bacon is touching but misguided. You are being badly advised."

"You leave him out of this," snapped Bacon.

"Leave him out of this? He's the heir to the throne. You can't leave him out of this."

Edward nodded, as if to concede that the Archbishop had a point. This only seemed to enrage Bacon further. His immaculate manner, so smooth and reassuring in the King's presence, was now a disciplined hardness, as though he were a devotee of a formal and demanding martial art.

"The King has a plan for the monarchy of Mars. Following his speech at the Mars House, he accepts that he is unlikely to take the throne of Mars himself. That is why he wants to promote Prince Edward's claim. When the moment comes he wants you to crown Edward as King of Earth and Mars."

Edward's eyes widened.

"Bacon, steady on!"

The Archbishop clutched his temples.

"But there is no throne of Mars! There never has been. There never will be. As for Prince Edward, I know that monarchy is its own enclosed little world, but come on. I doubt if Edward will even be King of Earth, let alone Mars."

Bacon's smooth face was now pale and mottled. The Archbishop's eyes narrowed.

"I don't think I have to tell you, seeing as you have been in the royal household for so many years, that Prince Edward…"

The bewildered young man watched the Archbishop pause and cast a sideways glance in his direction.

"Forgive me, Your Highness, but it has to be said. You have

never shown any interest in all the young ladies who have thrown themselves at your feet; not even in Lady Beatrice, who even a man of God like myself... well anyway, for a royal that is still a problem."

Edward now joined Bacon in pale blotchiness.

"I just want people to leave me alone. If you're suggesting anything else, then I... This is ridiculous. I don't want to be married off, that's all."

"There are equality laws, Archbishop," snapped Bacon.

"Equality? Since when has monarchy had anything to do with equality? This is the royal family, a throwback. Problems, which have disappeared for the rest of us, are preserved in the royal aspic. A royal needs an heir."

"There have been gay monarchs before. William II probably, Edward II and James I almost certainly. And King James I, if I can presume to remind you of your history, linked the crowns of England and Scotland. Edward could do the same for Earth and Mars."

"I am not gay!" squawked Edward.

The Archbishop shook his head.

"The kings you mention had the mystery of royalty to protect them. That mystery has gone. Edward will soon come of age and be fair game for the press."

"Is anyone listening to me?" bleated Edward.

Bacon stood up.

"I know things are not quite perfect at the moment, but with a little help from the Church we could start making progress."

The Archbishop stood up to face Bacon.

"Let's be realistic. The King has gone mad. His eldest grandson is gay. Mars hates us. Edward will never be King of Mars, and we'll be lucky if we make him King of Earth. In fact we'll be lucky if the monarchy survives at all."

Bacon approached the Archbishop, who responded. The two men were standing nose to nose, like two boxers before a fight, back when boxing was legal. Edward stared in terror at the sparring pugilists, looking around in vain for some kind of referee who would surely bring a stop to this.

"You have abandoned the monarchy," spat Bacon.

"I am the monarchy," spat back the Archbishop. "The King is nothing without me."

At this point, the door opened and a worried attendant, presumably concerned about raised voices, peered in.

"Get out!" screamed the Archbishop.

The door slammed shut. This interruption seemed to be enough to jolt the head of the Church back to a measure of control. With an effort of will, causing a slight shaking in an ill-defined frame, his tone turned from one of blazing anger to something closer to quiet threat.

"Age catches up with everyone in the end. We have to be humble. Consider carefully where your loyalties should now lie."

"My loyalties lie with the King. They have always done so and always will."

"Then you are a fool."

"We will see, Archbishop."

"Give my regards to King John. I bear him no ill will, you know. I feel sorry for him. If there is anything I can do, let me know."

"He does not require your pity. And he has already told you what you can do. Good day."

"I am sorry for this unpleasantness, Your Highness," said the Archbishop to Edward, once again screwing up his face in an expression of compassion. "This must be a difficult time for you; so much confusion."

Edward said nothing. Bacon guided him out of the room. The cowering attendant appeared from some hidden corner, ready to act as escort.

"We can find our own way out," barked Bacon as he walked with Edward, back past the ancient fig tree's sprawling knot of boughs and chaotic roots meandering through yellow leaf litter.

"Bacon, I am not gay."

"Just come on."

CHAPTER 12
(BROOKLANDS)

A petrol engine roar assaulted the ears of Prince James. Beside him, Boles, his hands spread expansively on a big, four-spoked steering wheel, moved with the car like a ballroom dancer with a perfect top line.

"This is good for you. Brooklands is home to the King's oldest friends. Get to know them. They might be of help to you. But be careful. Rather like this Bentley, they can be a real handful."

A gyrating cyclone spun beneath the long bonnet, squealing wheels sliding sideways on asphalt banking towards a blur of trees.

While James usually thought of painting to alleviate stress, it was difficult to think of that meditative pursuit amidst a terror of speed and noise. The only image James could hold in his mind was by Roy Lichtenstein. Fiery trails tracked rockets across a blue sky to an explosion beneath a crumpling aircraft. Bright yellow letters hung together within the flash of detonation just long enough to spell *Whaam!*

After giving the Bentley a good run, Boles pulled into the pit area. When four and a half litres of supercharged old-world power had churned into stillness, James sat for a moment within intensified silence. A mechanic in white overalls propped a jaunty elbow against the driver's door.

"How's she feeling, sir?"

"Wonderful. Very hard to drive. Just as it should be."

Acting like a man who had enjoyed a refreshing shower, Boles climbed out of the car, pulling off helmet and goggles. James took a few seconds to remove his own goggles, which seemed to have stuck to his face.

While mechanics busied themselves around the Bentley, Boles started to walk towards Brooklands Clubhouse. Pausing as James staggered after him, he reached out a steadying hand.

"Come along, sir. This is Brooklands. Pull yourself together."

"Yes, Boles."

"Lord Montagu won't take kindly to anything approaching the wobbly."

"No, Boles."

Boles led the way into the clubhouse, a building that took all its references from the horse meetings, golf tournaments and rowing regattas of what had once been England's sporting Season. That vanishing world remained unchanged inside this building, in the dark imaginings of people whose ancestors never wanted to let it go. James could feel a sense of loss, in pictures on the wall, in the way people dressed. The Birkin Suite was an exercise in aggressive nostalgia. Boles had warned him that it was time to grow up and meet some real men, but the general tone of the men here was one of arrogant youth, clung to long after arrogant youth should have been a memory, discussed with a gentle shake of wiser heads.

James nodded in acknowledgement to greetings, accepted handshakes, and tried to avoid the impression of taking guidance from Boles. The crowd was big enough for people to orbit one another like moons around planets, and for small planetary systems to circle around suns. James found himself thinking about a painting by Kandinsky, called *Several Circles*, where in an atmosphere of blackest space, planet-like forms spotted with unpredictable black nuclei, drifted and overlapped.

Astronomers observe black holes not by looking at those dark presences themselves, but by noting their destructive effect on anything close by. Similarly, in the Birkin Suite there were men who wore the most respectable of smart casual wear, whose danger became clear not in their own appearance, but in the cowering of other men around them, and in the interest of women wearing tea dresses, talking about horses and guns.

"Does Grandpaps really know these people?" James muttered towards Boles.

"The King lives in the real world. There are people in this room who saved the monarchy. Come and meet Lord Montagu."

James and Boles found Montagu beside a car, its elongated, silver bonnet folded back to reveal a stretched, V shaped mass of pipes and horns, like a musical instrument on which an absinthe-crazed, nineteenth century industrialist might play Bach's Toccata and Fugue. Montagu's jowly face was a combination of rough two-day stubble and smooth, grey, immaculate aviator shade lens. He wore a brown leather jacket, soft with age, over a white shirt untucked at the front. This casual untucking revealed a trace of hairy lower paunch. He looked like a boy in the body of a man, a man who had never really left behind the poor emotional control of youth. He smiled with adolescent charm. James had the feeling that this man ruled his playground like a charismatic tyrant, inviting people to belong in a way they had never experienced, at the price of throwing others to the wolves. If he didn't choose you for wolf fodder, you would have a great time.

"So, lad, what do you think of the Bentley? Was it like sitting on the top of Krakatoa?"

"Yes, it was most exhilarating."

James saw Montagu drop his head and study him. He felt like a defective part in a car engine.

"They tell me you like art."

"Montagu…" said Boles in quiet rebuke.

"Come on. If you like art, you'll love this intake manifold."

Montagu put his hand on James's upper back and started manhandling him towards the open bonnet.

"Montagu," demanded Boles. "We don't have time for this. I have come here to discuss important matters with you. Is it possible we can talk in private?"

Montagu, looking crestfallen, let his prey go.

"In private? Why?"

"This is a matter that involves the King and the succession."

"Why isn't John here anyway?" demanded Montagu, glancing around as if expecting to see him. He gestured towards a sofa that looked like the back seat of an old car. It was hardly the most secluded place to talk, but the crowd seemed to be circulating according to its own currents, and left the sofa in peace.

"He's not well," said Boles sitting down, indicating that James should do the same.

Montagu's face wasn't adept at looking worried.

"Not well? Didn't you tell him the Bentley would blow his cobwebs away?"

"Yes I did, and if there was any way we could have got him here, we would."

Montagu dismissed unwelcome news about King John's health with a wave of a hand. James noticed the hand was puffy and yellow. A plain, silver ring looked as though force and butter would be required in its removal. He was glad that hand was making careless gestures about the King, rather than pressing against his neck.

"Lord Montagu," continued Boles, "this is important. The King has some business to which he must attend. He wants to go to Vienna."

"Vienna, eh?"

"He has arranged for the Oxford Blue Boat crew to be selected in Vienna following the Danube training camp. He wants to be there. There are a few nominations that need keeping an eye on. The King also wants to see one of his doctors, and make arrangements for the future. Obviously, he will need you. You have the connections to influence what lies ahead."

Montagu said nothing. James felt now that power had little to do with the noise and show of the engine that had recently flung him around a racetrack. That theatricality was all just wasted energy. Real power was silent and hidden, and would involve quiet pressure exerted on people, perhaps already in this room, to support a continuation of monarchy when the time came.

"And there's another reason the King wants you to come to Vienna. For some reason he enjoys your company."

"Surely there must be more appropriate health professionals who could go with him; nurses, doctors."

The twisted tubes of a racing engine appeared in the silver lenses of aviator shades as they turned back towards their object of interest.

"I would remind you that without the King's protection you would never have been able to rebuild Brooklands."

The reflective glasses came off, James catching his breath at the sight of bloodshot eyes thus revealed.

"And I would remind you, Boles that without me and my father, the King would have gone the way of all other royalty, back when the country disappeared."

"Granted, but don't forget what King John has done for you, and what your duty in the future needs to be."

Montagu's demeanour suggested a man who, uncomfortable

with internal conflict, would rather explode immediately than put emotional energy to long-term use. Fortunately, Boles seemed to have prepared for this.

"It isn't as bad as you might think. The King still likes to have a little fun. He has asked to travel on the Orient Express. They are arranging a special train for him. He has suggested a race. We will be on the train, while the Duke of Devonshire and Lord March will be driving a classic touring van. Whoever reaches Vienna first gets in the drinks at the Schonbrunn Palace."

"I thought you said the King was ill!" yelled Montagu jumping to his feet. "This all suggests he is the same old superman he has always been. Best monarch we've ever had. Find me Devonshire and March," he demanded of no one in particular. "Christmas has come early."

CHAPTER 13 (TEMPLE ISLAND, HENLEY)

Edward, feeling the need for an emotional pick-me-up after his traumatic afternoon at Lambeth Palace, had presented himself at the door of Alistair's room in Longwall Quad, demanding festivities as soon as. Alistair wanted to discuss details. The carefree prince batted this suggestion away with a breezy reference to a pressing need to read the biography of one of his ancestors. He cast a merry "sort it out, there's a good fellow," over a royal shoulder.

Edward was not a details man. He felt his simple direction to hire Temple Island was clear enough. This was a place he had often used for entertaining, a sequestered Thames island near Henley. The island enjoyed the proportions of an Edwardian, Royal Navy battlecruiser, never used for the distasteful business of battle, always bedecked with shady awnings, required for showing the flag in hot climates. A mass of trees formed the stern superstructure, gathered behind a James Wyatt folly standing amidships, like the ship's bridge commanding a foredeck of mown grass.

Edward had faith that Alistair would get everything ready. It was a prince's job to simply turn up, arriving in his launch just as autumn dusk was gathering. The temple was already lustrously lit, and noisy with the sound of voices and music. There were repeated hurrahs, much backslapping, and raucous, politically incorrect singing of the old patriotic song *Jerusalem*.

Edward sang at the top of his voice, about those feet in ancient times walking on England's mountains green. Then a swing band started to sway, with mutes tipped over trumpet bells, and hats sloped over eyes. The face at the microphone, half hidden by a purple fedora, was that of Jerry Dramhaggle. Edward thought he saw a girl who looked like Caroline McMercy, playing clarinet. The prince didn't take much notice, what with the concentration necessary to gyrate to the sort of music that sounded young and modish in any era.

This outward show of carefree abandon did not give relief from the ache of worry that had beset Edward ever since meeting the Archbishop. In his heightened state, the world had taken on an unusual sharpness. Lights and torches lit up the trees, creating enormous fossil plants picked out on dark slate. Falling autumn leaves fluttered moth-like beside actual moths attracted by the illumination.

Feeling tired after fake revelry, Edward slipped away to stand on the temple's decorative balcony. Tiny paper boats of moonlight scattered across the dark river surface. For a moment, he was alone with the view up-river towards Henley. It was, however, almost impossible to be royal and physically solitary for any extended period. Matthew Nice soon appeared, followed by Alistair, who positioned himself in a shadowy doorway, drink in hand, one foot up on a white painted wall.

"So, let's get down to business," drawled Matthew, hands spread on the balustrade. "When the King came to see me in Oxford he said it was my job to help prepare you to succeed him on Earth, and on Mars."

"Oh, I know the old man is not very well, but he's as strong as an ox. He'll last for years yet."

"The time is coming, Edward. And when the moment arrives, King John wants you to take the throne of Mars as well as Earth."

Edward concentrated on the view up-river.

"You're not taking Grampap's mad idea seriously?"

"Very seriously."

Matthew occasionally put a shining drink to his lips but did not swallow. Edward was showing no such restraint when it came to the large glass in his own hand. The tinkle of ice accompanied each nervous gesture.

"How can it make sense, Nice?"

"Edward, old fellow, I have known you a few months now, and I see a man who has to face his destiny."

"My destiny does not include becoming King of Mars, surely?"

"You read the reports from Mars, I assume? You know about the Cinnabar Group? They have a lot of support. Those people don't view Earth as a quaint place with lots of history. For them Earth is the enemy. I'm told on good authority that an extreme element in the Cinnabar Group actually wants to get rid of Earth by redirecting an asteroid."

"Oh, dash it, Nice, that's just a rumour. I don't want to get involved with all that."

"Mars is in a dangerous state, Edward. We think you are the man to sort it out. You would be a perfect antidote to the crazy Cinnabars."

"But, Nice, being King of Earth should be enough to ask of any man."

"Duty calls, my dear Edward. We have to talk practicalities."

At that moment, Alistair left his spot in the doorway and walked out onto the balcony.

"Ah, Alistair old fellow, enjoying the party?" chirruped Edward.

"Yes, of course. Just thought I'd get some air."

"Is that so? Not ear wigging then?"

"I couldn't help over hearing; and I know we used to pretend you were a commoner at school, but things are different now. You are the heir. You have to do your duty."

"Why don't I get a choice in any of this?"

"You are one of the most famous people in the solar system. That simple fact means you could do useful work."

"Come now, Alistair, you know I'm not really fit for useful work."

"Just by being yourself you can be helpful to everybody."

"Oh, I see... Well as long as I haven't got to actually do anything."

A breathless Tarquin emerged onto the balcony. It seemed he had been enjoying swing music with more enthusiasm than might be expected from someone with a cool, young, vampiric bearing.

"Hello, you fellows. I must say, *Sing Sing Sing* is most invigorating."

Edward cast a sour look at the partygoer.

"What's the matter?"

"These two are telling me to be king of dozens of planets."

"Leave him alone. You know the idea of being king upsets him."

"Well that's a shame," said Matthew, "seeing as he's heir to the throne."

"Since when did you become such a monarchist anyway?" objected Edward. "Grampaps has really got to you. He's a persuasive old devil."

Matthew looked enigmatic.

"Maybe I should contact the King and recommend he goes with James."

"You can't do that," exploded Alistair. "That's not how it

works. Edward is the heir."

"Some heir he's turning out to be."

"It doesn't matter how good an heir he is," argued Alistair. "Don't you know anything about royalty? Who do you think you are? The King comes to Oxford and gives you a pep talk, and now you think you're some kind of privy councillor."

"Boys, boys, don't argue," pleaded Edward. "Tarquin, tell them."

Tarquin put a hand on Edward's shoulder.

"I think he's had enough."

"Yes I have had enough. You're all saying I have to be king, and there's that awful Archbishop saying I can't because...."

Edward stopped talking. An abrupt expression of cunning flashed across his worried and inebriated features.

"Maybe we should wait and see what happens," observed Tarquin. "That's what royalty seems to do. Do nothing for as long as possible."

Matthew was having none of this.

"Doing nothing is not an option anymore. The politicians have failed. There has to be a leadership that goes beyond them. The King entrusted me with the responsibility of making sure that Edward becomes a symbol of planetary togetherness."

"Dash it. I wish I wasn't heir to the throne. I wish I were a common working man. Oh hang it all. Come, Tarquin, I need to talk to you. We'll let these two argue."

Edward marched back inside the Temple. Pushing aside partygoers, he disguised forceful shoves used to make progress as the playful antics of royal horseplay. With Tarquin following behind, Edward made his way out to the quayside, where he climbed aboard his walnut launch. Clambering down a few steps into the cabin, he motioned Tarquin to join him and close the door.

There followed a royal declaration.

"Right, that's it."

"Sorry, old chap?" said Tarquin in his put-on Earth accent.

"I don't want to be king, and I want you to help me get out of it."

"Me? I don't see what I can do."

"I've been reading about one of my ancestors, Edward VIII. He married an unsuitable woman. A divorcee and an American, if you please."

"So, are you going to find yourself a divorced American? I don't think people mind about those things anymore."

"No, no. You don't understand. Divorced Americans might be alright now, but there is still such a thing as an unsuitable royal spouse. The Archbishop thinks I'm gay so I'm going to go with that. It's still a problem for the heir to the throne you know."

"Really?"

"Because of the need for an heir. It's frowned upon. And if I add Martian to the mix, so much the better. How about a marriage of convenience, Tarquers? It would just be for show. I know you like all the royalty stuff and you would be helping me out."

"You want me to marry you?"

"Yes, how about it? Even if I'm not king, I will still be royal. And if I'm royal, you will be too."

Edward, despite his panic, felt he was thinking with otherworldly prescience. He knew Tarquin had endured a difficult youth on Mars, son of a prospector who had finally struck it rich. He was the newest of new money, and those people were often keenest on the trappings of old royalty.

"I don't know what to say. I do like girls, Edward."

"Yes, yes, Tarquers, so do I, in moderation. You can do

whatever you like afterwards. That's one of the good things about life as a royal. Marriages of convenience are a tradition. They sort out the dynasty and whatnot. They don't mean anything."

People now began to surround the boat, drawn by the simple fact that Edward was inside. The prince could see his friend staring out at the multitudes, who were singing *Jerusalem* with sporting-event emotion. Tarquin looked back at Edward, a mixture of fear and astonishment on his face.

Edward still had a golden glass in his hand, and chose this moment to drain the last drop. His speech was a combination of slurred chat and declamatory singing:

"Bring me my bow of burning gold; bring me my arrows of desire... I desire not to be king, Tarquers. Help me out. We're young and we're free. No one is going to tell us what to do. What do you say? Do you want to live a life that others have chosen for you? Or do you want to ride into your own future on a chariot of fire?"

Edward spun around in a Bacchic dance expression of liberty, before slumping on a scarlet sofa in the warmly wooded saloon. Tarquin downed what was left of his own drink.

"I need to think about this, Edward."

CHAPTER 14
(ORIENT EXPRESS)

Prince Edward passed beneath the arched entrance of Victoria Station - or The London, Chatham and Dover Railway Station as King John liked to call it. He glanced upwards and saw Victoria's sculpted mermaids languishing in their grey stone sea, relaxing under the weight of a building resting on their bare shoulders. They ignored their latest visitors, concentrating their attention on protecting stone ships sailing beneath their time-ravaged arms, ships that sailed back to an era when boat trains left here for continental horizons.

The royal party made its way down Platform 2 towards a line of Pullman carriages, dark blue and cream paintwork glowing under yellow station lights. Edward paced at the back, worrying with his teeth at a small imperfection on a fingernail, periodically holding his hand in front of him to study his work. He watched on as King John stopped to speak with a dedicated band of Orient Express volunteers.

"It must be difficult keeping these trains running," said the King to a man whose timeworn face sat below a neat, pale blue kepi, and above the high collar of a crisp colour matched jacket with golden trim.

"Well, sir, it is hard to compete with virtual travel, but we do our best. Your contributions have been very welcome, and were the only reason we could continue a service last year."

"Absolutely marvellous, this is," boomed Montagu, who was using his reproduction, early twenty-first century smart phone to talk to March and Devonshire. Edward thought the idea was that they travel in the style of the twentieth century, but he wasn't going to quibble.

"You're where? They'll keep you wrapped up in red tape for hours, you poor sods." Turning to King John, Montagu chortled. "If they get out of London I'll be amazed. The documentation you need to get a car any distance today is appalling. I think we've got plenty of time to look at this lovely old train."

Montagu, seemingly confident in his competitors' problems, stopped with everyone else next to the rear carriage in a line of four. The elderly railway inspector explained that this was a display carriage used when Evening Star was on museum duty. There was a short tour of the exhibition, with Fred, an animatronic British railway worker, in an orange, hi-vis jacket, giving a cheerful and informative outline of the rise and fall of the railways.

After sloping around the museum car, Edward thought they were about to board the train, but King John led a detour down to the locomotive. Here it was necessary to admire Evening Star, built in 1960, the last of Britain's steam engines. Evening Star burbled and breathed, steam rising from her funnel, around wheels and from every seam and joint. It seemed that this machine was working hard just standing still. The sight of Evening Star even broke through the shell of anxiety surrounding Edward. It was clear that steam locomotives used only a small part of their energy on the mundane business of getting from A to B. There was plenty left over for drama and spectacle, with great scope for a demonstration of power in noise, heat, and mushroom clouds of smoke. Steam locomotives were like royalty in that sense. People liked them because they made power visible, even if this power was inefficient and could not compete in the modern world.

After looking at Evening Star, Edward hauled himself into the royal carriage, with the help of a pair of golden handrails each side of an open carriage door. The royal suite consisted of two linked lounges, four private bedrooms, a study and bathroom. In each sitting room, a red shaded lamp gave warm illumination at a window table. Edward made his way through to the second lounge area where he sat hunched and alone. He listened to Montagu in the neighbouring compartment talking to March and Devonshire on his mobile phone. Their conversation made it clear that the camper van had escaped London and was heading towards Dover to catch the Heritage Ferry.

Victoria retreated away, merging into the tapering world that follows railway tracks everywhere. This sinewy old railway district of narrow houses with elongated gardens riffled by, reminding the preoccupied prince of a Victorian seaside illusion, which bonneted ladies would spin with a crank.

It was just after Edward had flapped away a selection of cakes and pastries that the train pulled into a closed platform at Folkestone's Old Channel Tunnel Terminal. It was easiest to do what his grandfather wanted, and follow him along the platform to say farewell to Evening Star, which couldn't operate in the Old Channel Tunnel. Edward patted the slab sided boiler casing. Sensing weight beneath his hand, he knew that given time, even a world as substantial as this would melt away. The prince was on the threshold of a great change in his life. His former self would soon be an Evening Star, gone by morning.

Edward was back in his comfortable compartment, when a shudder of uncoupling and coupling gave notice that a newer locomotive had replaced the old. Movement away from the platform into the tunnel felt smoother, and sadder.

The train was soon speeding across wintry French countryside, pulled by a former royal diesel locomotive called Royal Sovereign. Edward could hear the King's enjoyment of the ongoing adventures of March and Devonshire in their camper van, who remarkably were also now in France and trying to get out of Calais. Montagu was in continuous and riotous conversation with them.

"Arrested?" he roared in delight. "You've got yourselves arrested?"

Montagu proceeded to provide an update of the bleeding obvious.

"They've been arrested. Some rubbish about incorrect historic vehicle documents. I'm telling you, a car these days needs an engine, four wheels and a lawyer. By next year they'll have closed the historic vehicle loopholes, and that will be the end of driving."

There was something very annoying to Edward about the ring tone of Montagu's phone. It was soon ringing again

"Where the Gordon's Gin are you now? Really? How? Paid them off? Wonderful. In the best traditions."

Edward stood up. He had to walk through the King's compartment to get to the corridor. His grandfather's eyes followed him, but he was enjoying himself, and probably felt that Edward couldn't get up to much mischief on a train.

Edward hurried down the corridor and into the dining car, where waiters were preparing tables for dinner. A maître d'hôtel answered his greeting with a bow from the chest.

Beyond the restaurant car, Edward reached Logistical Support. This was an office on the move, with press secretaries and administrators hard at work. Bacon was standing beside one of the desks, conferring with a darkly suited official. He looked up as Edward approached.

"Is everything alright, Your Highness?"

"Yes, Bacon. I just want to have another look at that museum exhibition. Jolly interesting it was. Do you think you can arrange for me to have some peace there for a while? I'm feeling a trifle overwrought what with one thing and another."

"Of course, sir. I'll see that you're not disturbed."

Edward fancied there was a glint of suspicion in Bacon's eyes. A railway museum was a strange place for a young royal to seek solitary reflection.

"Sometimes you just need to be alone, Bacon."

"Indeed, sir."

Edward, whistling *Jerusalem*, walked past the staff sleeping quarters and pulled open the door to the museum car. Here everything was as quiet as the past, a place where every uncertainty had played itself out. The past was like a kindly royal nanny, who picked up peace or war, happiness or sadness, and rocked it all to sleep. Edward reached into his pocket, taking out that same small, cylindrical, black object he had consulted during his evacuation from Folly Bridge. An outward finger swish soon increased the dimensions of this malleable device to that of an old mobile phone. Edward tried to steady his breathing.

"I'm ready," he said to nobody.

A shaky holographic image of Tarquin appeared beside him, dressed in a long tailed, formal jacket. He had never looked more like a young vampire. Edward muttered about second thoughts. The image of Tarquin flickered irritably.

"It's too late to back out now, Edward. My father has arranged everything."

"Right, marriage of convenience. Best all round. Everybody wins."

"Of course they do."

With Edward's last minute nerves apparently dealt with, the ceremony was about to begin. Edward and Tarquin stood side by side, with an appreciable gap between them, facing an open area in the middle of the museum car. A column of light appeared, guttered like a weak candle flame, and then vanished.

"Was that meant to happen?" asked Edward.

Tarquin was conducting urgent conversations with people faraway in his own reality. Agitated, he turned back to his intended.

"The link up with the minister has failed."

"What? Why?"

The distant conversation continued, with Tarquin reporting that seemingly a snowstorm and out of date hardware were responsible.

"Are we going to call it off then?"

Edward tried not to sound too relieved. Some determined people, however, were making their views known to Tarquin.

"Alright," he was saying. "I understand."

Tarquin pointed to the venerable shape shifter in Edward's hand.

"We can't link to your phone. Why don't you use a more up to date model?"

"I like this one."

"And you don't have any neural implants yourself?"

"No. The King doesn't like them. Not traditional. It was bad enough persuading him to have his memory boosted."

"Listen, can you find us something in here with nEXTsTAGE or above?"

"What? This is the museum car. There are old suitcases, timetables, station signs, pictures of Brunel. What do you want from me?"

Tarquin looked away, still getting advice from somewhere beyond his image.

"The android guide, you idiot. We're doing a search now to tell you how to connect to it."

Tarquin was nodding, intent on his continuing off-stage instructions.

"Ok, we're trying to access the guide."

"They will be wondering where I am soon. Maybe we should just forget it."

"Look under the clothing in the waist area."

Edward lifted up the hem of a garish, orange coat and felt around the waistband. Fred's unchanging expression seemed to convey disapproval. Finding a control panel, the prince followed some commands from Tarquin. Fred jolted under his hands, causing Edward to jump back.

"Dearly beloved," said Fred, his hands pressed together in front of him in a gesture of reverence. "We are gathered here in the sight of God and in the face of this congregation to join together these two people in holy matrimony, which is an honourable estate instituted by God himself, signifying unto us the mystical union that is betwixt God and the Church, which holy estate God adorned and beautified with his presence; and therefore is not by any to be enterprised, nor taken in hand unadvisedly, lightly or wantonly; but reverently, discreetly, soberly, and in the fear of God, duly considering the causes for which matrimony was ordained."

Tarquin told Edward to stand still. It had begun.

"I'm at a wedding presided over by a railway worker in an orange coat. Well that's a pretty picture."

Tarquin indicated that the prince should be quiet and recognise the importance of this moment. Fred looked solemn, as though he was about to announce a delay on all services into Paddington.

"I require and charge of you both that, as ye will answer at the dreadful day of judgement when the secrets of all hearts shall be disclosed, that if either of you know of any impediment why ye may not be joined together lawfully in matrimony, ye must now confess it. For be ye well assured, that so many as are coupled together otherwise than God's word doth allow are not joined together by God; neither is their matrimony lawful."

As he listened to this familiar litany, Edward could feel his ill-conceived plans unravelling. In his mind, he had foreseen a fuss, after which he would step aside for the planet's greater good, just like Edward VIII after his marriage to Wallis Simpson. Then following an amicable divorce, he pictured his respectable exile in Whitstable, living on the proceeds of his memoirs, a few light novels about badly behaved royals, and some after-dinner speaking. As he stood in front of Fred, Edward had the horrible feeling that his dream of shabby-chic, regal exile was not what the Martians wanted. Once they had their prince, they would not want to lose him.

It was soon over. There was an exchange of rings, followed by a difficult handshake.

"That's that then."

"My father will make an announcement in the media."

"No, Tarquin. Wait a bit. I want to tell my grandfather before anyone else knows. At least I owe him that."

Tarquin nodded, looking to one side for confirmation that this was acceptable.

"Alright, Edward. There will be no announcement for now. Tell your grandfather and get back in touch with us. You will then receive your next set of instructions."

Tarquin vanished, and Fred slumped back in his chair.

"What just happened?" asked the confused automaton, before his power saving systems shut him down.

Edward was alone with the neatly arranged debris of a lost

time. He stood still for a moment wondering what he had done, before starting to make his way back to the royal carriage. Bacon looked up as Edward wobbled through Logistical Support.

"Is everything alright, Your Highness?"

"Yes, Bacon, never better. A period of reflection has done me good."

"That is gratifying, sir."

Edward swayed onwards, through the restaurant car - the maître d' bowing once again - then back through his grandfather's compartment, to his own quiet sitting room. Edward sank down into his seat. He had made his bid for freedom, and freedom felt very much like entrapment. From the King's compartment, he heard a shout of triumph from Montagu.

"That's it; they're in a snow drift. They're going nowhere."

CHAPTER 15
(SCHONBRUNN
PALACE, VIENNA)

The camper van arrived at Schonbrunn Palace over an hour before King John's train pulled into Vienna's Westbahnhof Station.

"Never underestimate a classic car enthusiast with a shovel and some tools," the King counselled a downcast Montagu. "After all, you are one of them."

These words cheered the frustrated aristocrat. King John had learnt this trick long ago. The best victories are those that don't diminish those on the losing side.

Celebratory drinks were supposed to follow at the palace, but heavy security delayed the royal party at Westbahnhof. When King John finally reached the palace he was exhausted, and proceeded with Bacon towards his suite. Before he got there, an urgent need to empty his bladder necessitated a detour to one of the bathrooms. Emerging back into the corridor, he had the vague sense of Bacon's attention being elsewhere, something to do with a group of royal bodyguards pursuing an out of control android railway worker, who had jumped off the train yelling something about wanting to have his normal circuits back.

A gap in the King's memory opened up, a missing chapter in a story, which left him not knowing where he was. He wandered off in search of clues, finding a group of people who were in equal need of guidance. They were shepherded by someone who seemed to know the way.

"This is the room where, in 1918, Charles I of Austria gave up any role in government following the end of the First World War. And so ended one of the world's great dynasties. Charles was to fail in his long struggle to restore the Hapsburg monarchy. Perhaps he would have been happy to know that so many years later, the Schonbrunn did become a royal palace once again, donated to the world monarchy. It is now one of King John's most splendid residences; a fitting role for a former summer home of the Hapsburgs. The Schonbrunn of course is only one of many palaces belonging to the world monarchy. Upgrade to a membership pass today and you will enjoy access to the Hofburg here in Vienna, the Escorial, the Winter Palace in St Petersburg, Versailles, the Forbidden City, Rajasthan's Umaid Bhawan, the Tokyo Imperial Palace, as well as London's Buckingham Palace and Windsor Castle."

John shuffled along with the tour group, feeling in some vague way that all this had something to do with him. Who was this intriguing King John? Hearing about him was like listening to a familiar song, and forgetting the title.

The old man felt a hand on his shoulder.

"Your Majesty, come with me. You need some of your medicine."

"Are you a doctor? Can I trust you? Actually I seem to remember that I don't trust doctors."

"I'm not a doctor. Come this way, Your Majesty. Don't worry."

King John came back to himself in the suite of rooms that formed the Schonbrunn's royal residence. Returning memory brought back both happy and painful scenes. Of all the royal palaces, Schonbrunn had to be the most glorious. With a sigh combining profound thankfulness and deep regret, the King remembered that it was his favourite because it had always been his wife's favourite. She had loved the bright, sunny, yellow façade, and always tried to bring the family here every summer. In an unnatural rush of information entering his recovering mind, John found himself knowing the history of bereaved kings who destroyed palaces associated with their dead wives. Richard II of England ordered the demolition of Sheene Palace after his wife Anne died there in 1394. King John did not have any authority to destroy palaces, and even if he did, he would never think of doing such a thing to the beautiful Schonbrunn. This was a place to remember happier days. He knew he had been a distant father and grandfather. For most of the year, the press of work meant it was impossible to spend much time with the family. However, here it was different. Gruffness could not survive splashing games with the children in the Schonbrunner Bad swimming pool, closed on Tuesday afternoon for royal use.

King John had a study overlooking the Great Parterre. The day after his arrival in Vienna, he had come here at dawn, greeting his concerned night security team in the corridor outside his room with a crisp "good morning". It was unusual for the King to be up and about by himself, before his staff had brought him tea and his beloved paper edition of *The Times*. John told himself that he had to be up early to keep an appointment with his Vienna doctor.

While John thought he liked people who told him the truth, the doctor's words irritated him:

"I am sorry. While it is easy to hide the reality of your condition from the world, it is not right that I hide it from you."

Demanding that others face reality felt empowering. A similar demand coming in the opposite direction did not feel quite the same.

"I suggest you take a few days rest here in Vienna and then return home for Christmas. You should be able to enjoy the festivities normally. After that, things will become more difficult. We will then have a choice to make."

"This new thing you mentioned last time?"

"That's right. It seems to provide short-term improvement, sometimes of a dramatic nature. The downside is that it may shorten what remains of your life. The choice really is between quality and quantity. I am sorry there is nothing else I have to offer."

Following this brief consultation, King John spent a few hours in his study lost in reflection. Heated paving had cleared the Great Parterre of snow, and zonal temperature systems developed for Mars kept colourful garden displays on the Parterre in flower. Nevertheless, it could not always be summer. This sense of the brevity of human life was ironic when it seemed such a long time until lunch. A healthy royal had his time regimented so that it passed unnoticed. Illness had weakened that structure. There were now long gaps in the day, when all the King had to do was reflect.

Lunch came just after 1pm, a light meal served by Boles. Boles was now acting more as a nurse and care coordinator, while Bacon had taken over most business duties once attended to by the King. On the lunch tray was a document, which Bacon had prepared on old-fashioned, royal watermarked paper. Downstairs, Oxford's selection event was taking place, following final trials on the Danube's cold waters. Bacon's document was an advance copy of the crew list, with short explanatory notes.

The King indicated that Boles should sit in a chair beside him.

"Have our requirements been met?" he asked.

"I think so, sir. There was some negotiation, but Nice knows where his duty lies."

The King picked up the document and started to read:

<u>Oxford Crew</u>

Cox

Jerry Dramhaggle: a determined, straightforward, competitive Martian. Dramhaggle has spent two years at Oxford. He knows Earth well and has become something of an Earthophile.

Stroke

John Northcote: an Earth resident of American descent, who until recently was uncomfortable around Martians. He has overcome this prejudice through working with Martian crewmates.

Seat 7

Nico Wanyamwezi: reputed to be a descendent of a porter who helped British explorers in Africa. Wanyamwezi likes to say that his forebears weren't exploring; they were simply travelling with a few outsiders.

Seat 6

Harold Franklin: a son of the famous Franklin exploring family. Traditionally Franklins have a reputation for foolhardy daring. Both Harold's father and grandfather were lost in space. Harold himself is proving to be more cautious, while retaining a portion of his family's famous audacity.

Seat 5

Caroline McMercy: daughter of an entrepreneur who made her fortune in the drinks business, principally in exports to Mars. Caroline has spent time on Earth and Mars. Following a Martian hiking accident, she has received extensive medical enhancement.

Seat 4

Norbert Maanberg: born in a moon colony, Mannberg's family lost a fortune in the lunar speculative collapse, leaving him to pay his own way through school and college. Difficult early experiences have instilled impressive drive and self-discipline.

Seat 3

Prince Edward.

Seat 2

Tarquin Van Cello: son of the CEO of the most powerful mining company on Mars. The Van Cellos have strong links to Earth through their political influence in the Mars research domes.

Bow Seat

Matthew Nice (President): son of two career civil servants in the Earth government. In partnership with the coaching staff, he has shown admiral abilities in seeing through government plans for this Oxford crew.

The King looked up.

"Good. You've chosen well. I see Earth Mars links here, established space exploration families, and of course the young lady with extensive medical enhancement. All of that will be useful. I see they've given Edward seat three."

"Yes, sir."

Boles couldn't help a subtle clearing of the throat, which the King knew was as close as he would get to a chuckle when in his company and on official business.

"Inevitable really," said John nodding. "The gimp seat. They weren't going to give him anything else. I see that Nice has taken the bow seat. Odd that. I thought he would go at stroke."

"Apparently Nice prefers the bow because from there he can keep an eye on everything. He also has a perfect technique, which is so vital for the bow. Do you want him moved? Such is the importance of your role in the McMercy arrangement, they will do anything you say."

"No, no, leave him where he is."

"As you wish, sir."

"And what about Alistair Fitzwhistle? I thought he was in at seat four."

"You can, of course, override the decision, Your Majesty, but it was felt that Fitzwhistle is a rower and a student of average ability. As an old friend of your grandson, he was useful in settling Edward into the crew. Beyond that, the selectors felt Fitzwhistle had little to offer. They have, therefore, made the judgement that others show more potential both for the purposes of winning the Boat Race, and in supporting Edward into the future."

The King nodded.

"Can't carry dead weight. Shame though. I always liked Alistair. Put him in the second boat as consolation."

"As you wish, Your Majesty. I will confirm the crew with Nice."

"Good. Once you've done that, please get Edward up here."

"Of course, sir."

The King rested while Boles went downstairs with the final list. He must have dozed, because it only seemed a few moments before the prince appeared. Edward was his jovial public self.

"Well, Boles, who would have thought it? Me in the Blue Boat; there's a turn up."

"Indeed, sir."

"Life's a rummy thing sometimes, Boles."

"Very true, sir."

"Can't actually row very well."

"Indeed not, sir."

Once Boles had left them, Edward's sunny demeanour faded. The King gestured that he should sit down on a long, yellow sofa.

"Congratulations on getting into the Blue Boat. I know it will mean a lot to you."

"Oh, doubtless."

"This will be good for you. It will be useful preparation for what lies ahead."

"Ah, about that. I have something of an announcement."

"Tell me later. We have a lot to get through."

"No, I want to tell you now. Please don't take this badly, but I am married."

"You young people and your humour. Yes, all very amusing, but we have much to do. Let's get on."

"It's true. I have married Tarquin Van Cello. We had a virtual ceremony on the train. I have a certificate."

"What did you say? My hearing isn't as good as it used to be."

"Nobody ever listens to me, and asks what I want. Well, I've married Tarquin, and that will make it very difficult for me to be king."

Edward held up his certificate, displayed on his phone, the device enlarged so that an older person could make out details without too much strain. The King called Boles in and asked him to run a check on the identification number. Boles made a call, before confirming that the number was indeed valid.

The King sagged forward, before rearing up again.

"You fool!"

Edward pouted.

"I know this will cause trouble, but sometimes sacrifices are required. That's what you told me duty was. I have a duty to myself."

"Duty? You idle young pup. You have no idea what you've done."

"What I have done is find the courage to finally be my own person."

"By conducting a sham marriage with a Martian man?"

All of the words that the King now tried to say came out as coughs. Edward jumped to his feet.

"Somebody help him!"

Boles hurried to his master's aid.

"I'll leave you to it, Boles," said Edward standing in the doorway. "He seems a bit upset."

"Don't you go anywhere," shouted the King. "I'll talk to you shortly."

Boles slammed the study door in Edward's face.

It was in fact half an hour before Boles opened the door again. Edward was still there, standing to a kind of shocked attention. The King was resting on his yellow sofa, calmed with a combination of comforting words, sedatives, and some initial crisis planning.

"This situation was difficult enough. You have made it even more complicated. Now you will listen and do as I tell you. We have to buy ourselves time. Tarquin is the son of one of the most powerful families on Mars. My advisors consider it diplomatically unwise to give the impression that they are unworthy. Therefore, we have recognised the wedding, but we do not accept that the ceremony was fitting for an heir to the throne. I understand an android railway worker in a hard hat conducted the service. The Martians have agreed to keep quiet about this wedding. They are now under the impression that we are discreetly organising a ceremony of a more appropriate nature. I know Van Cello and if there's one thing he loves, it is respectability. This gives us time to talk to the lawyers and work out what to do."

The King wavered. Boles stepped forward in concern. A raised hand restrained him.

"You have created a mess here."

Edward looked at the floor.

"The Martians will keep quiet, and so must you. If you make any kind of announcement there will be trouble, with us and the Martians."

Edward said nothing. His grandfather judged that for all the boy's bluster he would welcome any delay in the storm of consequences which would soon fall on his head.

"Leave me, Edward."

With the prince gone, King John didn't look at his faithful companion. He was gazing out of the window.

"Boles, I don't intend to stay as long as planned. It's just going to be a few days. Please arrange for an early return to London."

The King continued staring out at the view. He could see a large group clustered around a camper van parked on the Great Parterre.

"You had better let Montagu know."

"Of course, sir."

CHAPTER 16
(ORIENT EXPRESS)

King John did not have much time to take the short rest in Vienna that his doctor recommended. He talked to lawyers and advisors in secret conclave. These meetings left him exhausted.

Journeying home, the royal compartment was like an empty goods wagon, filled with nothing but the rhythmically broken sounds of wheel upon rail.

The regular tones of an old mobile phone roused the King from a half slumber.

"Yes, Montagu. You did what to the van? Most amusing. Well I won't distract you while you're driving. That would never do. Keep your eyes on the road, Montagu."

An unsteady finger stabbed at the red end-call button.

"Not that I have breath to spare on giving useless advice," muttered the King.

"I am sorry Lord Montagu is not here," said Bacon.

"All that shoddy appeal to the sanctified privacy of health matters," scoffed the King. "The only strong emotions that man is capable of dealing with were those related to cars, sports, and food."

This was true. Yet the King found it hard to feel anything but affection for Montagu, in whose company problems seemed to melt away. The only thing was, when problems occurred,

Montagu tended to melt away as well.

As winter scenery flowed by, Boles and Bacon took turns to sit with their master. Nothing engaged him, except Bacon's announcement that the Cambridge crew list had arrived. Buckingham Palace had sent this on, following a selection event in Henley. While King John had been instrumental in Oxford's crew selection, he had also been talking to the authorities at Cambridge. He felt sure that the people James would associate with now would be significant in his life to come. It was important to control who those people were. As with the Oxford list, Bacon had provided accompanying notes.

Cambridge Crew

Cox

Marina Blackwood: born in Valle Marineris, daughter of one of the oldest Martian families. The Blackwoods, are as close as Mars comes to nobility. Her small stature belies a natural authority. Initially hostile to Earth, her view has changed since getting to know Prince James. Miss Blackwood is a promising candidate for queen consort.

Stroke

Francis Paulo (President): son of a planetary trading family. Paulo's family has impressive and historic trading connections with Mars, using a base on the moon of Phobos. He is a charming and effective entrepreneur.

Seat 7

Emilio Branson: a descendent of a family that made a fortune in private space ventures, when state support was lacking. Branson is self-contained, pragmatic, and ruthless when necessary.

Seat 6

Jocelyn Raymond: a refugee from a religious community on Mars. It is highly unusual for a member of one of these groups to seek an education outside their own nominated colleges. Jocelyn is socially isolated, and a good candidate for assimilation into the royal circle.

Seat 5

George Tyndale: a former musical director in the Coldstream Guards, recipient of a biomechanical arm fitted following an injury sustained in an accidental explosion involving faulty theatrical pyrotechnics. Following his army discharge, he became a celebrant for civil weddings and funerals, hoping to make enough money to supplement a grant the army provided to attend university. He has potential in the provision of a new direction in royal ceremonial.

Seat 4

Roger Nansen: a member of the Nansen computing and virtual reality dynasty. Nansen could provide James with useful guidance in the province of virtual reality.

Seat 3

Prince James.

Seat 2

Sarah Van Diemen: daughter of a family which made a fortune in exploration, designed for commercial gain rather than the expansion of knowledge. Sarah's quiet manner is deceptive. She is tough and resourceful.

Bow Seat

Constantine Moritz: son of one of the oldest colonial families in the solar system, with branches on most inhabited planets or moons. He is confident, wealthy, urbane, and a natural opponent of various moves for colonies to become fully independent. He thinks governments should run the solar system as a benign empire with highly educated and able people like himself in charge.

King John put the list down. He had arranged the pieces on his chessboard. Now the game would play out.

CHAPTER 17
(LONDON ROWING
CLUB)

At the London Rowing Club beside the Thames at Putney, James was hard at work on a rowing simulator. Everything about this experience was fake, except for one thing - the pain. Unfortunately, that was real.

"Typical," snapped Marina standing beside him.

James tried to listen but it was difficult to concentrate on anything beyond the growing agony in his body as he tried to maintain a punishing stroke rate. Nothing could compete with the hurt that is rowing.

"Typical."

The prince was able to manage a weak nod in reply. Spoken words were impossible.

"So, while he's been relaxing on a luxurious jaunt in Vienna, you are here training; and he's the heir and you're not. Monarchy is so unfair. Come on," urged Marina. "Break it down into packets of five strokes. Two more minutes. Pull harder. Harder I say."

It seemed cruelly ironic that Marina was taking out her frustration with the lazy prince on the hard working prince.

"The race is only a few months away, and Dramhaggle says Edward's been doing nothing... Come on, count it down...

And considering your grandfather's medical condition I'm sure Edward's poor attitude is something he could do without."

James could now barely hear what Marina was saying, let alone answer her. It would be so easy to stop. Everything was telling him that it made sense to stop. Marina failed to acknowledge any of his distress. She just launched into a general, anti-royal diatribe.

"Why do you still have a monarchy anyway? Surely, it can't go on. We need meritocracy where the best rise through talent and hard work. How can someone be entitled to prominent position through an accident of birth? Only on Earth could you even contemplate still having such a system."

James tried to listen but his senses seemed to be shutting down. All he could think about were the next five strokes. It would go on like this forever. Then very clearly, he heard Marina announce that he had done enough.

Collapsing forward, James heaved air in and out as hard as he could. He had the vague idea that this was the only way to stay alive. After a few minutes, higher functions began to return. He was able to straighten up. Another minute and he was able to look at Marina, who was studying him.

"Not bad," she said. "You demonstrate commitment even if you haven't much to show for it."

Within twenty minutes, the prince had showered, changed his clothes, and was having a drink. However, James was dismayed to find that, as far as Marina was concerned, this rapidly cooling beverage represented more training. Marina insisted they sit outdoors on a freezing balcony overlooking the Thames. She wouldn't allow a fleece hat, which meant that the only article of clothing keeping the royal head warm was a cap in London Rowing Club colours, dark blue with vertical white bars.

"We can go inside in a minute," said Marina. "But first you have to take the cold, and tell me why Earth still has its monarchy."

James clutched at the fading warmth of his mug of tea.

"Oh c'mon, Marina."

"No, you've got to be able to think when you're cold and exhausted. So tell me, the monarchy. Why?"

James thought for a moment, looking down at his drink, brown like Thames water, even as the polished perfection of its surface reflected winter sunlight. Then he started to talk, using a speech drummed into him by Boles for moments like this.

"Back in Earth's eighteenth century there was a man named Samuel Johnson. He was a very clever man, a writer, and compiler of the first English dictionary. One day he found himself arguing with a successful young author, a republican who showed no courtesy to noblemen."

"No courtesy to noblemen?" said Marina in mock horror.

"That's right. Now please don't distract me. Where was I?"

James took a sip of lukewarm tea and continued.

"Johnson told the disrespectful writer that he should think of a shoemaker. The shoemaker provides a vital service in the shoes he makes, but is not paid as much for his work as the writer. This is odd, since people could get along much better without the writer's books than they could without the shoemaker's shoes. So how do you grade what people do, and what they deserve? What we have is a continual struggle for precedence where there are no fixed rules for the distinction of rank, and where society can never come together in the celebration of something, or someone, that everyone feels is special. So here on Earth we have a stand in, which we call royalty. It is a distinction of rank universally accepted because we allow it to be accidental. I was simply born a prince and I don't have to argue whether I deserve to be a prince, or if I'm a good or bad prince. I simply am one, and when people all need something to celebrate together, I step into the breach and do my job of being a special person for everybody, or nearly everybody. I don't count you, of course."

The wind whipped across the Thames, its waters choppy and disturbed. Marina leaned forward as if about to say something, raising a finger to make a point, but never making it. She shook her head in something like irritation, tinged with grudging regard.

"Come on, let's get you inside. You look freezing, which is pathetic. If you want chilly, you should come to Mars."

"My tea's cold," grumbled James.

"We'll get you another one."

Nothing it seemed could keep James from seeking warmth on the other side of the door. Unfortunately, someone was standing in his way. The short peak of a London Rowing Club cap covered this stranger's eyes, leaving straight lips of a tense mouth in shadow. This mouth opened to speak terse words.

"Your Highness, please go back onto the balcony. I need a private word with you."

The cap moved upwards revealing the face of its wearer.

"Alistair Fitzwhistle? What are you doing here? And stand aside, old chap, I'm frozen."

"On the balcony if you don't mind, Your Highness. It's quieter out there. I have information for you."

Something in Alistair's manner made James turn his back on warmth and comfort. Alistair indicated a table at the balcony's far end. This area was as windswept and uninviting as the deck of a ship on an Atlantic crossing in winter.

"What's going on?" asked Marina.

The little group sat down, alone and exposed above the Thames. James pulled his cap in a futile manner down over the tops of his ears.

"What's this all about?" asked James. "Why aren't you with Edward? I know they dropped you from the Blue Boat. Don't take it personally."

"I don't care about that. Edward is in the crew, so how good a crew can that be?"

"Quite."

What Alistair said was true. Nevertheless, this level of candour was unexpected.

"Miss Blackwood," said Alistair. "Would you mind getting us a drink?"

Marina clearly didn't approve of this request, but with a glance from James expressing royal bewilderment, she disappeared back inside the building.

Alistair hesitated, and then in an atmosphere of conspiracy he said in a low voice:

"I come on the King's business. I do not come for Edward. He has abused the faith we placed in him."

"What's he done now?"

"Edward has got married."

James sat back in surprise.

"Married?"

"Married."

"I knew he and Caroline McMercy were unlikely friends. Or is it Lady Beatrice? That would be a feather in the cap for Lord March. I didn't think Edward liked her though. Still, he has done his duty."

"He hasn't married Caroline, or Lady Beatrice. He's married Tarquin Van Cello."

James was still in a state of shock when Marina returned with a tray bearing three mugs. She put the tray down on the table in what appeared to be as motherly a manner as she could manage.

"You boys alright?" asked Marina sitting down.

"I've just heard some news," croaked James. "I can't... I can't... But what does this mean?"

Alistair glanced at Marina. James noticed.

"She can be trusted," he said.

"I can be trusted with what?"

"This could mean the end of the monarchy," said Alistair not without a hint of satisfaction.

"It's not the King, is it?" asked Marina looking worried.

"No, he's fine."

"What is it then?"

With the King's welfare assured, James noted that characteristic Marina expression, which suggested he was a boy overreacting to some crisis related to a sports team.

"What's happened? I'm sure it can't be that bad."

"This could be the end."

"That's the spirit," said Marina, pushing a mug of steaming liquid across the table. "Come on. Get outside of that. You'll feel better. Now what is this news?"

"I still can't believe it," whimpered James.

"Just tell me."

"My idiot brother has gone and married one of the other men in his boat, Tarquin Van Cello."

There were expressions of disbelief, followed by solemn confirmations from Alistair. Marina took off her blue and white club cap and laid it on the table. She addressed her question to it.

"But will they make him king if he's done that?"

"He's never wanted to be king."

"I didn't think he had any choice. But now..." James saw

Marina's grey eyes glitter as they turned towards him, "you could be king."

"They will still try and find a way out," said Alistair. "We must not say anything. The King sent me here today because he thought you should know. It was considered too dangerous to tell you in any other way. Giving you this message ends my association with your family. I've had enough. I'm going to see a careers advisor. Maybe I can get something in the event organisation line."

"Would you like to work for me?"

"No."

Alistair stood up.

"Goodbye, Your Highness, and good luck. I think you're going to need it."

CHAPTER 18 (HENLEY)

Almost as soon as they arrived back in England, the Oxford crew went to Henley for a few days of winter training. On a freezing December morning, Oxford had been hauling down the long drag between Temple Island and Henley. Edward, grumpy at having to get up early on such a cold morning was in his usual tuck position, staying out of trouble.

"I don't know why I bother," he grumbled. "It's not as if I actually do much."

"You know why you're here," said Jerry's tinny intercom voice. "And you might not believe it, but we appreciate your cooperation."

Edward, looking at his shoes, tried to judge if this was sarcasm, deciding that it actually wasn't. With the race approaching, everyone knew that Caroline could win it for Oxford, and that her presence would not be possible without Edward. Fifteen consecutive years of humiliating defeat would be over. Rowers would inevitably come to appreciate anything that contributed to victory, even if it was a hopeless oarsman.

"Shall I help pull the boat in?" asked Edward.

"If you like," came Jerry's casual reply.

The boat reached Henley Rowing Club. Landing was difficult, due to a thick film of ice near the riverbank, early stages of a freeze that generally gripped the Thames from January through February. Leaden sky threatened more snow. Edward climbed out of the boat as quickly as his below-par coordination would allow. Once on the quayside, he noticed Caroline was having trouble. She appeared in pain, struggling to push against the gunwales. Edward looked around for someone to help her.

"Give Caroline a hand," shouted Matthew from the boathouse. Edward realised that he was the nearest person to Caroline.

"Me?"

"Yes, you. Help her out of the boat."

"Right ho."

Edward sauntered back towards Caroline, who had now levered herself halfway up, and was having a rest at that point. Edward put his arms under her shoulders, like a man with no previous parenting skills holding a baby for the first time.

"Ups-a-daisy."

The prince hauled upwards, and after a shaky moment when his efforts seemed about to topple them both into the water, he managed to help Caroline step ashore.

"You nearly had us in the river there, but thanks anyway," she muttered.

"No problem at all."

"Back's very sore." She put her hands on her waist, tipped herself backwards, forwards and from side to side. "Just have to keep doing the exercises."

"Personally I think doing less exercise would be the answer."

The crew now had an hour or two before going back to Oxford. This left time for lunch in Henley. Edward didn't want to eat with the others. Since their marriage, his dealings with Tarquin had become uncomfortable. A breezy friendship between two heterosexual males does not a marriage make, even if it is a marriage of convenience. Edward was lamenting what he thought had been a plan of immense invention. He decided to go for a solitary walk to mull things over, which his security detail assented to in a disturbingly casual manner. They still seemed to be under orders to stand back and allow life to toughen him up.

With a fur hood pulled around his face, no one was going to recognise a famous prince. Meandering along the river path, watching his step, he padded over frosted snow. Then, looking up, there was Caroline McMercy standing in front of him.

"Caroline, old fellow, what are you doing here?"

"I couldn't face lunch with the boys."

Edward didn't require any more explanation. He knew what it was like to be an outsider.

Edward found that he was going for a walk in the same direction as Caroline, which meant it would be rude not to walk together. Edward was usually adept at empty talk, having conversed with so many strangers over the years. However, on this occasion he felt awkward.

"I hear rumours," said Caroline, breaking a long silence.

Edward bowed his hooded head, lurking amidst fur trim like a cornered rodent. It was forbidden to discuss the matter to which Caroline alluded. But after that touching scene at the quayside where he had actually helped another human being, he was feeling strangely expansive. Caroline was the only person on the crew he felt he could confide in.

"If anyone asks you about these rumours, please say it is just gossip and falsehood."

"Of course…"

"It was just a ruse to get me out of being king. I mean Tarquin's a jolly fellow and all that, but it was just a trick."

"What was a trick?"

"Marrying Tarquin."

"You married Tarquin?"

"Yes. I thought you said you'd heard rumours."

Edward scrunched further back into his furry cave.

"I'd heard you had married an unsuitable actress."

"Ah, yes, the actress."

"You married Tarquin?"

"No, no, it was an actress; lovely girl, salty line in humour, no royal connections; involved in a few films early in her career which are not universally admired."

The phrase "gales of laughter" occurred to Edward as scudding clouds of vapour puffed out from Caroline's hood.

"You married Tarquin, and now you regret it?" said Caroline once she had recovered herself.

Edward realised that further dissimulation was futile. Besides, he didn't want to lie to Caroline.

"I do regret it, but I had to try something. I thought it would get me out of being king. My whole life I have felt this weight of expectation. It started when my parents died. Ever since then I have had no choice in my life. When I'm king that will be that. My days will be an endless treadmill of engagements that will continue until I drop dead, or some crazy anti monarchist, or Martian or whoever, shoots me."

Caroline, it seemed was not ready to give advice to a frustrated royal: but then who was? The future of a king was hardly a situation you dealt with every day. Wanting to fill the ensuing hiatus, Edward thought about what he knew of Caroline. He knew that she had medically enhanced arms.

"It can't have been easy coming back after your accident. Of course you might not want to talk about it."

Edward hoped she wouldn't. He had only been spooked into asking about Caroline's arms by uncomfortable silence.

"Nobody here has ever asked me about it, except the physio. My arms make me a necessary embarrassment, you see."

"Quite. I mean, poor you. I am also a necessary embarrassment, to cover up your necessary embarrassment."

"Well that makes us quits then. And yes, having the arms has been difficult. Everyone thinks you are superhuman, but it's not like that. You're sore, aching, and wrong and out of balance."

She touched her back as evidence.

"There's this idea I have an unfair advantage, but people don't realise how difficult it is to come to terms with enhancement. When I first started using my arms, I was like a toddler again. I'm still learning now."

"So why did you have performance arms fitted? Why not go for something closer to what you had before, a finesse model perhaps?"

"Because as usual I gave in to my mother, the famous Charlotte McMercy. Have you heard of her?"

"She runs a drinks business, doesn't she? I believe I sampled some of her work at the Temple Island party. Quite made me forget my troubles. Good stuff. Though come to think of it, that was the same evening I proposed to Tarquin."

"My mother's products were never designed to help people behave wisely."

Edward noticed that as she relaxed, Caroline was sounding just a little more Scottish.

"She tried to get into the Blue Boat you know, when she was at Somerville. Always was a formidable feminist. My mother thought it deeply unfair that men were stronger than women, and was actually one of those behind the rule change which demands at least one woman in the Blue Boat. She got her rule, but as you can imagine she upset a lot of people and was never selected herself. That's why she wanted me in the crew. I spent my childhood trying to please her, doing sports, going on expeditions, working hard at school. Then I got into Oxford, and was in line for the Blue Boat. It all seemed to be working out perfectly, until I got lost on a Martian hiking expedition in the Atlantis Chaos, got a wee frostbite and lost most of my arms. I thought that was the end of it. It was a relief in a way. But my mother talked me into getting new performance arms. At the time, they seemed like a good idea. Now I flick through medical enhancement brochures and look at the finesse models. They're, well, I know I shouldn't say it, but they're just right for delicate work like cross stitch, crochet and the playing of musical instruments."

"I didn't know you liked those things."

"Well I do. I've taken up the clarinet to try to help me with the fine control, but it's not easy. So, thank you for asking, and yes, it has been hard."

Edward was not one for sensitivity and discussion of feelings. Nevertheless, while he had feared a lot of emotional opening up, after an awkward start the chat now flowed, transporting them along to a diagonal weir stretching across the Thames above Henley, regulating the great river and allowing rowers to use it as their playground. Edward and Caroline stopped. They didn't have time to go any further.

"We had better go back. This was… nice," said Edward.

"What was nice?" asked Caroline.

"You know, talking."

"It was nice," agreed Caroline.

"When I say nice, I mean interesting."

"Yes, very interesting."

"When I say interesting…. I mean…"

At this point Caroline McMercy stepped forward and gave Edward a hug.

"Thank you," she said into the side of his hood. "Thank you for listening. I know the others think you're hopeless, but maybe you're not so bad. You're a little mad maybe, but that's probably down to your genealogy."

Edward just about managed a nod in reply. The hug's power meant he was unable to speak, or breathe. He felt it would be rude to try to struggle free. These ridiculous scruples meant precious seconds were lost. By the time it became clear that Caroline was crushing him to death, the strength to mount any sort of resistance was melting away.

"I hope this is okay. I know you're a married prince and everything."

To Edward's limp horror, Caroline interpreted silence as tacit agreement to continue the hug.

"It was so nice of you to ask about my arms."

Edward now began to droop in those mighty arms.

"Are you alright?"

Caroline released her grip, Edward collapsing in a heap at her feet, where he drew a desperate breath.

"Oh my God, I'm sorry."

Caroline knelt down beside the panting casualty.

"It's the arms. I forgot to control them. Where does it hurt? Do you need a doctor?"

"I'm fine. Think nothing of it; far worse used to happen at school."

After a few moments of shallow wheezing and chest clutching, Edward looked around, expecting security to come running. But there was nobody except Caroline to help him to his feet.

CHAPTER 19 (SANDRINGHAM)

Christmas can be a difficult time for any family, serving to push volatile material into critical proximity. Everyone goes home for Christmas, and for Edward, Sandringham, the old stately retreat in north Norfolk, played the role of home.

Edward tried to stay out of the way during those dark late December days. He looked on as King John had become increasingly ill, willing the old man to get better. His willing was in vain. The King's walks around Sandringham estate were now only possible with the help of exo-skeletal crutches guiding his legs. Edward tried to avoid news reports, but no one could ignore a pervasive feeling of anticipation, the sense that a significant moment in royal history was approaching. The focus of all this expectation was the King's Speech, broadcast every year on Christmas Day. Martian media had fuelled rumours that King John would use his speech to announce that he was standing down in favour of Edward. This rumour combined with others, like a howling dog joined by dogs in distant houses, brewing up a single pack of noise that hung in the air like some many-headed ghostly creature from Greek mythology. Whisperings spoke of strange weddings. Wild, windblown surmises hinted at abdications. By Christmas Eve, it was almost as though a dramatic announcement by the King was a certainty.

Edward had almost come to believe the hype that suggested

he might be king after Christmas. Robbed of sleep by terror, he had lain awake into the early hours of Christmas morning. Now, sitting down to his Christmas lunch, he found himself trapped with various dreary relatives, masquerading as countesses, dukes, earls and princesses. Most gallingly of all, dinner incarcerated him with James and his awful new girlfriend, Marina Blackwood. On his own, with no one to keep his feet on the ground, Edward ricocheted between inner foreboding and outward arrogance.

He looked down at his festive dinner, each element arranged like a political map, denoting region by colour. Across the centre of this world sat a row of three Yorkshire puddings. In Edward's fevered fancy, these puddings became craters, probably the result of asteroids hijacked by Martian activists. Cranberry sauce looked like an outflow of lava, spreading across a blasted expanse of turkey badlands, bordered by desolate roast potato mountains. A patch of carrots was a burning city. Edward had no idea he could be so imaginative. The turbulent prince lifted a slice of turkey to his mouth, only to lay it back down on his plate.

"Off your food?" asked Marina.

"No. All very tasty as usual," replied Edward.

"Why don't we pull a cracker?" suggested Marina, offering Edward one end of a golden tube decorated with sprays of tinsel. "Maybe you'll win the crown that way."

Edward paused, before taking his end of the proffered cracker. He stared into Marina's eyes.

"Maybe your prize will be a little compass," he simpered. "You could use it to find your way back to Mars."

Edward yanked the cracker, adding a sly twist, which after a sharp crack, and a shower of yellow sparks, left a roughly torn golden baton in his hand. A storm of barking erupted from royal dogs.

"Take those bangers out," shouted King John from the head of the table.

Edward, in an attitude of melodramatic gloating, surveyed his winnings - a diaphanous, yellow fortune telling fish, a joke printed on a strip of paper, and a flimsy, red tissue-paper hat, which he pulled onto his head.

"That's the only crown you deserve," Marina hissed.

James sitting beside Marina leaned over and said as forcefully as the need for discretion at a royal Christmas dinner table would allow:

"Will you two stop it. He'll hear."

Edward spent the rest of lunch amusing himself by needling Marina. He made repeated attempts to put a paper crown on her neat bob of red hair. A number of hats became coloured balls hurled back in Edward's direction. It took a sharp word from King John to put an end to this boisterousness.

The King's Speech was due at 2pm Universal Time as measured from Greenwich. Its content was a closely guarded secret. Not knowing what his grandfather would say, Edward was one of billions of people across the solar system sitting down in their party hats, watching news feeds, wondering if the King was going to step aside. In settlements on the Moon, on Mars, on Martian and Jovian satellites, on the flight decks of interplanetary space ships, displays that usually presented impenetrable data might now show King John ruining a young man's life.

The address opened with its usual calls for goodwill and decency, followed by reminiscences about lost friends and family, intercut with images of smiling kings and queens of the past. There were supportive sentiments for those staffing essential services over the holiday period. Then came the moment everyone had been waiting for. King John spoke words that reached out to Edward and the wider solar system.

"And now in these difficult and uncertain times, I want you

all to know that I intend to serve the interests of unity and peace for as long as may be granted to me. When the time comes for the torch to pass to the next generation, rest assured that the succession will take place with due regard for unchanging law and tradition. The great chain of existence that unites us, and calls all of us to our duty in life, will not be broken. Past and future, near and far, we are all together in the end. However you may say it, and however you may honour it, I say happy Christmas to you all."

At this talk of the great chain of existence exacting its duties, Edward uncurled from his slouch. He watched the Christmas cracker fortune-telling fish twist on his hand. Boles and Bacon stood by their king, Bacon leaning down to whisper something. The King's reply was clear.

"Thank you, Bacon. That went rather well, I think."

Edward tore off his paper crown, and threw both it and fortune telling fish down amongst gold and red debris strewn across the white tablecloth. Both fluttered in a mocking fashion towards the table surface. He felt it was time for a grand gesture, but the drama of storming out palled somewhat when the massive dining room door proved too heavy to slam shut, its oak mass swinging in a disdainful and leisurely fashion. It was necessary to haul the thing closed, leaving Edward winded on the far side. He wasn't going to be king quite yet, and should have been happy. But his grandfather had made it clear that his marriage plan wouldn't stop the usual succession. After Marina's jibes about paper crowns, it was almost worth becoming king just to spite her. Then as Edward thought of the overwhelming prospect of his accession, panic rose within him, accompanied by a potent mix of stomach acid and recently eaten Christmas dinner. The prince leant his forehead against the door's rough, carved contours, and wondered what was to become of him.

CHAPTER 20 (THE BLACK HORSE PUB, CASTLE RISING)

Sandringham estate was a place in limbo. James felt as though he might stand forever within the borders of Christmas and New Year. He tried to tell himself that given his uncertain situation,

spending an eternity between December 25th and January 1st wouldn't be so bad. Nevertheless, seasonal claustrophobia hung upon him. As well as the stress of the King's illness, Marina and Edward would argue almost every time they met. To escape all this, James walked under grey December skies, along Sandringham's snow-dusted woodland avenues.

Royal routine ground on, until New Year's Eve when, just after supper, the King called James to his rooms. John was sitting in a high backed armchair, looking quite comfortable. It was almost possible to believe there was nothing wrong with him. He always did well in a crisis.

"James, I want you to see Showertree. It will be useful for you to talk to him."

This was not good news. The King only consulted the royal astrologer in times of real trouble.

"As usual, it is advisable to play down our connection with Showertree, so I have asked him to stay at the Black Horse. Security would not allow any meeting if they knew. With

Marina here, they're nervous about protestors tonight and have people at the gates. We don't want you to use any transport that can be tracked, so take Merlin and head down through Wild Boar Wood. I know the officer covering that area. He will leave you alone."

"Yes, Your Majesty."

It made James feel better to be as formal as possible. Later it also made him feel better to be riding Merlin, one of his favourite horses. Merlin in horse terms was a grey, though if James were painting Merlin he would have used pure titanium white, to depict an animal passing through the late evening like a ghost. During this whole ride, he was quite alone.

The Black Horse, close to Castle Rising, lay just outside the southern borders of Sandringham estate. It was only a few miles, but this ride held a heavy significance. James had never ridden a horse before with any purpose beyond recreation. Tonight he was taking Merlin on an actual journey, which made the ride feel like no other he had ever experienced.

Crossing Sandringham's boundary at a little used forest gate in Wild Boar Wood, James followed country lanes until he found himself skirting Castle Rising Wood. Then, on a bend in the road, he came to his destination. Four evenly spaced, latticed windows were a checkerboard of yellow in cold darkness. Eyes, acclimatised to a Norfolk night, looked up from the homely pub glow to a distant perspective of stars in a cobalt sky. A full moon blazed over a landscape of silhouette and shadow. It was almost as if the sky remained white in its essential nature, though someone had spread a dark wash across it.

James jumped down from Merlin, tying his rein to a fence in the pub garden. There was a moment's hesitation at the door of the Black Horse, before James stepped over the threshold.

He sensed warmth, and threat. James had no security detail. In his nervous state, he saw big men gathered around the bar as rhinos around a watering hole. The barmen were crocodiles hiding in the water, not moving much, but with the potential to strike at all the creatures crowding in on the life-giving wallow. James nearly turned back, but it was impossible to return to his sick grandfather with news that he had not found Showertree. Pressing on, he knew that diffidence would call attention to his presence just as powerfully as overconfidence. He tried to gain that average of behaviour, not standing out by virtue of weakness or strength. In this way, he shuffled and dodged across the crowded room without incident. He saw Showertree sitting in a wooden alcove, which seemingly might have served as a stable for Merlin. On a round table of polish islands in worn wood seas, stood a full pint of beer in a dimpled mug, the room's yellow lighting refracting through it, like a cubist study in brown and yellow.

Showertree stood up. With large, jovial, whiskery energy, he clapped James on the back, and guided him into a chair.

"The police are nervous tonight," said the prince. "They think there may be trouble. They've sealed off Sandringham. I had to come here on Merlin."

"These are difficult times, but like all times they will pass."

James was soon sipping a drink, and chatting. Neither he nor Showertree were saying anything particularly notable. There was no clever study of planetary movements and their interaction. The conversation focused mostly on sports and horses. Showertree kept glancing out of the window to check on Merlin. They started talking about the King and his long reign. Time slipped by.

James relaxed, now feeling quite at home in a place where he had initially been a vulnerable outsider. It was after this long preparation that Showertree sat back with a more subdued air. It became clear that the astrologer hadn't been indulging in idle chat after all. This was just a way of steadying the emotions before their conversation took a more difficult turn.

"I have something your grandfather asked me to get for you."

There was much shuffling through pockets of a battered tweed jacket, before Showertree placed a small, blue velvet box on the sticky table.

"It's a gift, a good luck charm if you will, for what lies ahead."

James popped open the downy lid. Inside was a gold band, with a series of circular indentations at regular intervals around the outer face.

"What does it do?"

"Perhaps it doesn't do anything. Maybe this is a symbol that I am giving you; the gift of no real help, so that you have the chance to develop as a man."

James couldn't help feeling that it would be nice to get a gift that did give him some actual help.

"So what do think might lie ahead?" asked James, slipping on the ring. "Do you think they will make me king?"

"The picture is very confused, Your Highness. You should prepare for a great challenge."

"What sort of challenge?"

"That is hard to say. Saturn indicates a series of stern tests, which will require unusual discipline and commitment. I hope that as demanding Saturn sets tests, he also provides the grit to see you through them. It does look as though you will become king. But I would say the same of your brother. The stars are sometimes cruel to those who would wish to be guided by them."

There was a long silence. James was aware that Showertree's glass was now almost empty, looking like a pile of wet, silver pebbles.

"Well thank you for talking to me, Showertree."

James noticed the clock above the bar. It was close to midnight.

"Merlin doesn't like fireworks. And he'll be getting cold. I'd better be getting him back."

Showertree walked James out to Merlin, who he patted on his long, white nose. The prince mounted his horse, and with a final farewell, he wheeled Merlin around and cantered away.

James rode through bright moonlight, shining in from Aquarius, according to Showertree. He crossed back into the realm of Sandringham. The estate borders were no defence against the distant percussion of fireworks. Merlin flicked his head, but kept moving along at a steady pace. James didn't like fireworks either. He had once read about a festival held on November 5th in the old United Kingdom, recalling events on a dark night in November 1605 when plotters tried to destroy the King and his Parliament. That sedition had been defeated, but for centuries afterwards, fireworks had acted out its imagined success, with bonfires playing the part of Westminster burning down. People threw effigies of plotters on their bonfires, fooling themselves that this was a celebration of revolution's defeat, while in fact they acted out revolution's fiery triumph.

Nearing the lakes, images came unbidden into James's mind. He pictured Sandringham House burning all the way along her majestic length, domed towers on the façade's southern end flaring like Roman candles.

A few hours previously, Sandringham had stood solid, traditional and inevitable. Now as Merlin rounded the Lower Lake, the grand house presented itself to James's imagination as a black, burnt out shell, etched against creeping ground mist infused by moonlight. Weary illumination in the King's quarters mimicked whitewashed sky, peering through ruined, glassless windows. Even when he saw that the house remained unharmed, James couldn't get those images of destruction out of his mind.

CHAPTER 21 (THE FROZEN THAMES)

King John was enjoying his journey from Westminster to Putney Bridge.

"I feel better," he announced, giving Bacon a hearty slap on the back. Bacon staggered under the blow.

"That is gratifying, sir."

He really did feel better. This had nothing to do with putting on a brave face during a public event. Everything seemed more vibrant, the Thames icefield shining almost as if bathed in summer sunshine. John always told his grandsons that duty was acceptance of pain now in exchange for benefit later. Today's trade off worked in the opposite direction, but feeling as he did he could not regret his decision to accept the medication his doctor had talked about in Vienna, a treatment granting him fewer but better days.

The King surveyed the Royal Sledge, a fanciful creation, which wouldn't have looked out of place on a Venice canal. There was an open section at the bow, with a cabin decorated in red and gold dominating the stern. King John wiped away gauzy curtains of brume and looked out at London's wintry scene. A recent memory treatment had provided data about a climate shift, collapsing ocean currents and temperatures obliging countries to act as one to survive. In many ways, cold weather had created the world over which he was monarch. As usual, information could not be trusted without emotion. John recalled the way weather stirred passions. There was an image in his mind of the Archbishop ranting about divine judgement expressing itself in rain, wind and snow.

King John smiled, remembering with silky ease how changing weather had influenced rowing. Rowers continued to exist in their bubble even in those dark times. His glittering memory recollected an article he had once read, describing the salt balance of human tissue fluids mimicking the salinity of ancient seas out of which life first crawled onto the land. This made sense to the King, who knew that human ingenuity spends most of its time trying to keep life the same in changing circumstances. Following this deeply conservative instinct, rowers had sought ways to continue enjoying their sport on frozen rivers, improvising iceboats mounted on skids, with standard oar blades replaced by steel spikes. Steering slides replaced rudders. Using these converted boats, crews would race between Putney and Mortlake in a high-spirited prelude to the proper Boat Race, which would take place in April. For many, February's Ice Race was better than the real thing. Thousands of people would line the frozen course, or skate behind competitors, cheering their favourites on.

The King revelled in his memories of Putney's Royal Frost Fair, which grew up around the race start line. Quickly erected geodesic domes enclosed rinks, on which London theatre companies staged lavish skating productions. A multitude of stalls sold self-heated clothing and a range of memorabilia. Ice sculptures were popular, hermetically sealed in display cases using Martian thermal technology. London chefs provided hearty food from barbecues.

After arriving at Putney, the King enjoyed watching crews honouring pre-race customs. Oxford and Cambridge, wine glasses in fleece-gloved hands, toasted one another, whilst shouting robust abuse. Once everyone had vented all their darkest feelings, the starter issued a call to order, before throwing a jug of hot, blue coloured water into the air, which transfigured into a shower of cerulean ice. At this signal, two boats shot off along the frozen tideway, the royal sledge giving chase. There was nothing like a sporting event to give a calming sense of business as usual.

This year, however, business was not proceeding as usual. While Oxford and Cambridge skimmed towards Craven Cottage, King John began to sense trouble. He had been around crowds all his life and had an ability to read them, like a seismologist knowing the ground over a tectonic fault. Birds wintering in wetlands opposite Fulham took flight on a mass of anxious wings. Just beyond Harrods Village, Hammersmith Bridge came into view, its span draped with banners condemning rowing crews that combined Martian and Earth people. A number of protestors were abseiling down, avoiding police cordons. They landed on the racing line, wrapped in Earth's Blue Marble flag.

The King saw a rolling tidal bore of alarm spread through crowds lining the river. His attention jumped back to the ice ahead as Cambridge turned hard left, trying to avoid Blue Marble activists. Cambridge slid onto its side and into ranks of spectators. Oxford overturned almost under the bows of the royal sledge, which had to swerve to avoid a collision.

An emergency stop threw the King forward off his seat, leaving him winded.

The King was able to get himself up off the floor, despite the urgent attentions of Boles and Bacon. He soon saw through the smoke screen of pretense thrown up by senior officials and police officers, suggesting that everything was under control. An undertone of panic was clear in official voices as they argued over how to evacuate the royal party to Buckingham Palace now that London's transport control grid had just collapsed

"The trouble with you people," said the King, hands on hips, his voice strong with recreated vigour, "is that you don't know your history. Those who know history have a chance to repeat it."

The King looked towards Bacon who was ready with praise for the royal aphorism.

"Oh, very good, sir."

"Look to history, ladies and gentlemen. If the grid has failed then the answer is obvious. We will follow the river to Westminster Pier. Once there we will need cars free of computers to take us on to Buckingham Palace. Only one man can provide transport of this kind at short notice. Bacon put a call through to Brooklands. Give Montagu authority to bring a few of his vehicles down to Westminster."

The police did not argue. The King was more than a figurehead in times of stress, just as a cup of tea is more than a beverage when an emergency worker puts a blanket around your shoulders after an accident.

"It will take about an hour for Montagu to get to Westminster. We shall use that time to provide assistance."

Visiting disaster sites had always been part of the job. A lift provided access to the glacial Thames. Medical science thrilled through old veins as the King knelt down to give comfort to casualties and those who treated them. He was pleased to see James holding a makeshift dressing against a woman's bleeding forehead.

"Do what you can. Where's your brother?"

"He's over there."

Edward was sitting on a couple of rolled up fleeces, with a foil blanket around his shoulders. A bruised hand was holding a mug of steaming liquid. He had his left leg stretched out in front of him as though trying to distance himself from the troublesome limb. King John leant down and whispered in his ear.

"Get up and start helping people. If you don't, I will rip that blanket off your back and tip that nice hot drink over your head. Is that perfectly clear?"

The young man paused for a moment, sighed, and struggled to his feet. The King addressed a nervous looking paramedic, to whom he had handed Edward's drink and blanket.

"Do you require assistance in getting the injured to hospital? We have plenty of room on the royal sledge."

"There are a number of people waiting for transport. Are you going past St Thomas's Hospital?"

"Yes, of course. The sledge is at your disposal."

The King used his new strength to help embark casualties. With the sledge finally full, he saw that Edward had assumed there was room for him.

"You coming?" asked Edward, who appeared to be putting on a futile effort to saunter past his brother, when only his right leg was up to sauntering.

"I think we should stay here. There are still some walking wounded we can help."

"But I'm heir to the throne," complained Edward. "I've hurt my leg. There are security issues."

"He might be right, sir," whispered Boles in the King's ear. "We have police here, but the situation is unpredictable. Perhaps we should evacuate the boys."

"No, Boles. At Edward's age, I was flying lunar search and rescue missions. A little risk is good for him."

The King watched with grim satisfaction as Edward turned to members of his protection team.

"Oh come on, you chaps. Surely this qualifies as danger."

The guards remained expressionless, affecting the manner of Household Cavalry posted in sentry boxes at Horse Guards.

"Oh well, can't be any worse than school, can it. Let's see what we can jolly well do for these unfortunate people."

Without Edward, the royal sledge made a stately progress back towards Westminster, this dignified passage offering a rebuke to disorder. With casualties delivered to bustling medics outside St Thomas's Hospital, a short journey followed across the river to a scene of chaos at Westminster Pier. Three dark green Land Rovers, seemingly a short column of the 1950s British Army attending trouble east of Suez, pressed through a turbulent mass of unprepared police, protestors of varied hue, and curious onlookers. Lord Montagu opened the door of his leading Land Rover, pushing a few people aside with the door and his sense of entitlement.

"Get in," he yelled, standing beside the car. "Land Rover, Series 1. You'll love them."

Before security personnel could gather their scattered wits, King John and his renewed vitality had forced a way to Montagu's vehicle sitting rugged on the snow. Montagu held the driver's door open as his monarch climbed into a cabin, apparently fashioned from tent canvas and lengths of scaffolding. A royal sigh of satisfaction suggested Rolls Royce luxury.

"Your Majesty, what are you doing?" shouted Boles. "Wait for your escort. The officer in charge has not given us the go ahead."

Montagu was unconcerned.

"Who needs an escort when you have Solihull engineering to protect you?"

King John idled just long enough for Montagu to climb into a passenger seat rendered flaccid by time and the buttocks of stocky army officers, and for Boles and Bacon, now a couple of squaddies on manoeuvers, to scramble through the rear tent flap. Then, with a sound of ratcheting gears, rattling engines, and horns braying like aristocrats telling ramblers to get off their property, the Land Rovers pushed out from the turmoil of Westminster Pier. They slithered through Whitehall and down Birdcage Walk, the winter wilderness of St James's Park on one side, lines of Georgian mansions to the other, each one like the stern of HMS Victory.

"Want to go for a drive?" asked Montagu.

"I think I bloody well do," answered John.

With Buckingham Palace now just beyond the Victoria Memorial, it was easy to take advantage of chaos and turn away down Buckingham Gate. The ragged royal motorcade found itself in Chelsea, speeding past lines of snow encrusted silver pods, paralysed by a breakdown of their central control, pulled over to the roadside to make way for emergency vehicles, which were not working either.

Boles leaned over a craggy spare wheel, attached to the bulkhead between rear cabin and front seats.

"I must suggest that we return to the Palace now, Your Majesty."

The King sighed and admitted that at some point they were going to run out of petrol.

"Talking of petrol," said Montagu, "have they given you a top up?"

"They've given me some four star."

Montagu and the King bellowed with laughter, while Boles and Bacon bounced around like bits of old farm equipment. It was in Fulham High Street that the King finally hauled on a skinny steering wheel, swinging into a U-turn on ancient, leaf spring suspension. An equally ancient two-litre engine took one of its characteristic "egad, sir, you can't be serious," gear change moments, before grudging acceptance gave way to dogged urgency. The King was enjoying himself. His doctors had finally done him some good.

Fifteen happy minutes later, the remnants of a lost army, of a lost country, pulled into the enclosed quadrangle of Buckingham Palace, as though a changing world outside had closed in, and this courtyard was all that remained. King John slid back his window and shouted over towards a security officer rushing towards him.

"Don't know what happened there. Took a wrong turning."

A group of soldiers, who usually stood in lines wearing ceremonial red jackets and funny fur hats, now appeared much more comfortable in combat green and helmets. Looking at them, after his exhilarating drive, John knew he had to make the most of renewed health, and try to suppress renewed recklessness.

CHAPTER 22 (THE ASHMOLEAN MUSEUM)

As soon as possible after the Ice Race, Edward headed back to Oxford, wishing to evade the pressures of London where divisionary plans for his second wedding continued. This journey felt like an escape, until his train stopped unexpectedly at Kennington, just south of Oxford. Even Edward, who did not keep up with current events, knew that this was one of many transport failures. Like his fellow passengers, the prince walked the last few miles, a member of a straggling group making its way along the Thames path, back towards the centre of the city. Limping along, wrapped in the same hooded coat that had concealed his identity in Henley, no one took any notice of him. Every step aggravated his painful leg, injured in the Ice Race disaster.

Later that afternoon in his rooms at Magdalen, a sense of dislocation was undiminished. The university had suspended all lectures and seminars. Edward didn't generally attend them, of course, but they provided a nice background structure. Four o'clock when you should have been at a lecture on Renaissance art and architecture was better than four o'clock when you didn't have to be anywhere at all.

Unwilling to stay in his room, Edward pulled on his coat, wrapped a black and white striped college scarf around his neck, and went for a walk around Oxford. In the gathering gloom of late afternoon, he shuffled between patches of yellow light, shining from Victorian street lanterns once illuminating the way to Narnia.

Now what was he to do? He felt adrift. Cold was breaking through his boots, and his fingers were numb inside their gloves. Edward was in Beaumont Street, passing a building that made him think of a Greek temple devoted to one of the ancient world's more extravagant gods. Pale stone did its best to reflect Oxford winter murk as the commodious sunlight of Mediterranean climes. Hobbling up a wide flight of steps, Edward favoured his injured leg. The few lectures on Renaissance art and architecture he had attended told him he was passing beneath an entrance topped with a dramatic entablature, supported by Ionic columns, or maybe Corinthian. He couldn't remember.

Edward pulled back his hood, and found his presence not causing any kind of fuss. Perhaps people assumed that a young man on his own could not possibly be Prince Edward; or perhaps Oxford just didn't think that a prince was such a big deal. Edward kicked snow off his boots in the brightly lit foyer of what turned out to be the Ashmolean Museum. He had never been in here before. Trying not to limp too much, he started to have a desultory look around. Large banners announced an exhibition of the work of Canaletto. He wandered into the Canaletto gallery, only because a tearoom promising a warm drink lay at the far end. Edward aimed to walk straight through, but found his stride slowing. Against all expectations, one of the paintings grabbed his attention. It was called *The Thames on Lord Mayor's Day, Looking Towards the City and St Paul's Cathedral.* A glance turned into a stare.

St Paul's Cathedral dominated London's skyline, towering over a mass of red roofed buildings tumbling down to the river, where two magnificent royal barges rose like waterborne basilicas over a mass of smaller boats. All across the river, in splendid royal vessels, or on small pleasure craft, hundreds of oarsmen were rowing in unison, leaning back into their stroke, a forest of oars at an identical angle. Even the oars of a maverick crew going the wrong way lined themselves up with the oars of all those many boats going the right way.

Edward's attention then moved to a sailing vessel, central to the crush, which had turned awkwardly across the fleet's direction of travel, seemingly at the mercy of an unhelpful wind driving downstream. This same unfavourable wind carried a masthead flag - and dozens of other flags across the fleet - at the same angle as all those oars making their synchronised stroke. It seemed that even a contrary wind was part of things going the right way, blowing flags at the same purposeful angle as a host of harmonised oars.

Edward wasn't entirely sure how long he stood in front of Canaletto's painting. He seemed to disappear into it, and find comfort in a long lost Thames scene. It took a familiar voice to call him back.

"Hello, Edward. I didn't know you liked museums."

He turned and saw a bemused Caroline McMercy looking at him.

"Neither did I."

"So what are you doing here?"

"Well I thought I would pop along, to see the jolly old art."

"Is that so?"

"Well, no. I've hurt my leg and my staff has abandoned me." Edward's voice dropped in volume. "And the Martians are getting grumpy because they think the idea of me and Tarquin having a second grand wedding is a ruse to delay the announcement of our betrothal. I was just wandering around. This was somewhere to warm up."

"Poor little prince."

"And what brings you here?"

"I study history. I'm here quite a lot."

"History, yes of course. We have plenty of that at Windsor Castle: turrets, paintings, traditions and so on."

"I'm surprised they haven't given you a Gibbs Prize already."

Caroline abandoned her chiding manner.

"Sorry I nearly crushed you to death in Henley."

"No problem. It's forgotten."

"Can I buy you a cup of tea to say sorry? I know we haven't talked much since. I am embarrassed about the whole thing. It's not every day a girl nearly kills the heir to the throne."

"You don't have to say sorry. But you can buy me a cup of tea. And then, perhaps I could buy you one."

"Wow. That's like a relationship!"

Edward threw a nervous look at Caroline, who tossed it back with a naughty tip of her head.

As they walked together towards the teashop, Edward stumbled. Caroline reached out with tentative movements that suggested she would catch him if he fell.

Sitting in the teashop Edward once again found it surprisingly easy to talk to Caroline.

"The doctor says I've torn something in my leg. It could have been worse I suppose. That awful fellow run over by Cambridge, Nathan Balfour; he might lose his arm."

"Oh, he'll be fine. He's probably after some medical enhancement. He would do anything to get in the Blue Boat."

Edward was relaxed now, leaning in towards Caroline, sharing gossip.

"Balfour probably would have got a seat if it wasn't for me. I expect he was hoping that Cambridge would run me over, and then back up over my crumpled body."

"I expect so. But he should know that it's best eight not eight best."

Edward chuckled. Rowers seemed to face every unfairness in life with their best eight aphorism.

"Anyway, how are your supercharged aches and pains?"

"I'm fine. Well, not fine, but I have painkillers. What is really making me uncomfortable is hanging about. My lectures have been cancelled for the rest of the week. I can't settle to anything."

"At least it gives a chance to do a few things you wouldn't normally do. Please don't tell the other chaps, but I've been looking at a painting."

"A painting? How cultural."

"I know. For a while it took my mind off the less than jolly prospect of having to be king of two planets."

"I wonder what's going to happen to you."

There was a pause as Caroline appeared to be listening to some inner narrative describing the embarrassments that might lie in Edward's future.

A snapping sound and an explosion of tea interrupted Caroline's abstraction. Forgetting herself, it seemed that she had put too much pressure on the mug in her hands, which shattered, spilling tea and shards of china all over the table.

"Damn it. Sorry."

Edward looked around for someone to step forward to clear up the mess. No one obliged. Feelingly frightfully helpful, he grabbed a few napkins and started mopping.

"Please don't worry. It's easily done."

"Oh really? You try it."

Caroline pushed Edward's own mug towards him.

"No, I wasn't referring to breaking a sturdy china mug with one's bare hands per se. I was referring to unfortunate occurrences in general. One could have dropped the mug, or one could have knocked it over. Same thing really. Your unfortunate occurrence is merely more interesting than the usual, run of the mill drink-spilling accident. You mustn't feel bad about it."

As much busy wiping up of tea continued, Caroline reached across the table.

"One is being too kind," she said, squeezing Edward's hand. The squeeze actually wasn't very hard. In fact, it was a squeeze of perfectly acceptable pressure. Unfortunately, Edward had bruised his hand on Thames ice. He grimaced, and saw Caroline flinch back, as though she had once again misjudged her strength.

"Oh no, I've done it again."

"My hand is bruised."

"I'm so sorry I bruised it."

"No, no it's nothing you did. It was when I fell out of the boat."

"You're trying to be kind."

"No, really; I hit it on the ice."

"I must go. Sorry about all this. Sorry. Bye for now."

"Caroline, please…"

Edward tried to get up. Not thinking about what he was doing, a sharp pain shot through his damaged leg causing him to fall back down in his seat.

"You can't go because unfortunately I can't seem to get up."

Caroline returned to the wounded royal. She lifted him to his feet with the smooth power of a medical hoist.

"Where do you want to go? The hospital?"

"No. I'd like to go back to the Canaletto gallery. I'll show you that painting."

CHAPTER 23 (THE UPPER THAMES)

In the weeks that followed, Edward experienced gathering crisis in a strangely peaceful way. People told him that tensions with Mars had worsened. He tried to be positive, hoping that at least a good emergency might get him out of doing the Boat Race. His Majesty's Government did not want people moving about or forming large gatherings. Journeys, virtual and physical, were restricted to reduce strain on a damaged network. It didn't look like a journey necessary to get a rowing crew and its equipment to London would receive clearance.

Fate once again conspired to dash Edward's hopes, when King John intervened. It was his idea to circumvent the lack of normal transportation by using alternative and traditional means of conveyance. That was how Edward found himself sitting on top of a black and scarlet narrowboat. An arch of gold lettering announced Goblin, which was moving in a controlled drift along the Thames just downstream of Oxford. There was no computer on this boat, which meant it was immune to problems facing so many people outside the sanctuary of the Thames Valley. An eight man racing shell sat on Goblin's roof. Oxford's rowing crew had each found their place, whether it was in the galley or saloon, or perched on stern or bow decks. Edward could see Dramhaggle, usually a hunched presence in the cox's seat, sitting relaxed in the stern. He had one hand on a tiller bar, guiding his boat on its leisurely way. Looking back along the river it was just possible to see Petunia emerging around a Thames meander. Petunia carried Oxford's number two boat and its crew.

Winter's freezing weather was finally subsiding. Sunlight reflected on the creamy pages of a novel in Edward's lap. Network problems made this the only practical way to read anything. Caroline had given him the book just before they left, when he complained about having nothing to do. Edward didn't think of himself as a reader, just as he hadn't thought of himself as an admirer of art. Even so, he was soon enjoying *Three Men in a Boat,* by Jerome K. Jerome, about three Victorian gentlemen who decide to take a Thames rowing holiday. He was reading a passage where George, Harris and Jerome are trying to decide what to take with them on their trip. His own crew had faced a similar dilemma a few days before. They had instinctively ended up following George's advice:

"We must not think of things we can do with, but only of the things we can't do without."

Edward continued to read as Jerome reflected on all the silly things that people take with them on their journeys.

"How many people on that voyage load up the boat till it is ever in danger of swamping with a store of foolish things which they think essential… It is lumber man, all lumber! Throw it overboard… You'll find the boat easier to pull then, and it will not be so liable to upset, and it will not matter so much if it does upset; good, plain merchandise will stand water. You will have time to think as well as to work. Time to drink in life's sunshine…"

"Are you alright, Edward?"

Startled out of his reverie, Edward saw that Caroline had come to sit beside him. She always seemed to catch him when he was least expecting it.

"Oh yes, just reading that book you gave me." Edward closed the pages and felt his face becoming slightly cooler as he folded away reflected light. "Everyone out there is fretting and stockpiling fuel. And here on the boat everything's fine... Strange feeling."

"Do you think the race will actually go ahead?" asked Caroline, following another of those easygoing pauses that can only really be enjoyed on a narrowboat.

"It'll go ahead. Grandpaps is pushing for it. He thinks it will give the comforting impression of business as usual."

"How is business for you at the moment? How's the wife?"

Edward cast Caroline a weary look.

"You are not supposed to know about that. You haven't told anyone, have you?"

"No."

"Since you ask, marriage is not easy."

"Especially for a wee lad who likes girls, but has married a Martian man."

"Will you keep your voice down."

"Poor Edward. Can't face being king; can't face the storm when he announces he doesn't want to be king and has married a Martian man."

"One regrets one's actions."

Caroline leant forward and squeezed the royal hand, which rested on a sketched picture of three men in a boat decorating the cover of Jerome's book. A flash of worry crossed her face.

"Don't worry. Perfectly judged."

Caroline put down Edward's hand, as if it were a delicate ornament fashioned to commemorate some royal event of long ago.

Edward felt an unreal sense of contentment. The long, winding river world kept fears at bay. Those fears had only encroached when Goblin stopped at riverside pubs for its crew to enjoy an occasional meal. Even then, the pubs tended to focus their attention river-wards, which muted echoes of trouble. River life had a resilient routine which even interplanetary anxiety could not yet disrupt.

Caroline wandered off. The mellow tones of her clarinet practice were soon drifting like smoke from a comfortable campfire. It was fortunate that she considered her clarinet an item she could not do without. Picking up his book, Edward smoothed down a pleasingly silky page. Before he could get back to the nineteenth century, however, Tarquin's face reared up in the present. He wanted a private word. Grasping *Three Men in a Boat* like a lucky charm, Edward made his way forward to the bow alcove.

Tarquin looked seasick which was strange since Goblin was gliding along so smoothly.

"They've closed the border, Edward. It's too late to go to Mars now in the normal way."

"Perhaps best then if we just call the whole thing off."

"I'm afraid not. I've had a message from my father. He has an escape plan. It's to happen during the Boat Race itself. All we need is a convenient capsize. Hit Caroline's oar as it comes back towards yours. At speed that will almost definitely sink us. Then in the confusion my people will pick us up and take us to Kew where they will prepare you for the time when you become king."

"I wish we had never started this. I don't want to ruin things for Caroline. People have worked hard for this race. It doesn't seem right."

"Doesn't seem right? What's the matter with you? Since when did you worry about what's right?"

"A chap has pangs of conscience sometimes. I thought rowers were big brutes with whom I had little in common. But it turns out that they are good fellows."

"This is not the time to get virtuous on me. We were idiots getting married, but what's done is done. If you back out now, my father will make huge trouble for both of us. He didn't get to be the biggest mining contractor on Mars without a certain force of personality."

"I've just swapped my family telling me what to do, for your family doing the same thing. That wasn't the idea."

"Well that's just tough. You don't defy a father like mine, Edward. We just have to make the best of it."

"Yes, Tarquers, but surely…."

"We have to do what they tell us. There are powerful people involved."

"I'm a prince, doesn't that count?"

"We're talking actual power here. They say you can help with the troublemakers and their misdirected asteroid. There are many reasons why you should cooperate, all of them good ones. You just think about that while you are reading your ridiculous paper book."

Tarquin stalked off. Edward tried to withdraw back into *Three Men in a Boat*, but worries trapped him, preventing any decampment to the Thames of the nineteenth century.

Approaching London, Edward thought of George's boat trip advice: *"We must not think of things we can do with, but only of the things we can't do without."* With the looming, grey shape of Windsor Castle standing high above the water, Edward saw himself as the most superfluous of cargoes, like a bag with nothing in it. Yet into this vacancy, people poured everything they did not want to leave behind. Long lost myth and magic had gone into the bag that was royalty. Who would be strong enough to carry such weight?

CHAPTER 24
(EVENING STAR)

James had only ever seen steam trains in The Train Set Room at Buckingham Palace. This failed to prepare him for the real thing. Dispatched by the King to transport the Cambridge crew and their equipment to London, Evening Star hissed and burbled beside the platform at Cambridge Station. James felt the romance of steam, in the sense of delay and anticipation. You did not flick a switch with a machine like this. As James helped carry an eight boat along the platform, he watched Evening Star erupt with a flare of preparatory steam.

After helping to secure the boat on a flat goods wagon at the rear of the train, James made his way back up the platform to a line of three passenger carriages. Pulling open the first door he came to, he was confronted by bits and pieces of railway history, which had fallen through time into neat glass display cases, like prehistoric flies caught in amber. James realised this was probably the museum car where his brother's wedding had taken place. He shut the door with a heavy, fossil-fuel clunk.

James moved on to the next carriage where he climbed aboard. He knew that Edward had travelled to Vienna on the Orient Express. This train, by contrast, made him think of troops singing Vera Lynn songs. He ambled along a narrow corridor, just behind Marina who was trying to choose a compartment, seemingly thwarted by the fact that they were all the same. Making her choice, based on inscrutable reasoning, James was pleased that he and Marina had a compartment to themselves. Then the door slid open and Roger Nansen, heir to the Nansen computing empire, slouched in, folding his massive rower's frame down on the maroon upholstered bench opposite. He proceeded to unpack on old box of Cluedo.

"This is the only sort of gaming available at the moment. Let me explain the rules to you."

Roger then talked about Cluedo for about ten minutes, before a series of jolts announced that Evening Star was finally getting underway.

James, lulled into abstraction by Roger's characteristically absorbed rule lecture, found himself shocked back to awareness when the compartment door opened a second time. In teetered a railway worker, wearing a hi-vis jacket. He was suffering some kind of tic around the shoulders.

"Ah, a group of young people engaged in recreational activities. Wonderful. I recently had the honour of marrying a lovely young couple. Now I live to bring people together. I was briefly able to access the network this morning. Using a passenger list and publicly available biographical information I can say that compatibility data, while not being totally encouraging about Mr Nansen here, does have a number of good things to say about Prince James and Miss Blackwood."

"Who the hell are you?" demanded Marina. "And we are just friends."

James suspected that this odd figure might be the animatronic guide who had presided at his brother's wedding. Whilst reflecting on this, he still had a little attention left over to register surprise at Marina's reaction. He thought they had been getting on rather well, particularly since that day at the London Rowing Club when Alistair had revealed news of Edward's wedding. Even in Marina's jibing there seemed to be something affectionate going on. Perhaps he had misread things.

"Personality compatibility scores are higher than with your brother who ..."

"Please don't mention my brother," interrupted James, jumping out of his seat.

"Why ever not? People should be waving flags. There should be a parade. I haven't been able to share news of the royal wedding with anyone yet. For some reason our usual services have been cancelled. Now that we have a train full of people, I will get on with spreading the good news. And when we get to Euston there is a whole city to tell."

"No, you mustn't do that," pleaded James.

The sliding door moved aside once again, this time revealing an old gentleman wearing the black coat and field cap of the Midland Railway, slightly dusty, it seemed, from many journeys between Carlisle and St Pancreas.

"Fred," he shouted. "That's enough. Back to the museum car with you."

"Leave me alone, old man."

"Override command...."

"You can't remember the commands," taunted Fred.

"Just give me a moment."

The bizarre hi-vis jacketed figure turned his enthusiastic gaze back to James.

"Have you bought a ring yet?"

"I am terribly sorry, Your Highness. This is most embarrassing. Fred has not been himself lately. Fred, override command six zero."

"Wrong again."

"Why don't you try control, alt, delete?" suggested Roger Nansen with not a little sarcasm.

"I'm a heritage railway volunteer. I never wanted to manage

an automaton."

"The code is probably something familiar to you, like your birthday," counselled Roger.

"It's not that."

"Your child's birthday?"

"I have three children and nine grandchildren. Which one would I use? Hang on; it's to do with the train. Yes it's the number of Evening Star."

"Ok. And what's that?"

"Nine, two, two, zero."

The troubled automaton tilted just off vertical, the shoulder twitch ceased and his eyes were now like two shot glasses filled with murky water.

"That should hold him for the time being," sighed the railway inspector.

"What's going on?" asked Roger, his impassive face ruffled with bewilderment.

"This is Fred," said the railway inspector, "our animatronic visitor services assistant. He works in the museum car."

"Has he been hacked? Who would do that to a visitor services assistant?"

"I have no idea," said Marina.

"Kids probably," suggested James.

"Why is he fixated on marriage? He mentioned your brother. Why would he do that?"

James hesitated, wondering if he could trust Roger. This feeling of doubt only lasted a few seconds. To be part of a rowing crew is to learn trust.

"I am going to give you some classified information now, Roger. You might be able to help."

"What are you doing?" demanded Marina in an urgent undertone. "I don't think I need to remind you of the need for discretion."

"We have to do something. As soon as we arrive at Euston, our friend Fred wants to arrange a flash mob to publicise the royal wedding. Roger knows about animatronics and might be able to help." James faced the railway inspector, wilting by the door. "Is this the automaton that married my brother?"

"It is, Your Highness."

"Fred married your brother?" spluttered Roger.

"You're making it sound like Fred is Edward's husband," tutted Marina.

"Sorry. Fred didn't marry my brother; he presided at his wedding."

"He presided at his wedding? Oh well it all makes sense now."

"It's supposed to be a secret," continued a dogged James.

"I am trying to keep it a secret, sir," complained the railway inspector, "but Fred's software seems to have been scrambled. It's so hard to control him. Sometimes he even activates himself from partial power-down."

"Can't you get an engineer?"

"The activity log would give away what happened. And if I shut him down completely, an automatic alert would call for an engineer."

"Maybe Roger can help?"

"Maybe I don't want to get involved, thank you very much."

"I know this is unexpected news, Roger, but my brother has married a man in his crew, a Martian chap called Tarquin Van Cello. His foolishness could affect the succession and Earth Mars relations. The King doesn't want anyone to know about this until the time is right. It's a long story but Fred conducted the wedding, an experience that seems to have messed up his software. Can you tell us how to keep him quiet while my grandfather and the government work out what to do?"

Roger looked from James, to Marina, to the railway inspector and finally to Fred. He approached the slouched figure, lifted the hem of the hi-vis jacket and held his wrist against a polished metal plate. There was a click of connection, suggesting a magnetic attraction. Roger's expression of absorption deepened. His conversation with Fred had the appearance of a conversation with himself. He unclicked his wrist and turned to James.

"OK, now I understand. What happened was most improper, from a technical standpoint. Fred needs a repair. The Martian hacking was clumsy. It has corrupted his directives. If you say a factory reset is not possible, we will do a temporary reset. We need an authority figure. James, you must talk to him."

"But it's a machine," objected the inspector. "It won't understand."

"Fred is always trying to understand his customers. The problem is Fred doesn't know which aspect of human behaviour he is trying to understand. He has latched onto his most recent command sets, which involve marriage. We have to modify that command set. James, you must talk to Fred. Tell him your situation. He is looking for a directive. There is a good chance he will recognise your authority. I think he finds the idea of a prince romantic."

"Right, what do I say?"

"Just tell him about your problem and ask for his help."

"Surely this is an internal railway matter," blustered the inspector. "We don't have to trouble His Highness with this."

"He no longer recognises the authority of the railway."

"I suppose I'd better try then," said James, indicating that

Roger should do what was necessary.

Roger returned to Fred, reconnected his wrist briefly before standing back. The change in Fred was small but transformative, like pumping up a tyre on an otherwise perfectly serviceable bike. Thus reanimated, Fred beamed at James.

"Ah young love, I see it in you. There are personality areas where you and Miss Blackwood complement each other."

James glanced at Marina who was clearly unimpressed at the idea of a deluded railway worker robot marrying her off. Roger, standing behind Fred, waved a do-not-interfere finger at her. That warning finger then pointed at James, indicating that he should begin his pep talk.

"Fred, I am Prince James, and I have an important favour to ask you. Please do not mention to anyone that you presided over the marriage of my brother and Tarquin Van Cello. This has to remain secret for now because of the tensions between Earth and Mars. Can you help me with that?"

Fred appeared to analyse this request for a moment.

"But marriage is wonderful. Everyone should know and share in the joy."

"Yes, of course, but there are complications in this case. Revealing that you married my brother might imperil his wedded bliss. That wouldn't be good, would it?"

"I would never do anything to endanger a marriage, and a royal marriage at that. I will certainly keep quiet if that would help." Fred turned to Marina. "You must be so much in love with your wise prince."

James saw Roger staring at Marina meaningfully.

"Oh indeed I am," said Marina. Roger made a palm upward gesture, as though he were a conductor asking the string section in his orchestra for more emotion. "He's dutiful and has a quiet bravery," responded the string section. "Everyone seems to love his brother, but James is the one who has the qualities that would make a good king. He is also fairly good looking." Roger rolled his eyes. "What I am trying to say," Marina continued, "is that he is devastatingly handsome. You'll have to forgive me. The strength of my love is making me stumble over my words."

"I understand. Last time I was able to access the network, I found much data on the neural upset that love causes in humans. Say no more, my dear lady."

"So will you help?" asked Marina laying a tentative hand on an unsteady animatronic shoulder.

"Of course I will."

"Thank you, Fred," said Roger leaning in. "Thank you for helping the course of true love to run smooth."

Once Fred and his minder left to return to the museum car, James slid closed the compartment door, feeling rather pleased with himself.

"That was close; but we made a great team. Well done, Roger, and well done, Marina. Devastatingly handsome eh?"

James gave Marina a playful nudge on the arm, which she answered with a forceful, two-handed shove.

"Just to be clear; I am not marrying anyone, least of all you. I didn't study all these years just to marry a prince and hang around in a palace."

"No, of course not, Marina. Thanks for playing along."

James sank down on thick maroon upholstery. Roger took his seat opposite. With large, calloused rower's fingers, he picked up a conical Miss Scarlet from his Cluedo set and looked at her thoughtfully.

"Fred said my marriage prospects aren't good."

"You'll be fine, just as long as you don't talk about the rules of Cluedo," barked Marina, who from her standing position was able to look seated Roger in the eye.

"Thanks for that. Anyway, what's eating you?"

"Leave me alone."

Marina pulled open the door and disappeared down the corridor. Disturbed air seemed to rush into the small space where Marina had once been. Then there was silence.

James saw Roger looking at him.

"What?"

"I think Fred is right about you two. Don't take any notice of the anger and storming off. I was in the boat with Marina last year. That's just her way of demonstrating affection."

"Well, lucky me. She's very affectionate today."

CHAPTER 25 (PUTNEY TO MORTLAKE)

The King looked up as Boles came into the day sitting room, carrying a silver plate with a glass of water centred upon it, a large tablet resting on a linen napkin to one side. Dropped into the glass as a slice of lime might drop into a Singapore Sling, the white disc disintegrated in a cloud of mad Brownian motion. Despite gloved hands working like those of a magician, they could not hide the drink's true nature. King John drank with a grimace. He had to admit to himself that the tablets weren't working as well as they did when he drove a Land Rover out to Chelsea.

He stood for a moment, looking out at the view down towards the lake in Buckingham Palace Garden. Winter had only just faded into early spring, but even now it seemed impossible such a scene could ever change, that daffodils nodding by the water's edge should ever wither, or a cold wind blow through trees swelling on the far bank.

"Shall I turn the Boat Race on, sir?" enquired Boles.

"Yes of course." said the King, coming back to himself. "Is the television working?"

"Yes, sir, it is, surprisingly."

King John was having trouble getting used to his new 'television', which he insisted on continuing to call the device. He had hung on to his old one until they stopped its faltering signal. For the last few weeks, the new system had only been working intermittently. Today, however, global networks were stable. Boles waved towards portraits of George III and William V, behind which a kitchen materialised in what appeared to be a hidden annex. A number of famous people were engaged in lively cookery. Boles waved his hand a few more times. The kitchen disappeared, replaced by the southern end of Putney Bridge.

"Damn nonsense, Putney Bridge in my day sitting room."

"Yes, sir, but you must admit it is a convenient arrangement."

The King continued to grumble, allowing Boles to help him forward onto the road sweeping out onto a gentle rise towards the far bank at Fulham. A man with memory problems couldn't help worrying that once he stepped into a perfectly reproduced world, he might get confused about what was what.

"We can get back when we want to?"

"It is quite safe, sir."

The King shuffled forward, while Boles adjusted volume levels to his master's satisfaction.

Now that he was out here, King John concluded that maybe this wasn't so bad after all. He was part of an excited crowd rather than the object of a crowd's attention. This was an unfamiliar and wonderful feeling. His legs, or what counted for legs in virtual Putney, were the limbs of a twenty year old.

"A drink please, Boles."

Boles disappeared back into the palace sitting room, now hidden behind virtual people spilling across Putney Bridge. For a few moments, King John was, for all intents and purposes, standing alone, in public, in London. It was thrilling, yet also frightening. Boles was a welcome sight as he returned with a royal crested mug of tea, presented with due ceremony.

"That's better. Now tell me, is Bacon at Mortlake yet?"

"Yes, sir. He will keep an eye on things after the race."

King John raised his mug in appreciation, continuing to enjoy a crowd ignoring him. The one person who gave the illusion of registering his presence was that fellow who was always commentating on sports events. He was chatting about the crews of each boat, focusing on Prince Edward. Given the strict news blackout around the prince, his remarks were either blindingly obvious or romantically untrue.

"The Oxford crew has certainly taken their royal team mate to their hearts. The prince has endured a gruelling training schedule. He's had to juggle heavy training with academic work."

"No he hasn't!" yelled the King, pleased that he could still shout at a television. "What do you know?"

The presenter responded to this dressing-down by vanishing.

"Commentary off, sir," confirmed Boles.

Oxford and Cambridge sat on choppy water, moving in a brisk current. Both coxes held their arms up waiting for their boats to settle. King John could feel tension rising within him, and remembered his day on the Thames all those years ago.

"Come on, you young buggers!"

It was exhilarating that a monarch could say such things in a public place in west London.

After some coaching from Boles, the King realised he could choose to watch from many viewpoints - from the riverside, from chase boats, from the coxes' position or from aerial drones. It was only necessary to look where you wanted to go, and this damned clever device would find the closest available outlook. Concentrating on Jerry Dramhaggle, he was able to see the Oxford crew from a camera just behind the cox's head.

The King ran through in his mind the various factors that had shaped his crew selections. His memory was still effective when it came to sport. He started with John Northcote sitting at stroke in front of Dramhaggle. There were pleasing reports that this former Martianophobe was now a good friend to rowing club Martians. That had worked out well. If only he could put the entire population of Earth and Mars in a rowing crew together, interplanetary tensions would evaporate.

In seat seven, Nico Wanyamwezi had the confidence of a man whose forbears had guided explorers. His potential to guide the royal family in unfamiliar territory derived from the sense that he had already been where others were going; an air about him - to quote from the classics - that there was nowhere you can be that isn't where you're meant to be. This was very comforting to those around him.

As for Harold Franklin in seat six, Boles had given a positive account of this young man. Rowing seemed to have helped in the acquisition of control over the famous buccaneering Franklin spirit. Perhaps in years to come, Harold would assist the royal cause in going where it had never gone before, but be sensible and disciplined about it.

The King's virtual gaze now lighted on Caroline McMercy in seat five. Aside from her useful business connections, her medical enhancement would be a good way of getting people used to what was to come. And beyond that, she was a great rower, who might actually win this one for Oxford.

Norbert Maanberg in seat four had lost the chip on his shoulder and settled into the boat. A good monarch knew that overcoming a feeling of inferiority required a certain humility, an acceptance that you have a valuable role to play in something bigger than yourself. That would be a perfect attitude for a potential member of the royal circle. Matthew Nice in seat one was in a similar situation. After putting this group together, he now sat as just another crewmember waiting for the off.

That left Tarquin and Edward in seats two and three. The King had created this boat to mould Edward. All the way from

Windsor's royal nursery came an image of the Queen of Hearts playing croquet with unpredictable flamingo mallets. Anyone whose game in life is people will find that people have a life of their own. Edward had a life of his own. So be it. This game wasn't over yet.

The King then moved over to Marina's point of view in the Cambridge cox's seat. Directly in front of Marina at stroke sat Francis Paulo, with Emilio Branson in seat seven. These lads were entrepreneurs. They were not obvious choices for future royal retainers, but with the royal family having to be a commercial proposition, they could be very useful. The commemorative mug market needed a shakeup.

Jocelyn Raymond in seat six had fled a strict religious community on Mars. Jocelyn was running away from a backward looking, close-knit family, and finding another in rowing. He could find the same thing in the close-knit, backward looking royal family.

George Tyndale, in seat five was an interesting proposition. While the royal family was obliged to maintain strong military links, actual hostilities were unfortunate. Tyndale had the right background in military ceremonial to encourage a suitable balance between pageantry and fighting, with lots of pageantry and no fighting. His experience as a civil celebrant was also interesting. Who knows, for the purposes of formal occasions, he might be able to sideline the odious Archbishop of Canterbury.

Roger Nansen, in seat four, was heir to a virtual reality fortune. He looked inward. His horizons ended at the edge of an oar stroke. In many walks of life, this blinkered vision might have made Nansen a liability, but in rowing it was an advantage. The same would be true if he chose to make his career in the virtual reality world of royalty.

Then in seat three was Prince James himself. For him, rowing training had been a thorough grounding in the limitations of his role. James's coaches had told him in unequivocal terms to just go through the motions and absolutely do not get in the way. At Christmas, the King had overheard Marina telling James that he was a beginner, an amateur, a midget amongst giants, and in a world with any justice, he would not be in the boat at all. By accepting this, James could make his contribution. Most people knew that medically enhanced people competed alongside the 'able-bodied' in sport, just as it was common knowledge in a former age that amateurs and professionals competed together. James, like his brother over at Oxford, contributed to the boat by drawing a polite veil over truths we know about but would rather not acknowledge. Life is full of half secrets, known but unsaid, and it was James's job to smile and say nothing. This was perfect training for a royal future.

Secrets were also the key to Sarah Van Diemen crouched forward over her oar in seat two. Sarah's family was one of the most successful and least known space exploration dynasties. They had undertaken all of their journeys for commercial gain, any knowledge won kept confidential for its business advantage. Sarah was like that with her rowing. She guarded any information that she picked up in training. As a result, no one knew much about her. The trick with Sarah was to make it appear that her crew was a clandestine club, with whom she could share her secretive efforts. In years to come, the royal family could easily provide her with a similar closed environment. In return, she was the sort of person who would instinctively support the vital royal mystique.

Finally, in the bow seat, was Constantine Moritz, son of an old colonial family. Their philosophy held that only a benign imperial government could keep all sorts of different people together, when untrammelled democracy would only serve to widen divisions. The Moritz clan, hated by many, was expert in manipulating power from the shadows. They were a self-selecting elite which saw itself as existing above the fray. It didn't get much better than that for a potential future member of the royal circle, someone who could deal with the nitty gritty, while others got on with smiling and waving.

The referee was calling for both boats to stand by. Time slowed, reluctant to reach the moment it had long waited for. Marina dropped her arm indicating that she was ready. Over at Oxford, Jerry Dramhaggle did the same.

"Attention.... Go," shouted the umpire. With each crew hauling back on their first few strokes, the two boats shot away.

King John was in a chase boat. He was close enough to hear the coxes yelling commands, coming up with all kinds of strange phrases, which to an experienced ear sounded quite normal.

"Through the stroke, through the stroke. Hook flow, hook flow."

The boats were getting up to speed, their advanced hulls acting like rigid oil in the water. It was clear that the coxes were trying to judge when to order their crews to stop rowing. The King knew the technique - frantic activity to get to top speed, lean forward, oars into a streamlined position, then up and rowing again once speed started to drop. Competitive rowing was now like bob sleigh - run, run, run, tuck. The King revelled in the ease with which he could remember these sporting details. Different crewmembers would specialise in separate phases of the rowing effort, 'tyre smokers' generating an initial surge of momentum, before focus shifted to crew included for fast arm action – 'pianists' - honoured for their ability to combine strength with lightness of touch. The two princes lay in a third category – 'anglers' - who waved their oars above the water and hoped for the best.

Both boats went into lock down at about the same time, like an old-fashioned style of military jet, folding its wings into a streamlined position at high speed. Oxford flew along on the northern Middlesex station, which meant they were on the outside of the bend approaching Hammersmith Bridge. To King John's surprise, Dramhaggle decided to make up for this disadvantage by ordering his crew to put in a risky burst at near top speed. From the Cambridge boat only a few feet to the left, he could hear Marina's order as she responded:

"Okay, I need power now. Everyone stand-by."

Cambridge straightened up, oars unfolding like a Chinese fan.

"Get ready for power thirty five. Ready all. Row."

From Jerry Dramhaggle's position, the King watched Cambridge pulling hard, accompanied by cries from the umpire to provide more room.

"Cambridge! Cambridge!"

The King shared in Jerry's delight that despite their difficult outside position, Oxford pulled about a quarter of a length ahead. Things looked good for later on, when the river would reverse her favours.

"Steady on the stroke," yelled Jerry. "All the way through, all the way through."

At the twitchy margin of maximum effort, Jerry ordered his crew to tuck down in pairs. Oxford crept to almost a length ahead of Cambridge. The King knew that a lead of more than a length would allow the leader to choose their line, which represented a huge advantage. He switched over to Marina's position to see what the light blues would do.

"All blades ready," shouted Marina to her crew. "Be careful, James. I only want you pulling in the first ten strokes, then you're back into tuck position. Ready for power thirty. All ready? Row. Hook and through, hook and through."

James was giving everything he had, but his grandfather knew that at this level there was no way he could keep up. Marina was shouting at him to stop and tuck down.

James folded in his oar and crouched forward. His teammates continued to pull for twenty more strokes before they too tucked in. Marina did her best to maintain stillness in the midst of speed. The King had seen something similar at the Royal Ballet, when a ballerina spun on a pointed foot, never deviating from its tiny moment of contact with the stage.

King John switched his view back to Oxford who, despite Marina's efforts, continued to move ahead. It was obvious, however, that while they had a good lead, all was not well. Edward was slow to respond to orders to stop rowing, continuing to pull when the boat's speed had gone beyond his limited capabilities. Northcote at stroke was shouting at the cox:

"Keep him under control. He's going to sink us."

"I'm trying. You just concentrate on rowing."

Jerry steered on a curving line as they approached Chiswick Eyot. He called his crew up for another effort. As speed increased, the King could hear his frantic shouts, demanding that Edward tuck back down.

At this moment of greatest danger, the King saw it all. Edward successfully mistimed his stroke. His oar collided with Caroline's, creating a clash through the line of blades, like a frustrated author thumping his fingers down on the keys of an old typewriter. The shaft of Caroline's oar whipped back into her stomach, turning her upside down, before throwing her out of her seat. For a moment, speed turned water into a solid surface, a kind of rutted road after a rainstorm, across which Caroline somersaulted. As her tumbling slowed, the unyielding surface opened up and swallowed its victim. It was a few seconds before she bobbed back into view.

The King sat with Oxford as they headed away from Chiswick Steps down towards Barnes Bridge. The disruption of losing Caroline had unsettled the boat, which was slithering left and right, with Jerry straining to compensate. Jerry obviously had the option of ordering his crew to square their oars into the water and make an emergency stop, but doing that would mean the race was lost. Oxford still had their lead, and they just had to survive through this last section. Jerry hung on, trying to control the lurching turns of his slippery hull, over compensating as he did so. An aggressive adjustment right followed a vicious turn left. Throwing up a wall of water, Oxford collided with Cambridge coming up from behind. The King shared in Jerry's rush of confused impressions - chase boats, faces in the water.

"No!" shouted the King.

He scanned the water's broken surface. For long minutes, there was no sign of either James or Edward. Memories of the calamity that took the lives of the princes' mother and father swarmed up in John's mind and made him beg for forgetfulness.

"Please calm yourself, sir," said Boles beside him.

A wide-ranging point of view finally revealed James holding onto the upturned hull of the Cambridge boat.

"What about Edward? Can you see him? I'll never forgive myself if the boy drowns. Perhaps I have been placing him in too much danger. I did it for his own good. I don't feel well, Boles."

"I think I saw Edward pulled out of the water into Van Cello's catamaran."

"You did? Are you sure?"

"I think so. Are you alright, sir?"

Boles waved his hand in a dismissive motion, gesturing away the Boat Race as someone might dismiss a thought from their mind. The King only registered the return of his day sitting room for a moment, before seeing a burgundy-carpeted floor coming up to meet him.

CHAPTER 26 (MORTLAKE)

For Prince James, his individual disaster was part of a general breakdown. The grey light of a building without power infused him. A towel sat draped around his neck, marooned there when the energy required to rub Thames water out of his hair expired. This final outage coincided with Marina whispering details in his ear of Edward's sabotage.

"Not just an accident?" he asked.

"We think not. He was refusing to follow Dramhaggle's orders. And he was pulled out of the water by a Martian boat. They took Tarquin too."

Had Edward deliberately ruined the Boat Race? Was there nothing to which his disgraceful brother would not stoop?

Grubby from his immersion, James looked at the clubhouse. Everything took on a changed appearance due to a simple lack of illumination. This unfamiliarity provided a sense of dislocation. There was an ashen relief in the way James seemed to stand outside his predicament. It was as though he had become a member of one of those happy crews in pictures on the brown walls, who, after offering their strength in sacrifice to the river, now had a place in rowing heaven from whence they gazed down at today's crisis.

Oxford and Cambridge crews were scattered around a series of round tables. The roundness felt odd to James after all the straight lines of rowing. He registered ugly anti-Martian chanting from outside the clubhouse, accompanied by concussions of breaking glass. Flying stones didn't worry the prince. There was always the hope that a large rock in the form of that redirected asteroid everyone was talking about, would mercifully end his world. This would save him from the shame of his brother's actions.

James watched a senior police officer attempting to preside over an impromptu situation desk. He noted a crisp, black jacket, enlivened by scarlet and silver insignia on lapels and shoulders. This neatly tailored man was in conversation with a pair of Martian officers, whose appearance suggested an altogether more down-to-earth attitude to policing. Their black, nanotube-sailcloth overalls spoke of heavy work involving exposure to dirt and body fluids.

"Prince Edward is heir to the throne and we are responsible for his safety. If you don't place him in our control immediately, there will be consequences."

"That will not be possible, Chief Inspector Wembury," drawled one of the forbidding Martians. "Prince Edward has chosen to entrust his security to us. We have taken him to a Martian site. Considering the lack of security evident here, you can hardly blame him for his choice."

"I do not accept that this was his choice. Neither does the angry mob surrounding this clubhouse."

Wembury turned to a couple of officers working behind him.

"Get me Gold Control," he ordered.

James wondered in a tired sort of way what Gold Control was. It sounded important.

"I can't raise Control," said a young officer. "I was getting messages about network problems all over London. Hang on, something coming in. Sir, there's a report that Prince Edward has been kidnapped."

"Yes, I know he's been kidnapped. This man here just told me that."

"Sorry, sir."

Wembury turned to his Martian opposite number.

"This is ridiculous."

"Shall I arrest them?" asked a young, keen looking constable, loosening his tie slightly as he squared up to the Red Planet paramilitaries.

Wembury hesitated. It seemed he would have loved to say yes.

"You can't arrest us," smirked the Martian. "We have diplomatic immunity. You are obliged to protect, not arrest."

"You're right. We can't arrest you. But you can't stay here. We will take you back to Kew on one of our boats."

"I think it would be best if we use our own boat."

"He might have a point," admitted the junior officer. "The management computers on all our launches have failed. It's the same with our road units and helicopters."

"As I say, Chief Inspector, I think best if we use our own boat."

The Martians' manner suggested that Wembury's expression of contempt was nothing more than another helping of exudate brushing over nanotube sailcloth on a busy night outside a nightclub in an Elysium Planitia mining town. The Martians walked away with a swagger, suggesting full membership of Mortlake's Anglican and Alpha Boat Club.

With the Martians gone, Wembury addressed his group of officers.

"We are in a critical situation. We can't lose two members of the royal family in one day. Prince James has to be taken to a safe location."

Hearing his name served to pull James back from his illusory position as a distant observer. It hadn't really been a place of escape anyway. Sitting with the crews up on the walls gave his vision a kind of hard, bleached quality, which only served to reveal events more clearly. James stood up.

"I don't want to cause any trouble."

"Sit down. You will be told what to do."

The prince sank into his seat. He saw Matthew approach the Chief Inspector.

"May I make a suggestion?"

"And you are?"

"Matthew Nice, President of Oxford Rowing Club."

This was the first time James had seen Matthew since they all washed up at Mortlake. He had probably been dealing with an insurance claim for the Oxford boat, which was very expensive, and which his brother had caused to sink. James slumped forward, elbows on the table, hands cupped over his forehead and eyes. Through bunker slits between loosely knit fingers, he watched the junior officer reporting more news.

"I just had a short message from Control. They say the shelter in Whitehall is out of action - problems with the doors."

Matthew repeated his offer of help.

"May I make a suggestion?"

Wembury signalled with weary eyebrows that he was willing to grant Matthew a few moments of his attention.

"If we need a secure location why not take the prince to Windsor Castle? Windsor is a royal residence with security in place. It's also close to the river, which means we can row there. Rowing boats don't have computers. And as for security during the journey, the river itself will offer protection."

The narrow view between James's fingers acted like a pinhole camera, magnifying Wembury's glance over at his communications desk.

"No contact, sir," came a mournful announcement. "I'm not getting anything anymore."

"We've lost one prince," continued Matthew. "At least we can get the other one to Windsor. Think about it, Wembury. If Prince Edward's gone, that fellow over there could be the next heir to the throne."

Hearing this, James pulled a grimy towel collar over his head and pretended to continue drying his hair. He was actually hiding like a tennis player between tough games at Wimbledon.

"We would need an escort," said Wembury's voice through the towel, sounding louder now that James could not see the man talking.

"We can't use our launches, sir," answered the junior officer in a whiney voice.

"That's not a problem," asserted Matthew's insistent tones. "We will put the prince in a two man boat with our best rower. We will have the eights following as escort."

"I can row a bit, sir," piped up the keen constable.

"We will use our own crews. With respect, handling boats like ours takes a lot of training."

James lifted the towel away from his face and saw Wembury as a venerable and well-loved house pet, cornered by a street animal, seemingly as terrified of doing something as of doing nothing.

"There is the small matter that your boats are at the bottom of the Thames. And will you have enough people for your escort, when two have been kidnapped by Martians, and another will be rowing the prince?"

"Well, it seems that somehow Cambridge managed to get their boat back to the slipway. As for us, we have our number two boat. We can solve any personnel problems using our reserve crews."

Matthew gestured towards a group sitting around one of the tables on the far side of the room. Even in a circle, they sat in the same disposition they would have used out on the water.

"Fitzwhistle, Raeburn, Markov, you're up. Your boat is now the Blue Boat, and you three are in it."

Alistair Fitzwhistle stood up at the call. He wobbled for a moment and then sat down again.

After Marina selected a replacement for James from the Cambridge reserve crew, Wembury appeared to have run out of objections. A brick hit a window, broken glass spilling away from a web of traditional leading. Wembury nodded down into his chest, an ambivalent hand covering his mouth as though continuing to think about his options. If this was assent, it had been given in a manner that might allow denial later.

Matthew started to issue directions.

"Caroline, you are the strongest of all of us. Take one of the low drag double sculls. Get to Windsor as quickly as possible, but don't move too far ahead of us. We must be able to reach you if you need help."

James wanted to stay under his towel, but as ever duty called. He hauled himself to his feet and trudged out towards the slip. He could see Matthew in the boat storage area, who with the bravado of a man selecting a weapon from an armoury, lifted down a rapier two seater from the Mortlake racks. Cycloid scales shimmered on its low drag, snakeskin hull. Matthew swung the boat onto his right shoulder and carried it down to the water, steadying the shell as Caroline slotted herself into its rear seat. James faltered into the seat in front of her. He looked at empty oarlocks either side of him.

"You won't need any oars," said Caroline.

"Are you sure I can't give you a hand?"

"He means well," said Marina from the slipway. "Look after him."

James could hear Caroline settling herself behind him, adjusting the boat to her liking, as if she were doing up laces on her shoes. They waited for the eights to get ready. Marina was shouting directions to her crew.

"Okay, I want you ready for an easy twenty."

"Get ready for twenty" shouted Jerry Dramhaggle to his own crew. "It's a long way, and we'll be starting to run into the tide, so take it steady. Let's go."

Caroline pulled away from the two larger boats. The end of the Boat Race had turned into a trip to Windsor. James felt the reassuring rhythm of the boat beneath him. They were going into the great unknown, but at least they were rowing there.

CHAPTER 27
(RICHMOND LOCK)

The tide had turned and was running downstream. Caroline pulled the boat against a strengthening current. James couldn't help feeling he wasn't worth all this effort.

"I'm so sorry about what my brother did," he called back to his crewmate.

"He didn't want to be king."

"It didn't matter what he wanted."

"I felt sorry for him."

James assumed that Caroline would be furious with Edward. Strangely, she seemed more cross with the brother who had worked hard and done his duty.

"You felt sorry for him?"

"He didn't want people telling him what to do with his life. I know how he feels."

James was silent, watching the wide Thames roll away as Caroline sculled along with energy that was both emotional and mechanical, like an opera staged in the engine room of a steam ship. It seemed best to keep quiet. Failing in his usual strategy to see the world as a painting, the prince found himself musing on *The Wind in the Willows*, one of the few stories that he remembered his mother reading to him when he was young. Memories of his mother gave a sense of security and loss in equal proportions. When James asked that his mother take him to Toad's river, she said she didn't need to, because Toad's river was the Thames, which flowed through Windsor, one of the places that James could vaguely call home. James floated on sunny memories of much loved characters messing about in boats. The Thames was unending and unchanging, or so it seemed to James - who hadn't yet reached Richmond Lock.

It was there that his fond illusions evaporated. Initially, the centuries old, pale green and yellow iron sluice mechanism was another confirmation that this ancient waterway endured in a changing world - until he got closer and saw a flurry of lemon coloured jackets. A man in a white helmet was yelling down from the footbridge. Caroline turned the boat around to face him, her oars idling against an ebbing tide.

"Go back. We can't close the gates."

"I have to get to Windsor," shouted Caroline.

"Not today. We can't close the barrage. None of the locks are working."

"You don't understand. I must get to Windsor. I have Prince James in the boat."

"Well he's not getting to Windsor by river today."

"How else do you expect me to get him there? Have you heard the news?"

"I am the news. Go back. But be careful. London VTS is offline. There's nothing controlling river traffic."

James was shocked that the Thames seemed as badly affected by computerised mayhem as everything else. After a few moments thought, it all started to make sense. A long-established system of locks and weirs maintained the river beyond Richmond at a navigable level. Computers now supervised this system. The Thames locks created the delightful illusion of water always running at high tide, as though the fluctuating, tide-influencing moon had apparently ceased to change in its orb. Without Richmond barrage, and others like it further up river, low tides would drain the upper Thames, its majestic flow reduced to a stream running between muddy banks.

Caroline paddled back eastwards.

"It's no good," she called to the eight boats as they approached. "We can't get to Windsor. There are problems with the locks. We have to go back."

A confused waterborne conference followed, which consisted of people asking others what they thought. At first, everyone looked to Matthew, who in turn consulted the coxes. Those diminutive but tyrannical presences in the back of each boat were strangely quiet. The Cambridge president had nothing to say. For the others there seemed to be a small adjustment to the boat that needed attention, or something on the bank that had become interesting.

James realised that no one knew what to do. He had grown up with people who always had a plan - officers from the forces speaking in clipped imperatives accompanied by decisive hand gestures; or graduates from elite universities who had the entire literature of the ancient world lying behind each smooth decision. Now he sat exposed in a small boat, on a wide river pulling him back from the destination specified for him.

James heard himself making an announcement.

"We should go to the Tower. There are no locks between here and the Tower."

"Which tower?" asked Matthew.

"The Tower of London."

"The Tower is nothing but a tourist attraction. We should go back to Mortlake and let Wembury decide what to do."

"Don't be ridiculous, Nice," objected Marina. "Wembury didn't have a clue."

"He's the official in charge."

"He wasn't in charge of anything."

"Jerry's right," said James. "When we left Mortlake, the whole place was in chaos. We can't go back there. We will go to the Tower. Caroline, row us to the Tower please, while the others follow."

"You realise we have to register our boats if we take them into central London? Even if they let us in, it'll be like running around on the motorway."

"Just like you to raise a bureaucratic objection, Nice," sniped Jerry.

"The chap at the barrier said the control system was down. What did he call it?" asked James twisting around to address his question to Caroline.

"The VTS."

"Yes, the VTS. I'm sure the computer problems will mean the river is much quieter than normal."

James was relieved that a strength had risen within him. After a life of other people telling him what to do, everything changed. He had nothing and no one to feel intimidated by and beholden to. The lassitude and depression that had afflicted him since his boat sank now lifted. It was an abrupt change accompanying the loss of all hope that someone, somewhere knew what to do. Now there was nothing to say that his own decisions were inferior in some way. James sensed that every individual faces such a moment in life, and this moment for him came on the Thames at Richmond.

"We will go to the Tower."

"You want me to go back?" said Caroline.

"Yes."

"Back the way I've come?"

"Yes, sorry."

With a precise twirl of her left hand oar, Caroline pointed the boat's bow behind her towards London. James had no idea whether this plan would work, but he could feel the current underneath him, and they were now going with it rather than against it.

CHAPTER 28
(THE TOWER)

Keeping a steady pace, Mortlake soon came back into view. James noted that things there had not improved. Presumably, technical problems had afflicted riot suppressant equipment, because the police were using oars as pikes, as though they were a contingent of Royalists at the Battle of Edgehill. Staying in mid channel, the humble royal boat moved on towards central London.

It was a long journey back to Putney and then through Chelsea. The river was indeed quieter than normal, and no one challenged their progress. Eventually, after much wearying effort, the snakeskin boat slid past the Houses of Parliament on the left, with Big Ben's white face standing out against a light blue sky. Rich, solemn, composed strokes chimed the hour, suggesting that technical turmoil wasn't affecting E. Dent and Co.'s gravity driven clock mechanism. Gold and black filigree on Big Ben's face remained as intricate and organised as ever. Rowing under Westminster Bridge the story was less reassuring. People were parading in straggling groups. Remembering scattered bits of history he had studied at school, James felt these people marched in a manner that teetered somewhere between despairing retreat from Moscow and barbarian advance across the Rhine. It was remarkable that unhappy people still made banners for themselves. Thrown back on elemental emotions they turned to primordial means of expression, made with their own hands using their own bed sheets.

Beyond Westminster, James could sense that Caroline was getting tired. Her arms were relentless, but the rest of her body was weakening. Tyndale whimpering on a treatment couch in Cambridge had shown him that apparent superheroes were people like everyone else. Caroline's pace slowed as they moved past central London landmarks – the Old London Eye, Somerset House, and the South Bank Theatres.

Then the Monument came into view, indicating where fire had broken out in 1666, destroying London. The Monument told James his journey was nearly over. While Shakespeare's Globe Theatre crouched on the right, entering stage left was the Tower of London, grey and impassive, its four keep towers standing like pontiffs wearing the hats of an ancient religion.

All this time Caroline and her boat had been a bird in flight, a swan beating its wings just above the river's surface. Now, pulling up at Tower Quay, the effect was more London pigeon hopping about. Caroline scrambled ashore, and steadied the boat for her royal passenger. Together, they ran up towards the castle entrance, James wondering what he was going to say. Apart from a background noise of sirens, the immediate vicinity of the Tower was quiet. Despite what was going on in London, James was amazed to see a short line of people trying to get into the castle. Even at a time like this, a few determined souls wanted to go sightseeing. James had to overcome an Earth person's natural inclination to queue in an orderly manner. Remembering that they didn't have time for this, he began to push forward.

"Sorry, please let us through."

An imperious woman bustled over, a black cloak with red collar giving her the look of a conical shaped token used in Roger Nansen's game of Cluedo.

"I need to see someone in authority."

"We've just been told to close the castle. Please go home. All of you go home."

"I am here on royal business."

"This is an emergency situation. Leave now."

"It's because of the emergency that I need to see someone."

"I can call security, you know."

James, breathless and unkempt, realised that competing in a tough race, nearly drowning at Mortlake, and then making a journey in a small boat all the way from Richmond had left him looking a little less like his public self.

Clearly, it had been a long, hard day for Tower staff. Exasperated beckoning summoned a yeoman warder in full regalia - a deep blue, skirted, tunic coat with red trim on hems and panels, that same red trim spelling out J II R across the chest. The warder's duty until now had been keeping the queue amused. He appeared shocked that he was required to do something more serious.

"Is there a problem, ma'am?"

Caroline appeared to be restraining laughter.

"This is your security?"

The warder bridled.

"We yeoman warders have guarded the Tower since 1485."

"These young people are causing a disturbance," snapped the official.

"Oh, don't do that. You might get yourself locked up in the Tower!"

The yeoman warder chuckled at his joke, a rehearsed little routine, which James assumed he often used on naughty children.

"This is Prince James," insisted Caroline. "We need to get him to a secure location. None of the usual places are available."

"Oooh, street theatre," called out a tourist.

"This is not street theatre. I am telling you this is Prince James. We've just come from the University Boat Race."

James was aware of the yeoman warder studying him.

"I must say there is an uncanny likeness."

"It's a living history presentation," chipped in the tourist.

"No, not living history," said Caroline turning on her small audience, "history today, right now. This is the prince."

Turning back to the yeoman warder, Caroline made a last, impassioned plea.

"The Tower is still a royal castle. Prince James is asking for your help."

"Please, madam, don't make us call the police. They are already very busy today."

"We're getting to the good bit," chortled the tourist. "They'll lock them up in a minute."

"Go away," barked the Cluedo woman. "Go away all of you. I thought I'd have to avoid panicking you people. No need to worry about that, is there."

"Look," said Caroline pointing. "Here come Oxford and Cambridge."

James joined an enthralled queue of people turning to the river. A couple of eight-seat competition boats were making their way down the Thames towards the Tower. They pulled up alongside Tower Quay and their crews started to climb out. A feisty, elfin woman in a pale blue, waterproof jacket, directed operations, her leadership only equalled by that of a bantamweight boxer of a man in a dark blue jacket. James greeted the two exhausted coxes, indicating they should talk to the astonished yeoman warder.

"I am Marina Blackwood, cox of the Cambridge Blue Boat.

Prince James, a member of my crew, requests sanctuary."

"I am Jerry Dramhaggle, cox of the Oxford Blue Boat. We are here to tell you that Prince Edward, a member of my crew, has absconded to Mars, and it is your duty to protect Prince James."

James moved forward.

"I request sanctuary at the Tower of London, as Prince James, Earl of Europe."

The yeoman warder had lost his ability to speak. The game token official was similarly dumbstruck. Finally, it seemed that they saw through grime and matted hair.

"Do you grant my request, sir?"

"Yes, Your Highness. This is a great honour. Please follow me."

The yeoman warder stood at the Middle Tower entrance and ushered his new guests inside, the small cluster of tourists applauding. Perhaps they still believed this was street theatre.

"Please go home everybody," said James to his audience. "You'll be safer there. I think we are all in for a tough few weeks."

The dark, wooden gate swung shut.

CHAPTER 29 (KEW)

It had been like a massive beach party. Edward's experience of beach parties told him that they generally ended with a period of stupefied, late-night reflection around a fire. The same was true of this one, which had led, via raucous singing and dune buggy racing across Martian dunes, to a dell formed by two arms of a lunate sand ridge, now a glowing lagoon of yellow light centred on a burning pyramid of wooden stakes. Edward sat in a blue and cream striped deckchair, staring into an incandescent pyramid, slowly collapsing with the sound of rustling autumn leaves. Idle smoke drifted up about ten feet before whirling away in a spiral, presumably caught in the vortex of some kind of extractor system.

"An actual wood fire," said Tarquin in hushed tones.

"Huh?" said Edward.

"You imagine a ship straining into orbit with a cargo of wood. You imagine getting that all the way to Mars."

"It's heavy I suppose."

"On Mars we don't have many trees. Wood is a great luxury. And they're burning it for you."

The prince's royal marriage plan had without doubt caused his young Martian friend great stress, but at this moment Tarquin had the shiny-eyed air of a man sitting at the end of the rainbow.

"Pull yourself together, Tarquers," muttered Edward. "We're not actually on Mars. That's Kew out there."

The prince fell asleep in his striped deckchair. He dreamt that he sat on Whitstable beach, with a copy of *Three Men in a Boat* resting on his lap. He grasped tightly at this dreamy vision of Jerome K. Jerome's book. Tarquin had told him that the one thing with more mythic, and monetary, value on Mars than wood was a paper book.

It was the cold that slapped Edward back to wakefulness. The fire was a ragged circle of murmuring embers. Most of his fellow revellers had disappeared. Who were those people anyway? Staggering to his feet, he shivered. All he wanted was somewhere warm to sleep.

"The old man wants to see you," said Tarquin, who sat hunched forward, in a rainbow-striped deckchair, a style of chair that made hunching forward look particularly uncomfortable.

"Can't it wait?" moaned Edward. "I'm tired."

Waiting was apparently impossible. Tarquin led the way to a glass walled lift, which flew like a comet on gossamer supports to an accommodation area hundreds of feet up, tucked away against the curving dome roof. Lift doors opened into a comfortable flat decorated in a clean, understated Martian manner. Lighting was subdued, the furniture soft and inviting. Red planet scenes by well-known Martian landscape artists decorated the walls. Perhaps James would have appreciated them. To Edward, these artists just weren't a match for Canaletto.

The room also featured a tall display case with backlit glass shelves, exhibiting a collection of royal chinaware memorabilia. Smiling ceramic faces stared out of oval or heart shaped frames, flanked by protective lions and Scottish unicorns. Edward noticed the turquoise and gold carafe which had been produced in a limited edition to commemorate his birth.

"Oh look, there's mine - a particularly ugly example of the genre."

"Leave it," whispered Tarquin. "He likes them, and he's just out there on the balcony."

Tarquin pointed towards a set of dark, translucent doors, where panes of smoked glass held a small portion of a star display projected onto the dome's inner face.

"Come on," urged Tarquin. "There's no sense in putting it off."

Doors slid aside, opening a portal through projected star-scape. The happy couple walked through this tear in space to meet their fate. Edward saw a man in perfectly cut evening dress. Nevertheless, this courtly figure remained a Martian miner, someone who had made a fortune at the rock face of his business.

With queasy unease, Edward felt relentless eyes resting on him. It was even more unsettling to see a bow send that gaze to the floor. Dominco Van Cello then straightened up and looked out over rusty desert, sitting quiet and cold beneath the star display, a tiny portion of which now projected itself onto Edward's body. The prince felt like a misbehaving mortal, banished by godly decree into space. He had become a constellation, held forever by heavenly powers beyond his knowing.

Constellation Edwardius contemplated Mars. Silver marram grass pastures lolled to one side as though each stem were asleep. Stands of barrel cacti huddled together, waiting perhaps for an early morning visit from the dray. Tired eyes saw bundles of tumbleweed as sheep resting in Windsor Great Park. A bright, tenuously blue point of light sat prominent in an arching cosmos. Edward guessed this must be Earth.

"Not a bad view," said Dominico. "In time, you will come to our compound overlooking the Mariner Valley. Then you will see the real thing."

The enormity of what he had done settled on Edward, making his insides feel too big for his outsides. He had left Earth and gone over to the Martians. How had this happened? It had been his decision, but that did not make him feel any less of a passenger.

"Welcome to Mars, Your Highness."

Edward held up a polite hand to decline the offer of a drink. He felt it would just come back up again.

"It is a shame that our plans disrupted the Boat Race. Still, we all have to make sacrifices. We need you with us, Your Highness. We have important plans for you. There are people on Mars who want war. I have never liked war. It is bad for business. I am determined to bring Mars and Earth closer together, and you have a destined role to play in this process. You will play that role with my son. The people of Mars like to think of themselves as forward-looking. Your unconventional royal marriage is likely to play well with them. It will take a lot for Martians to embrace the monarchy, but we think you and my son are the key."

People had been telling Edward about his destiny since he was a toddler. It had gone to his head at play-school, where he had tried to have some of the other children arrested when they wouldn't share toys with him. At school, it had become clear that as well as having no power to arrest people, he had no control over basic life choices. Career advice was never an option for him. When other boys trotted off to discuss their future professions, the master left him sitting at his desk with his destiny. At Oxford, there had been a brief time of freedom. For a while, it was almost as though he would escape the fate that had dogged his steps since he was born. Right up until this evening as he sang about California Girls amongst Martian dunes, Edward had been kidding himself that once he got to Mars everyone would forget to make him king. Now, standing above a painted desert, it was clear that the latitude of his time at Oxford was over. He was like any other student who used this special interval to explore mathematics, science, literature, history; or to party and then find themselves thrown out following failed exams. Freedom by its very nature included all of these potentials. Edward, like his peers, was leaving behind a state of transient and blessed liberty.

"You know, of course, what this all means," Dominico continued. "It means that when the time comes, you are to be king of both Earth and Mars. Your grandfather wanted the dual throne. For him it will not happen. That fate now falls to you."

"I'll do my best," said Edward in a voice constricted by nerves and frigid air. "In the meantime do you mind if I pop back to the palace and get a few bits; toothbrush, change of clothes and so on?"

"I don't think that's a good idea. We can provide for your needs here. Many in the Earth establishment do not want you to join us on Mars. If you leave Martian sovereign territory, they will arrest you, and if that happens, your safety cannot be guaranteed. It is vital that you remain here. From what we hear from our friends in Earth's government, the King has suffered a collapse. We do not expect him to survive longer than a few weeks. I am sorry to be blunt, but these are matters of the greatest importance and we have to face them squarely. Following the King's death, we will proclaim your dual throne and stage your coronation with constitutional correctness here at The Mars House. Kew's ambassadorial status means Earth cannot interfere, and the distance to Mars protects us from our enemies there. Nothing will stop your historic mission. Much now depends on you. I wish you luck."

So, it had happened; his grandfather had finally begun to lose his battle. Edward felt a great space inside him, which the King had once filled. He realised that Dominico Van Cello, this man of immense power, felt the same emptiness. He wanted a King of Mars and if such a thing did not exist, he would bow down before a Martian monarch of his own making.

"Can I go to bed now?" Edward asked.

"Yes, of course. We are all tired. It has been a momentous night."

Tarquin led Prince Edward away to a small apartment with a view out over his future.

"How does it feel to be king of all you survey, including in this case the sky and the stars?"

"It feels bloody terrible, Tarquin. You have no idea."

CHAPTER 30
(THE TOWER)

James felt as though he was living in a medieval village rather than a castle. Half-timbered houses and a small church bordered a village green, over which loomed the White Tower, like an out of scale feudal office block that somehow got past a local planning committee. Around this askance village, layers of curtain walls had accrued over centuries, seemingly the reaction of modern London to a grain of something different in its midst.

Each evening James would meet with his Oxford and Cambridge colleagues, who had become what Marina liked to call 'the Privy Council'. They held their meetings in rooms on the White Tower's highest floor. Here they would discuss current events and their response, which was always the same - to sit tight and do nothing. James knew there was nothing wrong with this policy. It had served royalty well for a long time, and was the only course of action they could realistically adopt.

London was chaotic. The Boat Race Day digital breakdown had represented a significant and wide-ranging attack, with repairs proceeding slowly. There were unpredictable power cuts and communication outages. When news feeds did work, they concentrated obsessively on reports that the King at Buckingham Palace was very ill and not expected to survive. Somehow, however, there was a sense of cheerfulness in the Tower, the atmosphere of a warm hall on a bitterly cold night. James noted that yeoman warders, and other staff working at the Tower showed a muted delight in events. Only a week previously, these sentinels had been tourist strategy administrators, IT maintenance consultants, catering managers, visitor experience supervisors, or in the case of the yeoman warders, tour guides in silly uniforms. Now they were guardians of a citadel.

James had formed a close friendship with Swindon Hardy, who conducted him into the castle on Boat Race day. It was to Swindon that he turned late one night soon after arriving at the Tower. Unable to forget his worries, the prince had lain in bed for hours, before throwing off his duvet, getting dressed and opening the door of his room. Swindon was sitting outside on self-appointed guard duty. On a table at his sentry position, a few candles burned in darkness that recalled centuries before Martian settlement, before moon landings, before electricity. This was an ancient darkness, stretching back to the dawn of things, revealed by nothing more than a light going out.

"Can't sleep, Swindon."

"No, sir."

The watch was about to change. Instead of retiring to bed, Swindon offered the sort of companionship James associated with an old shepherd, or a family solicitor. They made their way up to the walls, the late hour lending an informal quality to their conversation. Swindon talked of his life at the Tower.

"I would have been retiring soon," he told James. "I have been doing DIY at a house in Ashford, for when I have to leave my Tower rooms. Now the Chief Warder has delayed my retirement indefinitely. As far as I'm concerned dropping dead on a night watch like this one would be the ideal way to end my career."

Swindon took James along the route of his regular watch. Flaming braziers lit their path. The City was quiet, as it was most nights, the result of a general curfew and power down. Swindon described how occasional sounds of trouble reached him. One night he had seen an orange glow to the south beyond

London Bridge.

James fell into a meditative state, brought on by extreme fatigue and worry. To the west, the Milky Way was a column of blue white smoke rising behind the Shard, billowing from a celestial fire burning more brightly as City lights had dimmed. To the east, a thin wash of emerald green hung over the black, blocky shapes of Docklands.

Prince and yeoman warder watched the sunrise. Strengthening light revealed tired lines on Swindon's contented face. A royal command ordered him off to bed.

James walked back to his quarters, aiming to sit for a while, catch up on reading his policy papers - which all advised waiting and doing nothing - and then attend a breakfast meeting with Showertree. He relaxed into a Chesterfield grandfather chair that wrapped itself around him. After what seemed like a few seconds, he found a loud noise jerking him awake. Opening his eyes, he realised that someone was thumping on his bedroom door. Responding to the summons, he saw Marina, looking smooth, blow-dried, tucked in and pretty.

"Bad night?" she asked.

"Oh, you know," came the vague reply.

"Well I thought I'd better remind you about the breakfast meeting arranged for this morning."

"Yes, I was just getting ready for it."

"Really?"

This single word served as a mirror in which James saw his puffy face and tousled hair.

The prince indicated that Marina should come in.

"So you're having a breakfast meeting with an astrologer?" said Marina, who appeared to be trying to make her voice more questioning than scornful.

"He's an old friend. He has come from the Palace and will be able to tell me how the King really is."

"You realise he may have bad news. Do you want me to come with you?" James hesitated, casting a wary look at Marina. He knew that she wouldn't have much patience with astrologers. "I just think you might need some company."

Another knock on the door interrupted their conversation, three respectful raps with two seconds between each. Swindon's knock was easy to recognise.

"A Mr Showertree to see you, sir."

"Thank you, Swindon. Show him to the Martin Tower. I'll be there in a few minutes. And, Swindon..."

"Yes, sir?"

"Please go to bed."

"Of course, sir. I just need to feed the ravens first."

James usually had breakfast at the bustling New Armouries room. Today he was using a private dining area in the Martin Tower, which was the massive White Tower reimagined as a modest townhouse. Showertree was sitting at a table by the window on the second floor.

"Ah, Your Highness."

Showertree stood up and shook James's hand, using both of his hands in a gesture that turned a handshake into a kind of hug.

"And this lovely young lady must be Marina Blackwood."

Showertree produced another of his handshake hugs.

"I have heard a lot about you from the King. He comments approvingly on your spirit. Of course spirit is usually dictated by where your Mars lies, but when you're from Mars Earth takes that role."

James watched Marina's sculptured eyebrows arch a little. This wasn't a good sign.

"We don't quite know what to make of astrology on Mars, Mr Showertee."

"It's the same as astrology on Earth, my dear. It's just looking at the same thing from a different place."

James rather wished now that he had come alone.

"Let us get some breakfast," he said, making shepherding movements towards the buffet. Fortunately, with power restored, there was a range of cooked items, which Showertree placed in liberal quantities on his plate.

"So, my dear boy, how are you?" asked Showertree as he tucked into an ample sausage.

"Not too bad, considering the circumstances."

There was a pause for appreciative sausage chewing.

"Things are not easy. A moment of great change is approaching for you, and for all of us."

"How long does my grandfather have?"

"Probably closer to hours than days. I am sorry, Your Highness. But just remember while human life seems to end irrevocably, everything else in the universe goes in circles - seasons, orbits of planets, hands on a clock, all of the wheels that take us on our journeys and bring us back again. It would be strange if human life didn't follow the same path. There is the darkness of night, and then we have breakfast. So tuck in both of you. You'll need your strength. This food is excellent."

James took a mouthful of toast. Showertree shovelled in some bacon, combined on one fork with a generous helping of egg. Glancing at Marina, James could see that she was appalled that such breakfast eating gusto should accompany news of

King John's imminent demise.

Once he had dealt with the important business of his cooked breakfast, Showertree dabbed his mouth with a napkin and put cutlery, yellow with egg yolk sheen, down on swirling brush marks of toast pulled through tasty juices. James knew that this enjoyment of breakfast was simply a relish for life. Showertree felt the continuity of existence as a breathing reality. That meant he could be worried about the King, while still enjoying a hearty breakfast.

"Your grandfather has told me I am to discuss your future with you." Showertree turned to Marina. "Now, my dear, I know what you're thinking. You're wondering why Prince James is talking to a silly old fool like me at a time like this. All I can say is that we stand in a moment of doubt. As we look ahead, the only patterns we can truly predict are the movements of planets and stars."

Marina pulled a taut smile, while James poured out some tea.

"Do you have any advice for me?"

"Your Highness, there is no denying that things are difficult. Pluto, Uranus and Mars are in play, which is always going to be challenging. As for your personal chart, I confess I have nothing new to tell you. Your chart is poised between two outcomes, and it is not easy to see what will transpire. There seems to be the promise that you are about to fulfil a new stage in your destiny, which will have far reaching consequences for you and many others. In fact I would have said that you are about to become king. Yet there is something else. Jupiter is expanding your house of career and ambition, while Saturn squashes it down. Saturn has a dominant emphasis in your birth chart. There is much weight of responsibility here."

Marina sucked in her cheeks, as though pulling back words that longed to escape her mouth. James tried to ignore these omens.

"So, how do you think my brother is getting on?"

"Ah, Prince Edward. Now there's the thing. He has a difficult square of Neptune and Saturn. His Mars is retrograde in his twelfth house, and will be there for an unusually long time. I would say there is something hidden going on, a secretive plot which will change his life. Whereas you have an emphasised Saturn, your brother's chart hangs on Neptune, the planet of illusion. He has been deluding himself and is now coming back down to Earth, or Mars, with a bump."

"We hear Edward is hiding on Martian territory at Kew."

"The day your brother was born, I looked at his chart and knew he was a difficult case. Both of your charts seem to indicate that this is your moment. As I said back in Norfolk, it's almost as though you're both going to be king, each in your own way."

"Oh come on!" said Marina, as though she had been holding her breath and could do so no longer.

James absorbed in what Showertree was saying, looked around in shock.

"What's the matter?"

"I don't want to appear rude, and I'm sure you're a very nice man, Mr Showertree, but isn't this an old trick? You're being vague enough so that you can claim success with any outcome."

Showertree opened his arms, as though Marina was a child running towards him.

"The stars don't care if I look stupid. I can only tell you what they say, and they seem to say that both Edward and James will be king."

"But how can that be? And why can't Edward and James simply choose what happens to them?"

James choked on a triangle of toast when he heard this.

"Choose what happens to us? You really haven't got used to

this whole royal thing, have you?"

The astrologer smiled a soothing smile.

"We are destined to be free, and freedom is the harshest master. I am sorry I cannot be clearer."

James gave Marina a hard look. He then turned back to the astrologer, who had drunk the last of his tea.

"Are you going back to the palace now? Security won't let me go. It must make me look like a coward."

"No, my boy, you are not a coward. The time for bravery will come, but now is a time for caution. It is not safe in London. It is best if you stay here. Besides, the authorities are keen to make it appear that they planned your arrival here. The fact that you washed up at the Tower like some driftwood would be embarrassing to them. They want you here until your moment arrives. It won't be long in coming."

"I understand, Showertree. Tell my grandfather I wish I could be with him."

"He knows that, Your Highness."

Showertree stood up. He shook Marina's hand just as warmly as before, which made her look uncomfortable, and a little ashamed of herself. James was pleased if she felt this way. She had a lot to learn about life as a royal. Marina cast an apologetic glance in James's direction, and reverted to courtesy.

"Thank you for taking the time and trouble to come here. Please take care on your way back to the palace."

"I will, Marina. Lovely to meet you. I am sure I will see you both again soon. Good luck."

Showertree walked to the door. He didn't look back. The lack of his usual 'toodle oo' parting wave impressed James with the gravity of the situation more than anything else.

CHAPTER 31 (THE THAMES)

On the evening of the King's death all trouble ceased in London. Although James guessed that the sudden return of electrical power would not last, the illuminated City was like a Viking long boat in flames drifting away on a midnight tide. Billions of people shared in James's private loss. The prince, seeing images of the Mall packed with mourners, guessed that their loss was also personal. King John had been part of their lives, a reassuring presence in the background, which they would now have to learn to live without.

The following evening, with stars once again bright above a dark London, Francis Nurhaci, came to the Tower for a meeting. Greeting him at the Byward Gate, James noticed that his old boss was limping, an infirmity that had never been apparent during those distant work experience days. James changed the venue for his meeting from the White Tower's upper-most floor, to the Martin Tower.

After formal expressions of sympathy, the sheen of convention began to crack.

"Your Highness, it is my unpleasant duty to inform you that following recent disruption of vital services, the government has lost a confidence motion and resigned an hour ago. While it cannot be denied that mistakes have been made, calls for administrative stability at this difficult time have fallen on deaf ears. Consequently, I am now acting head of what can only be described as a caretaker administration. Formal permission from the monarch is required to form a new government, but I don't need to explain to you the difficulty of fulfilling that duty, following the King's death and the disappearance of his heir. As the most senior royal figure now available, I come to you at this difficult time."

Nurhaci then explained to an unresponsive carpet, with side notes to the wall just behind James's head, what ardent supporters of the royal family he and his colleagues were. He admitted, however, to a crisply trousered left knee, that carefully organised plans for what he called the 'exequies of the King,' had been thrown into turmoil. There was talk of wider considerations, of republican pressure groups who felt that the monarchy summed up everything that was wrong with Earth. There were evasions, caveats, and - recognised from James's training in public speaking - use of passive voice. Nurhaci concluded by saying something that made James catch his breath:

"Perhaps, sir, this is a time for leadership from yourself."

It was apparent that Nurhaci did not know what to do about King John's funeral. Following his moment at Richmond, this was the second occasion when James felt entirely alone with his own resources. Nurhaci, usually so assured, now presented himself as an exhausted old man. James knew that desperate politicians often came to visit his grandfather. Now the prince found himself playing the role of last resort. It was a lonely place to be. In a vertiginous moment of realisation, it became clear why monarchs had always been associated with religion. James never had time for the spiritual flummery that came with his position. He had been dutiful about it, while always keeping his own counsel about how absurd it all was. In this moment, however, as Nurhaci talked to him, with no other human agency to turn to, James came to understand the deistic nature of royalty.

Immediately after the meeting, James called Alistair and asked him to arrange a visit to Westminster Abbey where King John was to lie in state. After rushed discussions with officials, they agreed that a short visit to Westminster would be acceptable. Alistair assessed that the safest route to Westminster was the Thames, using a vessel with no technology to fail.

The royal row barge Gloriana came down from its mooring at St Katherine's Dock. A few hours later, with Oxford at one bank of oars and Cambridge at the other, Gloriana approached Westminster. One day was merging into the next as Big Ben cast out twelve doleful tolls, as if presiding over an apocalypse that somehow repeated itself twice a day with smaller disasters every hour and pessimistic editorials in the Times every fifteen minutes. This huge sound was oddly reassuring, suggesting that disaster was merely part of the daily round.

Alighting at Westminster Pier, James walked to the Abbey, massive and melancholy as a Whistler nocturne. The surrounding area from Whitehall to Millbank stood in silent isolation behind security cordons. With his entourage stopping at the West Entrance, James walked on alone, coming to a reverential standstill beside King John's coffin at The Crossing. A series of towering candles around the catafalque cast a peaceful glow on stone pillars, and on Guards officers who maintained a vigil. With great bearskinned heads bowed, they held themselves motionless and silent, gold buttons on black Hainsworth cloth twinkling in candlelight.

After a nebulous time had passed, Boles and Bacon appeared beside James. Hanging their heads together for a few moments, they all turned away and paced back to the West Entrance.

"Your time of duty has come, Your Highness," said Bacon. "Your first obligation is to arrange a fitting funeral."

Returning to the Tower in the early hours, James, knowing

time was short, called an emergency meeting. He was reluctant to drag everybody up to their accustomed meeting room in the White Tower. That choice of venue now seemed more a triumph of drama over practicality, back when they had nothing to do but talk. Instead, James set up operations in the Royal Regiment of Fusiliers Room. Another power failure saw a line of candles scattered along a table running the length of this narrow space. Portraits of generals and field marshals stood back in half darkness, as if declaring that they had done their bit for a country that did not exist anymore, and they were having none of this new trouble.

"We need a code word for the funeral," said Alistair. "Traditionally the name of a bridge is used."

James thought for a moment.

"Putney Bridge," he said. "And perhaps we should have King John interred here at the Tower. It has been a sanctuary for us. Come to think of it, the church beside Tower Green is the resting place of Lady Jane Grey. She was queen in the sixteenth century. Her reign only lasted for nine days. In a strange sort of way, it makes sense to me to have the monarchs with longest and shortest reigns together."

Alistair frowned with thoughtful concentration, as though these remarks must have a deep royal meaning. James was aware of this change in the way people treated him since his grandfather's passing. There was a sense that there was some new direction in what he said or did. James had given voice to a vague idea that had popped into his head. He was still adrift, as he had been on the Thames at Richmond; but those around him seemed to feel the tide flowing through him.

James joined Alistair in musing over a map of London, found by Swindon in the Royal Armouries Library, now spread out on the long central table. While many aspects of London had changed since this map had been printed, the river's meandering blue line remained constant, running north past Westminster, then turning east through the City, before its great ramble around the Isle of Dogs.

"The most difficult part of the operation will be securing a route between Westminster and the Tower," said James. "Perhaps it would be best to use the river again. The Thames was once a natural focus for all of London's great ceremonial events. It might be time to restore that position?"

James could sense Alistair taking the words *might* and *perhaps* out of what he had just said. Alistair wanted to know what to do, and James realised he had just told him what to do. The King's resting place was going to be at the Tower. There was going to be a river-bourne funeral procession. James knew the monarchy was of a constitutional nature and played nothing more than a symbolic role. Yet with the passing of his grandfather, he had experienced heart-stopping moments when the representation of power became actual power.

The following morning Matthew and Caroline rowed down to Thames Police Headquarters at Wapping. It was clear they faced a tough meeting. An influential group in both government and police felt that rolling technological emergencies left no resources for a public funeral. In their favour, James knew that Chief Inspector Wembury had some influence, and was solid in his support for the young men and women who had helped him at Mortlake, and who had played along with the subsequent charade that James's evacuation to the Tower had all been part of a plan.

The prince was in the Royal Fusiliers Room when Matthew and Caroline returned. Caroline simply said:

"Putney Bridge."

Three days later at 11am, King John began his last journey in Gloriana. He would have loved it thought James, who in tribute was rowing in the Cambridge Blue Boat, stationed on the barge's south side. On the north side was Oxford. Many other varied craft joined Gloriana on its voyage, some in an official capacity, but most present in an informal, democratic kind of way. A word of mouth campaign started by Wembury had gathered a fleet of old, small or otherwise humble vessels, immune to computer failure.

James felt events had borne out the wisdom of pressing ahead with a state funeral. Even though a bushfire of technical problems continued to burn, ancient ceremonial coincided with a calmer atmosphere in London People in their thousands crewed the fleet, and watched it go by from bridges and embankments. While Alistair and his team had been improvising on the run, behind this rush job was a tradition of water parades stretching back to London's earliest times. Somehow, people knew what to do. A folk memory offered assistance, as though the past came back to help the future.

A monarch never retires. Even their funeral is a public duty. James knew his grandfather would have hated retirement. King John had found rest in the same endless work that now stretched ahead of his grandson.

CHAPTER 32
(THE TOWER)

When the funeral procession reached the Tower, a team of yeoman warders brought King John ashore. His funeral pall was a yellow savannah across which three lions passant guardant leapt in unison, turning their blue claws and furious, blue-eyed gaze towards onlookers. The warders carried their burden through the main gate to Tower Green, laying it with gentle respect on a raised dais.

James noticed Alistair beside him, studying the congregation, as though trying to gauge its mood.

"Maybe we should have gone with the Archbishop of Canterbury."

"No," said James, his voice fragile with emotion. "Not after the way he treated my grandfather. If the government doesn't want to be involved in this funeral, then I am going to get an oarsman to say goodbye to the King. It would have meant something to him."

George Tyndale stood up beside the coffin and gave a eulogy that was homemade and heartfelt. The King was laid to rest. There were tears in James's eyes, which he shed for both the King and himself. He glanced at Marina beside him. At their first meeting back in his room in Cambridge, she had been a fiery, Martian republican. Now he could see her fighting grief for a difficult old man she had known for only a few months.

Afterwards there were refreshments for mourners in the New Armouries Room. This was a space formed by rugged walls of rough stone. Ceilings, joists and pillars were all fashioned from the sort of wood that once made Royal Navy ships. Over this ancient fabric lay a lacquer of newness. Blocks of pearly furniture surrounded a silver bar glittering in washes of chromatic light. James sank down into a moulded polymer chair, its beach-pebble modernity smoothed by fashion's rolling waves.

People talked in an atmosphere of regretful, placid cheeriness, appearing to take refuge in memories and the reassuring continuity of the day to day. James wanted to sit and recover with his friends, but he knew he would only have a few minutes.

Alistair whispered in his ear that the Accession Council had issued a summons.

"They want to see me now?"

"They are finalising some details. Then they will want you. They'll be doing it by immersive link, because of the security situation."

Alistair took James to the corner designated for the link, where they began rehearsing a speech. They hadn't made much progress when the call came. James accepted pats on the shoulders, handshakes, and hugs from Tower staff, and from both Oxford and Cambridge crews. The connection went live and James was standing in the Picture Gallery at St James's Palace, an image disrupted by occasional flickers and elongated distortions. The Lord Mayor of London, the Archbishop of Canterbury, Nurhaci, and a few dignitaries from Earth's government sat at a long table draped in the same sumptuous scarlet cloth that appeared to adorn the walls. This robed table stood in front of two deeply recessed white doors with panelling outlined in gold. It was as though the seated figures were guardians of a border, preparing to send James through one door or the other. Here in fate's antechamber, James was aware of paintings in heavy frames, depicting smoke from red-coated battle rising skywards to blend with a natural tumult of cloud in stormy skies.

"I wish to address the council before it begins its work," said James, preparing himself for the speech he had partly rehearsed with Alistair.

There was a flutter of alarm among council members.

"Why do you wish to address the council?" Nurhaci asked. "That is not required."

"I wish to say that I apologise for my brother's behaviour. I hope you will bear in mind the long years of service given by my grandfather, and the valuable role he played in world affairs for so long. King John contributed greatly to peace and stability, and I believe the monarchy, in whatever form you now wish it to take, will continue in that work."

"I also have something to say," said a ghostly figure sitting close to Nurhaci. This wraith was the Archbishop of Canterbury, his face inflamed with chimeric fury.

"I am declaring ex cathedra that the burial of the King in a civil ceremony with a celebrant outside the Church was unconstitutional and an unforgivable break with convention."

"We had to act quickly," said James. "We had a celebrant with us and asked him to help. You have to understand the pressures we were under."

"It is unacceptable, young man," shouted the angry prelate. "In fact I would argue that the King's burial is void ab initio."

"Preposterous," snapped Nurhaci in a high voice. "A burial is a burial. It can't be void ab... Just because you say something in Latin does not make it right."

Nurhaci was shaking. Visual echoes in the unsteady link-up image shimmered each side of his quivering form.

The Archbishop stood up. He leant forward, his fingertips resting on the table, the posture of a man about to launch into a vigorous defence of whatever was on his mind. Nurhaci's voice strayed towards the shrill.

"This discussion is not appropriate for the council."

The Archbishop dropped his head, rocked back and forth on those outstretched fingers for a few seconds, before sitting down. He leant back in his chair, hands behind his head, elbows stuck out wide, like a tropical lizard puffing out a colourful dewlap. The chief minister took a moment, as though trying to gather himself.

"We are not here to talk about the King's funeral. We are here to talk about the future. The Accession Council usually sits in a ceremonial capacity only. However, on this occasion circumstance dictates that the council has real decisions to make. Prince James, you are obliged to abide by those decisions, which represent the will of your serving government."

Nurhaci started to read from a formal, archaic, hand written page.

"We, the Accession Council of Earth's monarchy are here to confirm the identity of our new sovereign following the passing of His Royal Highness King John II. In this matter we note that heir to the throne, Prince Edward, Earl of Australasia, has left Earth for Martian territory at Kew Gardens. It is noted that Prince Edward has been unilaterally declared King of Earth and Mars by certain Martian ambassadorial parties at Kew. Since Earth government jurisdiction does not extend to Martian territory on Earth, the council is obliged to accept that Prince Edward must be regarded as His Royal Highness King Edward IX in Martian diplomatic territory on Earth, namely ambassadorial and research properties at London's Kew Gardens, the Eden Project in Cornwall, the Orto Botanico di Padova in Padua, the New York Botanic Garden in New York City, the Jardim Botanico in Rio de Janeiro, the Trelew Dome in Wales, and the Martian demesne of Monaco. I have here a letter received from the Mars House containing Edward's written Accession Oath which is correct in all points."

Nurhaci held up the letter. Something about the way he grasped it between finger and thumb at one corner, told James that deckled edges, embossed coats of arms and pompous jargon did not change his low opinion of a distasteful document.

"As for Edward's wider claim to the throne of Earth, the council asserts that while Prince Edward has a theoretical right to the throne, it is clear that this government, under precedent set by the Declaration of Rights of 1688, has final authority in royal matters. We, therefore, find that Prince Edward has abdicated his responsibilities to the Crown by leaving Earth territory. On these grounds, the council decrees the exclusion of Prince Edward, Earl of Australasia, from the succession to Earth's crown beyond the aforementioned Martian territories on Earth. Prince Edward will not be permitted passage to Mars at this time. We see his removal to Kew as entrapment and believe that misleading Martian influence has impaired his judgment. Should Prince Edward attempt to emerge from Martian territory he will be taken into protective custody. The council further decrees that Prince Edward's younger brother, Prince James, Earl of Europe, now has priority."

At this point Nurhaci's voice changed to a strange monotone, which he obviously thought fitting when announcing the accession of a new king.

"We the lords spiritual and temporal of this realm of Earth, assisted by members of his late majesty's privy council do hereby with one voice publish and proclaim that Prince James Henry Lippe Lakota Saxe Qing Coburg Yamato Montezuma Imhotep Romanov Khan Hapsburg Windsor, by the death of our late sovereign of happy memory, is hereby declared His Royal Highness King James III. His lieges do acknowledge all faith and constant obedience, beseeching fate to bless King James III with long and happy years to reign over us. Given at St James's Palace, this twelfth day of May, in the year...."

The broadcast faded for a moment. There was silence. Then from back in the Tower, James heard a chorus of voices shouting:

"Long live the king."

In the Picture Gallery at St James's Palace, James stared at people who had just changed his life. Alistair had warned him that something like this might happen. Edward was king of a few research domes. He, Prince James, humble younger brother, opener of smaller spaceports and more minor underground mass transit systems, was king of everything else.

James noticed that the Archbishop was getting restive.

"We should now hear the Accession Oath," demanded the Archbishop.

James regarded the oath, to serve and protect the established Church, as more of the usual royal religious extravagance. Yet after his recent meeting with a traumatised Nurhaci, he was accepting of what the oath stood for, understanding now more than ever, the deep-seated need for a symbolic authority beyond the imperfect counsels of humanity.

"I, James profess, testify and declare..."

Before he could continue, the Picture Gallery began stretching, everyone in it coming to resemble those elongated Plantagenet lions on the royal funeral pall. The link lasted long enough for James to see panic on the Archbishop's distended face.

"The oath!" shouted the Archbishop. Then the Council was gone.

Later that evening James was talking to Marina and Alistair in his room. James was now officially King of Earth. For a few hours, he doubted whether this could actually be true, since he did not recite the oath fully; but a message from Nurhaci to Alistair provided firm assurance that the decision stood. The government had enough trouble giving an impression of competence, without having to admit to procedural confusions during James III's accession. Proclamation usually followed oath. In the stress of events, the council had muddled its order of proceedings. Nothing more would be said.

"There's no going back. The deal is done," said Alistair. "Edward pushed it too far. He had to go. Now you are king, and everything will just rub along."

"I've got to rub along as King of Earth, have I?" said James.

He had coped well with the day's pressures so far, but now in private, the young monarch's resolve was at breaking point. It was clear that the oath problem wasn't a technicality that would get him out of his responsibilities.

"You are more suited to kingship than Edward," reassured Alistair.

James saw Marina looking out of the window at scattered groups of people milling about on Tower Green.

"Don't you think it's interesting that they're trying to get the Martians on Edward's side?" she said. "That's rather clever."

"On Edward's side? How do you work that out? The Martians will go crazy when they hear they have a king, even if it's a king of a few research domes. They'll rebel, use military action. They'll redirect that asteroid everyone has been talking about. They'll shoot any member of the royal family they can find. Oh, Marina, it's not safe to be near me!"

Marina looked impatient with this outburst.

"I know Mars people and if there's one thing they don't like, it's having Earth tell them they can't have something. Edward is not arriving to take over his kingdom, expecting everyone to bow and pay homage. No, the King of Mars is a fugitive at Kew. Mars will be furious at having their man locked up. They'll see it as a slight, and will fight to get him out and have him recognised. Before you know it we might actually have a King of Mars who the Martian people themselves have fought for. I didn't know your grandfather for long, but I saw enough to persuade me he was a clever man."

James tried to slow his breathing.

"He liked talking to you. Did he tell you anything? He spent a lot of time with Devonshire in the last months, and that man is a strategist if ever there was one."

"No, he didn't tell me anything. I've just got a feeling that he had a plan."

That night, to calm himself, James imagined he was back in the Blue Boat, counting strokes instead of sheep. He concentrated on the mental image of each stroke, and tried to imagine where he was on the Thames as the boat moved along. He was still awake when Putney Bridge loomed out of the mist of his imagination. That night he rowed the tideway many times.

CHAPTER 33 (KEW)

"This is ludicrous," spluttered the Archbishop as he unpacked his ceremonial robes. "I should be doing this in Westminster Abbey, not in a big sandpit at Kew Gardens."

These complaints were addressed only to himself. There was a distressing absence of Lambeth Palace staffers, who usually facilitated such venting.

The Archbishop relived that moment of horror, when Nurhaci announced that not only was he refusing to reconvene the council to have James recite a proper oath, he was also going to insist on a religiously neutral coronation for King James III. This was in response to various religious groups seeking to fill Earth's power vacuum. The government had asked George Tyndale to preside, since he was Earth's only civil celebrant with experience of royal ceremonial.

Civil weddings and funerals were bad enough, but a civil coronation was a disaster. Losing the coronation was a fundamental loss of political and symbolic power. The Archbishop shuddered at the memory of those dark hours, wondering whether he would be the last of a line stretching back to 597AD.

There was, however, an alternative to James III in the guise of King Edward IX. After a long night of spiritual struggle, it had become clear that the Church's only option was to offer ecclesiastical backing to Edward. Compared to those apostate coronation plans for James, a king crowned with holy rectitude would be a potent force. Personal consequences did not come into this decision-making, because there weren't too many personal consequences to consider. Leading the Church was an all-consuming career.

For an old man who relished his routine, it was profoundly disorientating to be ironing his robes in the Mars Dome at Kew. It helped to recall the sequence of events that had brought him here. On the night of departure, he had decided against trying to find a Vox Pod that worked. Specifying a restricted area as a destination would have invited unwanted attention. Instead, he had called Equus Events, a wedding carriage hire company, with whom he had a discreet financial understanding. In this way, only a week after that fateful Accession Council gathering, the Established Church's senior prelate lowered curtain blinds and sat back on a velvet seat, in a claret and cream landau, listening to a rolling cadence of clipping hooves on London's night-time streets.

Arriving at Kew, the comforting sounds of horse drawn travel dissipated into a nervous clatter of horses pulled to a halt, when they would much rather have kept going and arrived at some place less worrisome. The border checkpoint between Earth and Martian territory lay in Lichfield Road. Floodlighting illuminated a barrier running from pavement to pavement. A solider raised one hand, while the other rested on a weapon slung across his chest. This reincarnation Check Point Charlie could not resist God's work. A believer in Immigration and Interplanetary Settlement had filed all necessary border-crossing permissions. A waved arm gestured the visitor to proceed.

That moment beyond the cordon sat in the Archbishop's mind in images bleached by floodlights and stress. Only then did it become clear that there was no going back. This was a journey across the Rubicon, an advance on Rome in defiance of all convention. The Rubicon in this case was Kew Gardens' Victoria entrance - a pair of black, wrought iron gates, supported by two Portland stone pillars engraved with a crown and the letters VR.

The two white horses trotted and fretted towards the Mars House. A member of Martian staff gestured towards a humble side entrance, opening into a cavernous cold store, filled with trough planters blooming with frost-hardened juniper. Anxious equine breath condensed in chilly air.

All this happened only the previous day. Now, after a few hours' sleep in an unfamiliar bed, the Archbishop was about to crown King Edward IX.

Dominico Van Cello's face appeared around the door of this fertiliser storage area designated as a dressing room.

"All ready?" he asked.

"Won't be a minute."

Creases in a gold and red cope, packed hurriedly, weren't coming out, despite the efforts of a self-guided iron zipping about on fabric more suited to carpeting than clothing. Pushing the scuttling iron to one side, the Archbishop pulled the cope around his shoulders, letting it slump into place. Now fully armoured, he made his way to what counted as Edward's dressing room, improvised against a background of dripping hydroponic Martian plant cultivators. Edward was sitting on a plastic chair. He looked stiff and uncomfortable in a splendid ceremonial outfit not designed for sitting.

"Are you ready, young man? You are about to embark on a historic reign. As head of the Church, I wish you every success."

Edward stood up, and surprised the Archbishop with a hug. Hands, heavy with rings, patted the royal back. Perhaps Edward thought these hands reassuring but they were actually saying, "that's enough". Edward stepped away, an apostolic grip on his shoulder holding him at arm's length.

"Do you recall our meeting at Lambeth Palace? God tested my faith on that occasion and I'll admit I was found wanting. But tests are only designed to make us stronger in the long run. In crowning you, the Church is obliged to do something it once opposed, which just serves to demonstrate guidance from a higher power. God arranges pragmatic manoeuvers to buttress the cathedral of faith. The correct course of action has been revealed to me. King John wanted you to take the throne of Mars. He believed in you, Edward. There are people who would deprive you of your birthright. I am here to stop them doing that."

"I always thought my grandfather preferred James."

"No, he wanted you."

"But why would he want me? Why?"

The Archbishop grabbed a wilting young man by both shoulders and shook him.

"You are the first born. You are the rightful king and no one can change that. You have been chosen."

Men in red robes were standing nearby. They had come for Edward.

Prelate escorted prince to the Mars House foyer where the claret and cream landau stood ready, its image shimmering in Martian Liberty's reflecting pool. Only a subtle shake of Van Cello's head stopped the Archbishop climbing into the carriage after Edward. Thwarted in this regard, he made sure his impressive ecclesiastical form was heading the procession following the coronation coach as it proceeded along an improvised ceremonial way across the Mars House plain.

At a predetermined point, narrow steel-rimmed wheels crunched to a halt on red flagstones. Edward climbed down backwards, reminding the historically minded Archbishop of Neil Armstrong descending Eagle's ladder in 1969. This felt like a moment for wide-ranging thoughts and connections, a moment when even someone who had trouble empathising with others was quite sure that everyone under that recreated Martian sky shared in something bigger. They were part of history, and did not stand alone in west London with sand on their shoes.

It was this sense of irresistible destiny that now forced the Archbishop to continue with his duties. He had assumed there would be some kind of church in the dome, or at least an altar. Instead, he found himself led out to a pink stone circle, modelled on Stonehenge. No one had told him about a stone circle, at least not until he was walking with Dominico Van Cello in the procession. A new planet loved creating a past. Martian engineers had erected this ceremonial shrine with stone brought back from Olympus Mons. How they managed to do this was a matter of endless conjecture. As usual with religious buildings, said Van Cello, the trick was to create something that looked as though only God himself could have built it.

A programmed morning sky gave an illusion of sunrise between the Martian standing stones. These pagan overtones were appalling, but there had been no rehearsal and no time to object. The moment had arrived. Everyone present was a small part of a big story, and no one was in a position to bring proceedings to a halt.

Only a few minutes before, back when Van Cello had been making hard-boiled remarks about God working as a building contractor, this ceremony had all been part of a political game. Now things were different. This was a culmination, one of those moments when individual choices come together in a broad sweep of events.

At the stone circle's exact centre sat Edward's coronation throne, hewn from rose marble. On a neighbouring pedestal rested a crown of cast, milled and polished ingot. Before touching it, there was the matter of the oath, that vital pledge the Accession Council had so foolishly neglected.

"Is Your Majesty willing to take the oath?"

"I am so willing."

"Do you, Edward, solemnly and sincerely in the presence of

God profess, testify and declare that you are a faithful follower of the Earth Church, and will according to the true intent of the Church enactments, which secure the succession to the throne of your realm, uphold and maintain said enactments to the best of your powers according to law?"

"I am so willing."

"Will you maintain and preserve inviolably the settlement of the Church of Earth, and the doctrine, worship, discipline and government thereof, as by law established on Earth? And will you preserve unto the bishops and clergy of Earth, and to the Churches there committed to their charge, all such rights and privileges, as by law shall appertain to them?"

"All this I promise to do."

God's chief representative experienced a thrill of vindication in hearing fittingly dull and lifeless responses. Priestly fingers, dipped into a pot of Martian camelina oil, touched the royal head, hands and heart. At this point canopy bearers lowered a fringed screen of finest Martian fleece over busy ceremonial, like nurses pulling curtains around a procedure.

Then with the canopy carried away came the moment. Hands, oily from anointing, lifted the crown, dense in symbolism and atomic number, from its pedestal. It was necessary to hold this amalgam of terrestrial and Martian precious metal close to the body, to avoid unbecoming arm shaking and potential back injury. With a grunting clean and jerk, an offering of industro-decorative expertise rose towards a flushed sky. Lowering was slow, with a loss of control at the last moment. Red-rimmed eyes widened under a heavy impact. The Archbishop bowed to Edward IX.

"I, as Archbishop of Earth, promise to be faithful and true, and faith and truth will bear unto you, our sovereign lord, king of this realm and defender of the faith, and unto his heirs and successors according to law. So help me God."

From his position of submission, he glanced up at Edward's face, and saw a single tear running down his cheek. It was understandable. Compressed vertebrae are painful.

CHAPTER 34 (WESTMINSTER ABBEY)

King James III's coronation was to take place at Westminster Abbey, with George Tyndale officiating. During preparations, George's role had been subject to an official complaint lodged by the dean. Alistair had taken the dean aside and reminded him in as friendly a way as possible that Westminster Abbey was a 'Royal Peculiar', a place of worship under direct royal jurisdiction. If the Crown wanted to conduct a civil service at Westminster Abbey then it was entitled to do so. His Majesty's Government did not want an overtly religious coronation, but they did require a sense of tradition. In the spirit of compromise, Alistair suggested using Poet's Corner for the service. This was Westminster Abbey's most secular quarter, laden with memorials to writers, expressing spirituality in its widest sense.

Standing at the West Door, Alistair directed everyone through the nave's towering symmetry to Poet's Corner. Once everyone was in, he joined the congregation, standing at the back. He felt like one of those watching statues. Even though various writers in their sculptured form tried to appear intellectual and wise, a certain raffishness still came through. It was like the green room at a time travelling Royal Variety Performance. The writers might have written the script. Now they had to stand back and watch the show going on without them. Alistair had often felt like this, standing unnoticed at one of Edward's grand parties. He had made it happen, but no one was ever looking in his direction.

As Alistair tried to gather himself and concentrate on this historic moment, he became aware of a presence beside him.

"I've been looking for you, Alistair Fitzwhistle."

"Lady Beatrice."

"Don't act so surprised, darling. I was on the guest list. No doubt you put me there."

"I felt it was only right and proper that the House of March should be represented."

"I bet you did. Anyway, thanks for inviting me."

Beatrice was right. This daughter of Lord March, a futile torchbearer for Edward, had long been an object of affection for Alistair. As he was doing most of the work organising this coronation, he thought he might as well enjoy some benefits.

"So there he is, King James III. Who would have thought it? I went after the wrong prince."

"You might not realise it, but you are well out of it."

"I know that. Tell me; is it true that most people meet their future spouses at other people's coronations?"

"Beatrice, you're just emotional because a king you are not married to is getting crowned. Don't tease me."

"This isn't teasing, you silly goose. This is seduction."

"I don't think this is the time or place…"

"We are in the back row. Being nobodies, no one is looking at us. That has advantages."

Before matters could proceed any further, George Tyndale began his opening preamble. Alistair felt an odd combination of relief and disappointment that Beatrice's frank wooing or whatever it was she was doing, should be interrupted. George had begun with an informal speech. He was talking about Poet's Corner, and the wide sense of spiritual enquiry it represented. Then he spoke of royalty rising above narrow affiliations to reach out to a wider world.

"A coronation is a turning point in the life of one person, and a time when we are all given an opportunity to re-examine our lives. Royalty is a kind of historic mirror in which we see ourselves. We cannot know all of history for everybody, so we know royal history as a representation of the whole. Today is a special day. It is the day we crown King James III, and the day we are offered the chance to mark a new beginning in all of our lives."

Alistair had tried to turn his back on royalty when Oxford cast him aside, his usefulness to Edward seemingly at an end. Now here he was working for James. He couldn't help it. In a strange kind of way he felt like James himself, who couldn't help the fact that he had to be king.

George picked up St Edward's crown, sitting on a table beside the throne. The upwardly curved bell shape of its golden, jewel-peppered frame seemed designed to sit easily in the hands of someone lifting it, and awkwardly on the head of whoever wore it. Without more preamble, without holy oil, scepter, orb or ceremonial canopy, George lowered the ancient crown onto James's coiffured hair, where it perched top heavy, demanding an upright posture.

"I pronounce you King James III. Good luck, King James. Good luck to us all as we begin a new chapter in our lives. Long live the King."

These words came back as a massed reply, filling the great perpendicular space.

"Oh, coronations are wonderful," said Beatrice in a teary voice.

Alistair dropped his head, uncomfortable with a knot of emotion sitting like a medical condition in his chest. He put an arm around Beatrice. Staring at his feet, he realised that he was standing on the memorial to Lord Byron:

"But there is that within me which shall tire

Fortune and Time and breathe when I expire."

CHAPTER 35
(THE TOWER)

Back in his rooms at the Tower, King James still felt the burden of his unwieldly crown, sitting like an empyreal halo around his head. There was also the weight of news that the Democratic Conservatives had finally managed to oust Nurhaci. People who faced complex situations with easy answers now controlled government. Tomorrow James would have to endure a trial his grandfather had faced many times - meeting unpleasant leaders and showing them hospitality.

He wanted to be alone, but solitude had always been a luxury. On this occasion, James had an hour of retirement granted to him as a kind of parting gift to help a young man over the threshold into his new life.

The Tower walls were a good place to walk and brood. Illumination came from braziers, found in a Tower storeroom. It was in ardent firelight, felt as much as seen, that King John's ghost appeared. He stood framed in the arched doorway to the Salt Tower.

"Don't worry, my boy," said the King. "This is a holographic file recorded about two months before my death, as far as the doctors can judge anyway. They have programmed me to appear using a device in the ring that Showertree gave you at the Black Horse. I have returned one last time to offer help with your new responsibilities. If all has gone well you should be seeing me on the first occasion when you are alone for an extended period following your accession. The recording will stop playing if anyone approaches. I hope you are not in the toilet. The toilet was about the only place I was ever alone."

James looked at Showertree's ring, glowing blue on his finger, and glanced around in vain for a witness to this overwhelming event. His only companions were flame and shadow. James stood in fervid isolation with a royal mirage, feeling the anxiety that he had always experienced in his grandfather's company. There was also a joy, which could only be compared to the exaltation of a devotee.

The King burped. He hesitated after this gastric mishap. He seemed to be toying with the idea of starting again, before changing his mind and pressing on.

"I am here to explain our plan regarding your brother. We want Mars to have a king, and we want to persuade the people of Mars that they want one. By now, Edward should be monarch of Martian territory on Earth, and will have taken refuge somewhere in his new domain. That was the agreement I came to with our constitutional lawyers, and with Dominico Van Cello. Van Cello thinks the Martians, while not initially welcoming the idea of a king, will be very angry at having a king of theirs confined to a few research domes. Eventually we are hopeful they will make such a fuss that the government will transfer Edward to Mars as a new monarch. But of course we don't want Edward to establish a separate dynasty. It is crucial that in the long term we have a joint crown shared between Earth and Mars."

The King paused. James took this moment to remember that he had a clever girlfriend. Marina had been right about the manipulation of Martian sentiment.

"A monarch," continued the King, appearing to lean against a parapet, "is the focus of constant problems. There are no solutions except those provided by difficulties. One difficulty that robbed me of sleep over the last few years has been Edward's lack of resolve. I thought this would make the succession difficult. As it turns out Edward's awkwardness could prove useful. He might not last long as king. Certainly, his foolish attempt to evade his responsibilities by marrying Tarquin Van Cello will make a rightful heir unlikely; particularly as Tarquin's father has assured me he will never agree to a divorce. We are hopeful that when the time comes, you or your children will inherit the throne of Mars, just as our forebear, James VI of Scotland, inherited the throne of England in 1603 to create what was once the United Kingdom. We are royalty, James, which means that we are playing the long game. This is only the beginning of our effort to create a new United Kingdom."

The next pause was lengthier. It seemed that the effort of talking, and remembering what to say, was telling.

"Right. Last bit. Hope you're still concentrating. Assuming that Edward eventually travels to Mars, we want a group of good people to go with him. We placed candidates for this group in the Oxford boat. Send Edward his Oxford crew. The months of training and team building will make it likely they will answer this call. I can think of no force in the universe other than the camaraderie of rowing that would persuade a group of decent young people to work with Edward. How you get these people to Edward will be your decision. I don't know your current situation, so it will be a matter of thinking for yourself. To help you do that, now and in the future, I have provided your Cambridge crew. I selected them to go forward with you into your life as king. Rowing introduced me to Bacon and Boles. I hope the friends you have made in your Blue Boat will be as good as the friends I made in mine. That is all I have to say. Now my time is over, and yours has come. There will be occasions when you will not be able to see a way forward. Just remember, for the monarchy it is all just business as usual. Good luck, Your Majesty."

The vision of King John began to fade. As it did so, Swindon Hardy came running from the direction of Lanthorn Tower.

"Halt! Who goes there?"

"It's alright, Swindon."

"But I saw someone, Your Majesty. It looked like..."

"Please don't talk to anyone about this."

Swindon appeared to be struggling to regain his breath and remain dignified at the same time.

"So I did see something, sir?"

"Yes, you did. It was a holographic file left by my grandfather. I'm asking you not to mention it to anyone."

"No, sir. Of course not."

"He had advice for me. In the days to come I am going to need all the advice I can get."

"You will be fine, Your Majesty. We all believe in you."

James felt how lonely it was to be the object of belief.

CHAPTER 36 (THE EDEN PROJECT)

When Martian officials presented him with the plan for his traditional dominions tour, Edward was not in the least bit enthusiastic. What exactly was the point when his royal domain consisted of a few domes and the Martian Demesne of Monaco? And was it safe to leave Kew? Edward was counselled that yes, the trip was important, and yes it was safe, since Earth based Martian transport enjoyed diplomatic immunity; and no, refusal wasn't an option if he wished to retain the goodwill of people who fed him, kept him warm, and prevented his handover to Earth's vengeful authorities.

It was thus that Edward found himself at the Eden Mars Dome, which squatted in a huge worked-out Cornwall clay pit close to the original Eden Project. On a precipitous wall above a line of welcome desks, visual displays weaved their way around various remarkable Red Planet facts - highest volcano in the solar system, biggest sand storms and so on. Beneath this revolving journey through Martian extremes, Eden Mars Dome staff in traditional maroon fleece formed a line along which Edward and Tarquin had begun walking, shaking hands as they went. The new king noted with wry amusement that Tarquin Van Cello appeared to have found his niche as a royal consort.

"Delighted. Hello. Wonderful to meet you."

King Edward, meanwhile, was master of the bright greeting. While Edward's conscious mind was telling him he didn't want to be king, he had a dim awareness that some kind of royal id, honed over generations, had him pausing at intervals asking staple questions of the royal walkabout:

"How long have you worked here? I expect you have met a lot of interesting people."

Children, twisting from side to side on nervous heels received extra, eye level attention.

A round of applause accompanied the royal party through to vistas of red sand. This place conveyed Martian immensity just as a cathedral roof suggests height more powerfully than the sky above it.

King Edward stopped to look at a recreation of the original manned Mars landing site, listening to a nervous curator presenting some well-rehearsed history. Viewing the interior of an original landing vehicle, he made a comment about how small and cramped it was.

The walkabout then continued along the Mariner Valley path, which after following a coral coloured river, turned behind a thundering waterfall. Emerging from this cascade, his face damp and pink with atomized water, Edward admired a Martian eight boat sitting beside a representational slipway. He listened to a story he already knew, of Martian rowing having its origins in a publicity campaign designed to show that there was water on Mars. All it needed was some atmospheric engineering to set it free.

The path zigzagged up steep valley sides, reaching a region of dusky steppe. An Eden official explained miniature weather systems and their mechanics. A small Martian twister did a dance around a rocky tor.

Edward's journey ended back at the manned landing site memorial. Here the Dome's director presented his new monarch with the Mars Medal, awarded to people considered to have made a significant contribution to Red Planet culture. Gathered press hustled in to record this historic moment.

Edward then experienced his own version of the Newtonian carry-on that throws rockets into space. His lunch fell downwards as his equal and opposite body went the other way, riding on a lift curving upwards along the warp of the dome's pink cloud-strewn inner surface. Eden's interplanetary elevator deposited him in a lofty platform area, known as Deimos. Here he listened to Dominico Van Cello giving a speech to gathered dignitaries and press, calling for the release of Mars's new monarch to his home planet.

That evening in a private guest room on Deimos, Edward collapsed onto his bed.

"My hand hurts," he moaned, looking at purple bruises indicating countless handshakes.

"You did well today," said Tarquin at the wardrobe, checking suits. "Keep it up. The Italian dome tomorrow. The Cupola Marte. Read those notes I gave you."

"Yes, yes. But, Tarquers, after Italy then what? Brazil, South Wales, New York?"

"No, the people at all of those domes are a bit edgy about security."

"So Italy and back to Kew then? What happens after that? This monarchial carry-on is onerous enough when my realm consists of a few domes. How do I jolly well cope when I'm king of two planets? I won't have a hand left on the end of my bally arm."

"You'll get used to it. Think of this as a training course. Learn your Martian history, and get on with memorising those Martian dialect phrases as well."

Though Edward prickled and huffed, he did indeed start running through phrases he might need on his next walkabout. The path of least resistance was to slip into the role expected of him, even if he had to shake people's hands until he tenderised his own.

CHAPTER 37
(THE TOWER)

Matthew spent vague hours of lassitude reading in his room. Alistair Fitzwhistle, a man who hadn't even made the Blue Boat, was now chief aide to King James.   Matthew Nice, President of Oxford Rowing Club, found himself ordered about - told to go rowing down to Wapping to see Wembury, or to undertake various menial jobs organising King John's funeral procession. He didn't know if he wanted to do this anymore. Maybe it was time to go back to Oxford and get on with his life.

The summons was unexpected. Matthew had been sitting in his room, researching heraldry, preparing for another of his lowly tasks - a planned meeting with a journalist who had questions about the royal coat of arms. Swindon interrupted this arcane work with an announcement that Marina wanted to see him in the Royal Regiment of Fusiliers Room. Getting there, he saw Marina sitting at the end of the long table, like a cox in her seat. He sat down at stroke.

"So, what's all this about?"

"I am here to offer you a proposition, Matthew. King James would have talked with you about this himself, but he has been called away on government business. Can I begin by asking how you are?"

"Well if you want me to be frank, I am looking forward to getting back to Oxford and doing some normal things. I assume we're not all obliged to stay here?"

"No, you are free to go. The security situation is still precarious, but I am sure you are beginning to feel that you do not need or want to live at the Tower any longer. The police agree that if you wish, you and the rest of your crew can return to Oxford. There is, however, an alternative."

Matthew put his hands together in an attitude of tentative prayer, resting his mouth on the tips of his fingers.

"What kind of alternative?"

"Nurhaci still has a channel of communication open to us. As you know, the planetary border is closed. Nevertheless, the Martians are still hopeful they can get Edward off planet in the near future. When he gets to Mars, the Martians will probably recognise him as their king."

Matthew's swaggering kingmaker confidence was long gone. His boat had sunk beneath him. Any directive that he mould future monarchs had expired.

"I know I used to believe in the idea of Edward as a Martian king. King John could be very persuasive."

"You're right, King John could be persuasive. He continues to be so, even now. It's no accident that we have a monarch presiding over a small piece of Mars in Kew Gardens. Many Martians are already identifying with Edward's plight, seemingly imprisoned at Kew. He is symbolic of a struggle against Earth, rather than a symbol of Earth's colonial power. By the time we get Edward to Mars the authorities there probably won't have any choice but to make him king. When they do, he will need a staff. We want the Oxford crew to form that staff. This all began with you helping King John place Edward in the Blue Boat. Would you like to join King Edward and continue what you started?"

"I'm sorry?"

"Would you like to go to Mars, to help establish the monarchy there? I know it's a lot to take in."

Matthew had no words. He stood up, which felt as wrong as standing up in a boat. He sat back down.

"A lot to take in? If we do this, we might never see Earth again. We're in the middle of our degrees. You just want us to up sticks, leave everything we've ever known...."

"Take your time," counselled Marina, as though she were steadying her crew out on the water.

"But why us? There must be better qualified people available."

"Surely you know a little about Edward by now. Beneath the image of carefree privilege he likes to display, he had a very tough time as a child. His mother and father both died when he was young, and his grandfather was a stern man who sent him to a hard school in Scotland. He got through on his charm, and with the help of his friend Alistair Fitzwhistle. It seemed like the same sorry pattern was going to repeat itself at Oxford. As it turned out Edward joined the rowing club, where he was eventually accepted. I am telling you now, Matthew, if there is anyone King Edward will want with him on Mars it is you and the rest of the Oxford crew."

Matthew knew that Marina was playing with the instincts that bond rowers. Rational parts of his brain struggled with primitive lobes dealing with sports.

"Don't forget he sank the boat. Why should we show loyalty to a man like that?"

"The Martians forced his hand. Our contacts at Kew have told us Edward argued with Tarquin Van Cello, while you were on the Goblin. Our source says he came to see you as good chaps who deserved respect."

"He said that? He said we were good chaps?"

"Yes, he did. The Martians had to threaten him before he gave way. Do you think the old Edward would have made that stand on your behalf? We both know that rowing made him a better man. You did that for him."

"Changed him? I think he's still the man he used to be, only with a little more strength behind his capacity to make trouble."

Matthew's internal struggle continued. It was a scuffle between instinctive hatred of someone who had damaged the team, and an impulsive loyalty to crewmates. Fighting himself to a standstill, Matthew decided to retreat for a moment into practicalities.

"You still haven't explained how all this would be done. Edward is at Kew surrounded by police and soldiers."

"We believe the Thames is the safest route. Should you choose to go, you will make the journey using the same boat that brought you here."

For long moments, Matthew looked at the little Martian woman who was saying strange things.

"You mean we'll be rowing to Mars?"

"Yes, that's right. Your boat is fast, and has no computers to fail. You stand a good chance."

"Well that's some plan... And if things don't go well, what then?"

"That is a fair question, and you have to be clear that this is a risky proposition. The border at Kew is under heavy guard. Any attempt to reach Martian territory without authorisation is an offence under the Emergency Powers Act. You must understand the risk you will be running in trying to break into a restricted area."

Matthew knew all about the new legislation. When not studying heraldry, he had read about the Emergency Powers Act in his Tower bedroom.

"On a more positive note, Chief Inspector Wembury is sympathetic to our cause and will do what he can to help. We will also get some assistance from the Martians. I can tell you that on the day, network problems will worsen. Police launches will be compromised, and it would be a brave officer who decided to climb into an aircraft."

Matthew massaged his temples. He wished he had never put Edward in the Blue Boat. If any one of dozens of deserving candidates had taken that seat, he'd be back in Oxford, enjoying early mornings on the Thames. Instead here he was, planning a rowing trip to Mars.

Matthew pressed his fingers against closed eyelids, opening them to see Swindon placing a delicate cup of tea on the table beside him.

"I thought you might need that," said Marina.

"Yes, us Earth people do enjoy tea."

"We're beginning to take tea on Mars too. We are growing low temperature versions. This is in fact a Mariner Valley Sochi Oolong. Try it. Due to the lack of cows on Mars, it is traditionally taken without milk."

Matthew sipped his tea, and tried to hide his disapproval of its smoky taste. Keeping his face impassive, he used the drink to give himself more thinking time. Despite losing faith in the idea of a Martian king, a rowing crew's loyalty had him in its grip. This devotion even extended to a hopeless oarsman. Matthew needed to believe that Edward had not wanted to cause the fatal oar clash. Marina was right; rowers and prince had come to accept each other. If Edward had come to respect his crewmates, they in turn had come to appreciate Edward's good humour and friendly manner. Though no rower, his effort to escape the life planned for him by his elders allowed Edward to worm his way into the affections of the crew, who as young people were all trying to find their own way. Matthew felt loyalty towards a man who could not row and had sunk the boat. This must have been what King John wanted. Resistance now was as futile as it had been on the terrace at Magdalen.

"I'll see if I can get a crew. I'll talk to them. If they say yes, when will we go?"

"One week from today."

Matthew assumed the interview was over and got to his feet.

"Matthew, there is one more thing I would like your help with."

"Oh yes and what's that?"

"It has been decided that James and I are to be married, to demonstrate a firm link between Earth and Mars. We plan to do this within a few days, here at the Tower, so that those in government who would stop it won't have a chance to interfere. I hope you will have some time this week to help us with the necessary organisation."

Matthew had reached his limit. He was going to Mars in a rowing boat. Marina and James were getting married.

"Fine," he heard himself saying.

Matthew deep in thought, turned to leave, only to hear Marina calling to him as he reached the door.

"What?"

"Your cup," said Marina. "It's from the royal collection. They'll get cross if you go wandering around with it."

Matthew looked at the white bone china cup decorated with a unicorn rearing up on its hind legs. He noticed a golden chain, snaking from a crown-like collar down to a ring anchored in a figurative mound of grass. He knew from his heraldry reading that the invisible arbiters of myth judged a free unicorn to be highly dangerous. This animal was white, demonstrating a purity so demanding, so resistant to compromise, that it all came out as something wild and primal. In the United Kingdom's ancient coat of arms, a tethered unicorn represented Scotland. Now, Matthew saw the unicorn as his old self. He had been clear and certain about himself and his direction in life. It wasn't possible to be like that anymore. It was all about adapting, and compromising, and going to Mars in a rowing boat if that's what life offered you.

CHAPTER 38
(BROOKLANDS)

In the Brooklands Clubhouse, Edward said he would do the talking. Donning his protective coat of charm and humour, he turned to his hosts and described what happened.

"We were just about to leave for Italy when we had news that Martian Diplomatic Transport might no longer be secure. The plan was to come straight back to Kew. So, we were west of London when our smooth passage was rudely interrupted by some bally shuddering and shaking. We were certain Earth authorities were trying to bring us down outside Martian territory, so they could take me into what they charmingly call 'protective custody'. And while Tarquin and the other chaps were all wondering what to do, cloaking our position with technical what-nots, I casually suggested dropping in on old Lord Montagu."

Edward gestured towards his small entourage, consisting of Tarquin and a couple of Martian bodyguards, who might just as well have been another couple of Guards officers determined to ignore Edward completely.

"Montagu will give us a warm welcome, I said. If there's one welcoming place west of London where a king can land quietly and find a hiding place, it's Brooklands. It would be just a matter of parking next to that Wellington bomber in the air museum, sticking an information board in front of us, and no one would be any the wiser."

Montagu laughed; Devonshire tapped a finger on his cheek just above the corner of his lip where a smile would be if he went in for that sort of thing; March hee-hawed merrily.

"I do know a few things, you chaps," said Edward, feeling more than a little vulnerable behind his full armour of hail-fellow-well-met, nonchalant caricature.

"Well you're not King John with your man marrying, but you're not a bad lad. So what are you going to do? Flee the planet? Never saw you as king material."

"Never saw you as lord material, Montagu."

"Ha! You're right there."

"I haven't much choice but to flee the planet. If the Earth authorities get hold of me, I'm in prison. And I admit I've never been king material, not least in never wanting the job. Nevertheless, I find myself where I find myself, and who knows, if I get to Mars I might be able to do some good. I don't want the Martians to destroy Earth with an asteroid any more than the next man. They say just by chatting to people and being pleasant I can help avert that, so in my own way I will do my very best."

Lord Montagu gazed at Edward for a moment. Then something remarkable happened. Montagu dropped his eyes and bowed his head.

"I will try to help, Your Majesty."

This drop of the head astonished Edward. It was extraordinary to witness a frightening man such as Montagu engaged in early stage bowing and scraping. Some people no doubt would have enjoyed the experience. To Edward it was as though Montagu's dark strength had left its host and was floating towards him like a fell creature of myth, a parasite looking for a new home. He tried not to let it distract him.

"I have to get back to Kew, Montagu. You were always good with planning a daring prank. Now I need your most audacious mischief. We've had a think and there seems to be only one solution. You have to drive us to Mars, in old-fashioned cars without computers that can be hacked, tracked and otherwise interfered with. What do you think? Can you do it?"

Montagu looked shocked, and then delighted in quick succession.

"I've got just the thing. What about three Mini Coopers, red, white and blue, driven by myself, March and Devonshire?"

Edward's caricature slapped Montagu on the back.

"My God, Montagu, that sounds splendidly reckless."

At this point, a certain air of regret clouded the royal features.

"If you do this, they will know you have helped me. What other fellow has the gall to drive three Minis through west London? The new government is hostile to Mars, and is not interested in any idea of sharing the monarchy. They will label you a collaborator and treat you as such. You could lose Brooklands. Your only option if you help me escape is to escape with me. Does that bother you? I mean, it's only polite to ask."

Montagu, hands on hips, leant backwards, as though he had been studying this problem at his desk for a long time and felt the need to loosen up.

"Earth is not what it was. As for Brooklands, I think she is lost anyway. What about you two?" said Montagu, turning to his fellow nobles. He didn't give them a chance to answer before turning back to the King.

"We will help, Your Majesty."

"Are you sure? I'd have thought there'd be wives and children and so on?"

Montagu snorted. Devonshire wore the blank expression of a man more interested in cataloguing things than human relationships. He reached up to straighten a yellow bow tie that was already straight. March's eyes tipped down yet further at their sad edges. Perhaps March enjoyed romance more than the life that came afterwards. Edward had heard one of March's favourite anecdotes, describing the origin of his family in a liaison between the charming, if wayward, King Charles II and his mistress Louise de Kerouaille. The present Lord March, it seemed, recreating this original act of genesis, enjoyed the lonely charm of a number of relationships. He was generous to all and yet couldn't avoid an accusation of selfishness. Edward understood. No more need be said.

"Once you reach Mars I'm sure you'll love it. In some ways, Mars is Earth as it used to be. They have proper motor racing there now, with danger and everything."

Montagu walked out onto the clubhouse balcony, looking behind in a gesture that invited Edward, Devonshire and March to join him. They stood together with hands resting on white painted railing. Early motor racing enthusiasts, blinking in the light of a new motorised dawn had built this clubhouse on foundations of what they knew from their old sporting worlds, using an architectural style derived from them. Edward felt kinship with those original motor racers who, even as they looked out over the future, tried to arrange for their eye to stray once again over Ascot turf, the Thames at Henley, or Sunningdale's eighteenth green.

"Nothing lasts forever, Your Majesty."

"No, Montagu. I wish it did."

"There's no money now," continued Montagu. "We made money in the same way that old motor racing teams made money. Big corporations gave it to us to have their names associated with old world glamour at Monaco, at Goodwood, and here at Brooklands. We spent other people's money. We often spent it before they actually gave it to us."

Edward tried to rally flagging spirits.

"Maybe you'll all build a new Brooklands on Mars. And there'll be a new Goodwood and a new Monaco."

Devonshire tapped his smiling place; March's hands ran through straggling hair, his face a theatre mask of happiness and sadness; Montagu slapped the white clubhouse railing.

"My God, you're right. We could build a new Brooklands. Now there's a prospect."

CHAPTER 39
(THE TOWER)

"You couldn't find a better place for a royal wedding really," mused Marina as she swished around in Queen Victoria's wedding dress. "Experienced caterers, a license to conduct weddings, and a celebrant with royal ceremonial experience; and lucky us, the Tower was staging a royal wedding dress display. It's like fate."

Even a no-nonsense girl like Marina couldn't help enjoying the romance of saying dreamy things about fate. Caroline McMercy, tall and beautiful in Queen Katherine's wedding dress, giggled. With the Tower closed to tourists, Marina and her new friend had Earth's finest wedding dress collection to themselves. Thanks to the best in textile repair and conservation, every thread shone as brightly as it once did on a long lost wedding day.

Informed by the curator that she was free to choose any gown she wanted, Marina faced a reality where her freedom of choice wasn't as unrestricted as it appeared.

"Well I can't have any of them, can I? I'm short, so Queen Kate's frock is not going to fit."

Marina gazed down at Queen Victoria's cream satin dress, appraising lacy ruffles, voluminous skirt, and a tight bodice defining the curve of her waist. It was as though Honiton lace and silk satin portrayed a symbolic bottleneck, a crisis rendered in fabric through which she was moving between one stage of life and another.

After swirling for a while, the girls flopped into seats at a table in the gallery teashop, still wearing their favoured outfits. They decided to have some tea while they talked. This turned out to be difficult. Network problems meant that the digital drink dispenser, capable of providing from a catalogue of forty synthesised beverages, stood helpless on a deserted servery counter. One forlorn question, 'milk and sugar?' showed on its customer interface. Just when it seemed that they would have to abandon the tea idea, Caroline spotted a cylindrical object hidden behind some storage boxes.

"We could use this."

"What is it?"

"It's a kettle. People used to use it for boiling water. They'd fill it up, boil all the water and then just use a cupful. This is an old building, so we should... Yes, look an electricity socket. As long as it is still connected to something, we are in business. Who says the study of history isn't useful."

After some rinsing, a crackling, roaring sound filled the kitchen. Marina looked worried.

"It sounds like it's going to explode."

"I'm sure it'll be fine."

While water was coming to the boil, Marina rummaged in a cupboard.

"There must be some real tea leaves here somewhere. Swindon made us some tea using them. Ah, here we are."

Marina placed two dumpy, black caddies of tea on the work surface. Wondering if a Mariner Valley Oolong might be of interest, she pulled off a tightly fitting lid, and held rustling purple fronds under Caroline's nose.

"Yorkshire Breakfast please," said Caroline.

Marina spooned a generous portion of Yorkshire Breakfast into a florid teapot, procured from an exhibition case of fine china given as royal wedding presents. She ignored a crazed fridge door display, which was suggesting that its supply of milk and fresh herbs would make a nice dill sauce to pour over a chocolate cake. This same overwrought display claimed that the milk had yet to reach its use-by date. Whether this was true was anybody's guess, but a quick smell test suggested the risk might be worth taking. A few minutes later the girls were drinking tea from a pair of royal wedding commemorative mugs.

"I'm sorry about what happened in the race. You should have won it really," said Marina.

"It doesn't seem to matter much now, does it?"

Marina looked at Caroline and realised she agreed with her - all that effort to do something which, after all, didn't seem to matter. So what mattered now?

"Do you love him?" asked Caroline.

"I'm Martian. He's from Earth. It could be like Romeo and Juliet."

"Yes, but is it?"

"Well no, not really. I'm not that sort of girl. Nurhaci told me it would be a politic match, something he could use against the Democratic Conservatives who want to isolate Earth from Mars. That's how it is with royal weddings."

"So you don't love him?"

"I've never been interested in that sort of thing, and I certainly never imagined I would marry a king. At first, it felt like a trap, especially when Nurhaci sat me down and told me it was necessary to consider the fate of humanity. I could have said no of course, but when the time came it was just impossible. I have come to appreciate what James does and how difficult and valuable it is. I was one of those who wanted an end to the monarchy, which gives me some insight into winning over the sort of person I used to be. Besides that, there's a feeling of not wanting James to face everything alone. That's the thing. He seemed to be so alone. I just couldn't bring myself to leave him there by himself."

"It's like a pity thing then?"

"Yes, the poor lad, with his lovely clothes and big palaces and no money worries; but someone has to marry him. I've come to see that the wife of a king is an important job. This isn't a fairy tale, and James's wife should not be someone whose head is full of unicorns and fluffy clouds. Someone like that would be wrong for him."

Marina gazed at the couple on the mug in Caroline's hand. The man wore an ironic smile, angled away from his partner's demure sincerity.

"Thou still unravished bride of quietness," said Caroline. "Thou foster child of silence and slow time."

"Sorry?"

"It's just an old Earth poem."

The young woman on the mug reminded Marina of a picture she had once seen of a stewardess, blue jacketed with matching gauzy scarf, welcoming people aboard a journey that went no further than some other spot on Earth. The stewardess leant towards the retreating shoulder of the man, who, in white shirt, dark tie and blazer, looked like an old-world airline pilot, ready to fly around the hamster wheel of his tiny journeys, which in those days stood in for long haul.

"I don't know if you have ever heard of Lady Diana Spencer?" asked Caroline.

"Can't say I have."

"Twentieth century Earth royal history is a bit of a niche subject. Anyway, poor Diana was a daughter of the Althorp family, linked with the British royal family for generations. Left to her own devices she would probably have become a posh nanny or nursery school teacher. As fate would have it, Prince Charles, came a-courting. Unfortunately, Diana had a view of love coloured by the reading of romantic novels. By the time of her royal wedding to Charles, she probably realised there would be no fairytale with her prince, but by then it was too late."

"Did she wear that ridiculous dress back there with the train that goes all the way across the gallery?"

"Yes, that was her. I ask you; is it better to blunder into a fairytale that never existed, or go into these things with your eyes open. I'm with you on this, Marina."

Marina distracted herself from emotional complexities in the ruffles of her dress. She looked at Caroline, who appeared to be trying to sort out her own mind as well as sift through all the odd information she had just received about marrying a new king.

"Anyway, what about you? I hear that Edward likes you."

"Oh he's adorable" swooned Caroline. "I would have married him in an instant. But he's already married."

"Hang on. What happened to all the going into marriage with your eyes open stuff?"

Caroline shrugged her shoulders, a movement which in her case had an intimation of immense power, like the flick of a lioness's tale. That mechanized twitch made Marina, feisty leader of a rowing crew, feel like a domestic kitten beside a pride leader who sat in the sunshine not even realising her power.

"When I first met Edward, they handcuffed us together, at the club ball we went to just after starting at Oxford. He was drunk and needed the toilet. I know you don't have any time for him, but he's different once you get to know him."

"He neglected his duties as heir to the throne."

"Put yourself in his position. Wouldn't we all feel

apprehensive about the prospect of being monarch of two planets? I enjoyed his company, and felt very bad when I nearly crushed him to death at Henley, by accident, with my arms. It was terrible."

Marina sniggered at the thought of a crushed prince. Although Caroline joined in with the tittering, one of her mighty, mechanical, manicured hands, which had nearly squeezed the life out of Edward, came up to her mouth in a gesture of distressed embarrassment. Caroline's eyes were shining. Taken-aback by this and not knowing what to say, Marina once again rearranged Queens Victoria's lace ruffles on her shoulder.

Interrupted in her musings, Marina looked up to see Sarah Van Diemen from the Cambridge number 2 seat, make, what can only be described, as an entrance. Sarah was an imposing young woman, her muscular lines soothed by a high-collared dress of exquisite lace. On her long dark hair, she wore a lace cap from which hung a gauzy veil reaching to her waist.

"Sarah," said Marina. "I thought you said you didn't want to come to our little trying on session."

"I changed my mind."

"That dress is stunning," gasped Caroline.

"It's the wedding dress of Grace Kelly. She wore it to marry Prince Rainier of Monaco in 1956. It's on loan, apparently, from the Philadelphia Museum of Art. I came to the conclusion that there is no reason to give up on delicate lace just to fit in with the boys."

"It's good to get away from them," said Caroline. "You should have come to see us more often."

"Well I'm here now."

"Can we get you something to drink? We're having tea made with a kettle."

"Have you got something cold?"

With one hand gathering the skirt around her legs, Marina, shuffled to the crazed fridge and found something on a door shelf, describing itself as Victorian lemonade. To make sure of meeting the cold requirement she found some ice cubes in the freezer compartment.

One hand controlling the skirt, the other holding the drink, she returned to her odd fancy dress party.

Taking the offered glass, Sarah swirled her yellow Victorian refreshment, eyeing a school of bobbing ice cubes.

"This ice has been frozen in a freezer. Do you see how cloudy it is? The freezing process has taken place from the outside in, shunting air and impurities towards the centre of the cube. Directional freezing, by contrast, forces out the air bubbles and gives clear ice, which takes longer to melt. Ice is fascinating; or rather, the water that makes it is fascinating. We row our boats on something profoundly odd, an other-worldly material that expands when it freezes. This property means water's solid form is, quite incredibly, less dense than its liquid form, so that solid ice floats on liquid water."

The rustle of fabric upon fabric filled the awkward silence that followed.

"Okaaay," said Caroline.

"We scientists find poetry in natural phenomena," said Marina. "Isn't that right Sarah?"

Sarah looked furtive.

"Ice is certainly very interesting."

If this was a conversational gambit, it was difficult to follow up.

"I don't suppose there's any harm in telling you," said Sarah. "It doesn't really matter now the race is over. I know about ice because we worked with it at the Cavendish. We used a type of enhanced ice in the buoyancy project."

"The buoyancy project? You mean the one for the boat?" said Marina.

"Yes."

"Why didn't you tell someone?" asked Marina.

"I wasn't supposed to. But it doesn't matter now."

"What's this buoyancy project," asked Caroline.

"Just a little something we used to try and keep up with you, Caroline. I don't know the details, but the boat builders used a material that allowed the hull to stay high in water no matter what the conditions. Until just now, it was hush hush. But it seems that Sarah here was the buoyancy genius."

"Oh I wouldn't say genius. It just took a little feminine intuition and a lot of work."

"You know what," said Caroline, "between the three of us we owned that Boat Race."

Two days later, Marina Blackwood, wearing Queen Victoria's wedding dress, walked down a grassy aisle towards King James on Tower Green. The congregation included James's royal family members, minus brothers who had absconded to Mars. The blockade had marooned Marina's family on Mars, which was a shame because her mum would have loved this. Still, she had Caroline, Sarah, and a railway automaton wearing a morning suit with a yellow carnation buttonhole.

Marina travelled a symbolic route to the future, her journey accompanied by a jazz band led by Jerry Dramhaggle. He stood with his band in a democratic kind of way, conducting audience and musicians alike. Marina could hear Caroline's clarinet saying a melancholy goodbye to the past, and a thoughtful greeting to the future. With a semicircular movement of his arm, Jerry collected the music up and put it away.

George Tyndale began his address.

"We are gathered here today in the presence of friends to celebrate the marriage of King James III of Earth and Lady Marina Blackwood of Mars. I don't need to remind you how they met. Marina was cox of the Cambridge Blue Boat, and James was a member of her crew. Those of us who row will be aware that a boat is a collection of individuals pulling as one. In a rowing crew, our differences complement one another to make something better than individuals can manage alone. It is best eight rather than eight best. Perhaps there has never been a better model for marriage than that. So it is my great pleasure to ask James and Marina to join hands in front of us today and share their vows of marriage."

Marina looked up at James as he turned towards her.

"Marina, I promise to honour the way you are different in our common effort, and to continue to realise how special you are to me even when you become the most familiar and reassuring part of my life. I will help and support you in good and bad times. I wish you to be my wife."

Now it was Marina's turn. She felt tight around her middle, a product of both apprehension, and Victoria's dress.

"James, I promise to share my life with you. I marry you for who you are, not what you are. I promise to help and stand by you in good and in difficult times. I am fortunate that you joined my boat, and I wish you to be my husband."

George Tyndale then made his way through a section of standard text that for all its easy familiarity held lurking danger.

"I require and charge of you both, here in the presence of these witnesses, that if either of you know any reason why you may not be lawfully married you do now confess it. And I require that if any of you here can show any just cause why James and Marina cannot be married, speak now or forever hold your peace."

This marriage was a revolution. Apart from Edward's shambolic train ceremony presided over by Fred, this was the first royal wedding conducted by a civil celebrant, and the first between citizens of different planets. Marina, standing at this crisis point in her life, actually expected someone to raise a voice in objection. But the great rhetorical question of marriage never is answered, no matter how well matched, or madly incompatible, people might consider bride and groom to be. Events had passed the point of no return.

"In that case I pronounce you man and wife."

Spontaneous applause broke out, growing louder. Then cheering began. Marina turned with her new husband to face their friends. Winning an Olympic gold in rowing must be like this, Marina thought to herself. The cheering went on and on, joy feeding itself. The band struck up again, Dramhaggle leaning sideways into a song about a crazy little thing called love.

Marina walked with James into her married life. The arch of oars created by Oxford and Cambridge was a passageway through to a new world of beginnings for the most traditional family on planet Earth.

CHAPTER 40
(BROOKLANDS)

Three Minis – Mark 1 Cooper S - sat on the tarmac outside Brooklands Clubhouse, each one glazed in a single elemental colour - red, white, and blue. Edward was listening to Montagu telling him about Troy Kennedy Martin's historic film, which had seen three similar Minis used as getaway cars following a gold robbery in Turin. This time, said Montagu, the Minis would not be stealing gold; they would be stealing freedom.

Edward stood in what he hoped was a dashing manner beside the red Mini, one hand resting on its roof. With a regal smile never wavering, his worried eyes surveyed hordes of excited people. This scene was more suggestive of a motoring festival than a clandestine affair. The car enthusiast community was, in Montagu's words, insular, backward looking and suspicious. Even so, Edward had come to realise that Brooklands' security - even with Martian technical assistance from Kew - was a ramshackle affair based on a gentleman's word and a lady's discretion. A Members Only policy would not offer protection for long.

Montagu was buckling a helmet strap in preparation for a practice session around his beloved circuit. Pointing to the red Mini's boot, he said to March:

"Will it take the weight of my luggage? Will it take the weight?"

"Yes, yes it'll take the weight, Charlie," answered March, trying out his best cockney accent.

Montagu, appearing satisfied with this answer, folded his portly form into a compact driver's seat. Edward saw Montagu studying him through the Mini's open window. For a moment, it seemed as though he was going to say something like, "get in, lad". But once again there was evidence of that unsettling deference.

"Shall we give it a go then, Your Majesty?"

Edward pulled on his own white helmet, and climbed in beside Montagu. A tuned, 1.1-litre engine nickered into life, whining with irritable intent in response to Montagu's prodding right foot. Car fans straggled aside to allow a dramatic pull away across a wide concrete apron towards Member's Banking.

They made two circuits before sweeping down onto the infield, where various obstacles provided experience in dodging and swerving. Edward's casually irresponsible nature now stepped up and allowed him to enjoy this wild ride. He shouted with delight, which earned a broad smile from Montagu. Edward realised that aspects of his personality he had assumed to be faults, had become qualities in the strange world of Brooklands. All of his brother's sensible caution, which made him popular with officials, would have been useless here. Reckless disregard for consequences made Edward a good king in this Mini, in the company of a powerful aristocrat, who would do anything to get his monarch to Mars.

After the second hour of dodging and swerving, however, Edward and his sore bottom came to realise that this enterprise wasn't just about recklessness. This impression only deepened after three hours in what Montagu called the Surrey Simulator, a virtual reality car experience, programmed to allow practice on Surrey byways unsuitable for car travel. Though not a deep thinker, it did strike Edward as ironic that truly rash behavior, the sort of behavior that allows people to tumble on trapeze or walk tight ropes between high buildings with no safety net, or drive Minis along an improvised route from Brooklands to Kew, required meticulous planning. It was clear that Montagu was a skilled driver. It was also clear that he, Devonshire and March were planning the operation with great care. Edward, who would be in the lead car with Montagu, had been given the job of navigator, and was busy learning the route that would take them to Kew. He had been conscientious in pouring over paper maps of Surrey and west London - which would be the only guidance available once the Martians took the network down on the big day.

While personal growth was always something he had tried to avoid, Edward, in a rare moment of insight, realised that his development as an instigator of rash acts also involved the maturing of his self-discipline. His dream of taking one bound to freedom was never going to come true, now that he appreciated the endless work that went into planning such a bound. He was so enjoying the work, however, that it didn't seem to matter.

CHAPTER 41 (WATER GATE POOL, TOWER OF LONDON)

Shrouded in morning mist, Oxford's Blue Boat sat in the Tower's restored Water Gate pool, a dark place, designed to intimidate those who entered here. Gazing down from above, James saw the pool as a Lilliputian dockside, busy with tiny re-enactments of preparation for long-lost sea voyages. A rigger devoted himself to adjustments beside number two seat, a distant echo of work carried out at dizzying height above tea clipper decks. Light-duty stevedores loaded miniscule cargoes into bow and stern sections.

Finding a crew had not been as difficult as James imagined it would be. Perhaps he shouldn't have been surprised that everyone wanted to go. Rowers trained to work as one, and it was their greatest comfort to be in a boat, a place where they knew exactly what they were doing.

While it had not been difficult to find people to put in the boat, this led to painful decisions about who to exclude. Before he died, King John had stipulated that each former prince would need one of his aides. As Edward was to have Bacon, a seat had to be reserved for him. Caroline was also back in the boat. This left only seat three, once occupied by Edward. With room for only one of the Mortlake stand-ins, Matthew Nice had called Fitzwhistle, Markov and Raeburn into a meeting, where Raeburn got the nod. Markov took his exclusion calmly. Alistair was not so accepting.

James didn't have time to worry about Alistair now. He walked out onto a raised walkway above the Water Gate. Earth's new monarch was about to give the first speech of his reign. Beside him stood Cambridge friends, and yeoman warders in their formal state dress - a scarlet and gold coat, an immaculate white neck ruff, all topped by a flat brimmed, black velvet hat encircled by red, white and blue rosettes. The Oxford crew had stopped what it was doing and stood in a ragged line, looking up.

"I have come to wish you well on your journey. You were our enemies on the river, but I hope you will go forward with the knowledge that only together could we make a race of it."

James's words were shaky at first, but he kept going, his voice growing stronger.

"What you face now is a race. Our discussions with the government to organise your peaceful and orderly transfer to Martian territory have failed. This means we have a race on our hands. I will not try to hide from you how difficult this might be. However, while our enemies know of our ambition to get you to Mars, they don't know how we propose to do it. They don't suspect that you will row there!"

James was gratified that his joke evoked cheering. He felt like Henry V giving his men heart in the dawn before Agincourt. He descended a flight of stone steps to stand with his soldiers. He was acting a role, which didn't make his performance any less sincere.

"The fact is they are watching. Once you row out onto the river it won't take them long to work out what's going on. We do have allies in both police and government, but we have powerful enemies too, and they will oppose any attempt to reach Kew. You can expect a good race. But I tell you this my friends, as one who has raced against you, I know that you are equal to the challenge."

James paused as Oxford applauded.

"For all of you this journey will mean giving up a great deal. It is not clear when you will be able to see Earth again. I salute your sacrifice, and trust you will find much that will make up for what you have lost."

James now moved amongst the crew, picking out individuals with handshakes and pats on the shoulder.

"Dramhaggle, a great cox and a fine leader; Northcote, Wanyamwezi, and Mannberg, so solid and dependable in setting the stroke; McMercy, possessing a strength that goes far beyond her arms; Franklin, the buccaneering spirit; Nice, the brains and the planning. And Bacon, of course, always there for my grandfather, and now bravely setting out on a new journey with a new king. Finally Raeburn, noble enough to accept not having a place in the original Blue Boat, and big hearted enough to step in when called. You are the dramatis personae for the latest act of the royal story on a new stage. Please accept my thanks for what you are to do. You go to help create a new monarchy on Mars. It might seem to be a rival court, but I hope that is not how it will be. Please remember that Oxford or Cambridge, Mars or Earth, we are competitors on the same river. So good luck my friends, and good racing."

"Three cheers for the King," shouted Matthew Nice.

In answer to throaty hip hips, the pool's echo threw back a refrain that sounded like 'away, away, away'.

The crew climbed into their seats. As they did so, James turned to a quiet young man who had been helping prepare the boat.

"Markov," said James. "I am sorry you are not travelling today. Though Bacon has a place you might have filled, obviously this has nothing to do with the quality of your rowing."

Bacon clapped Markov on the back.

"Best eight, not eight best," said Bacon.

Markov carried on with what he was doing, using a small spanner to make a final rigging adjustment.

Meanwhile, James tapped Bacon on the shoulder.

"Bacon, I have someone here who has come to see you off."

James stood aside and allowed Boles through. He looked on as the two men exchanged a hearty handshake. For a moment, James thought the unthinkable might happen and a hug would follow, though dignified as ever, a mutual bowing of heads sufficed.

"Are you sure you want to do this?" asked Boles.

"I have to do it. My duty to the King continues. I have given my life to the royal family. They are my family. That's why I believed the King's death would be my own. But the dynasty goes on. Perhaps my time is just beginning."

"That's quite a thought at our time of life. Take care of yourself."

While this conversation was taking place, the crew had been taking their places. Only Bacon's seat now remained empty. James helped Bacon into that empty seat. He then pushed Oxford's Blue Boat out towards the Thames. Dramhaggle had timed their departure to run with an incoming tide, which was already pulling the boat westwards towards central London. Eight oars unfurled, reaching back into their first stroke.

James ran up to the wall, where he had once walked at dawn with Swindon. He swept a one-handed wave of farewell in a wide arc above his head. When this gesture could not contain sufficient emotion, he raised both arms and held them there, fingers outstretched, which would have looked decidedly awkward if it wasn't for the overwhelming strength of feeling evident in every gawky muscle. The King's gaze followed Oxford as the boat ran between two parallel lines of disturbed water, under the guns of HMS Belfast and out of sight beneath London

Bridge.

CHAPTER 42
(BROOKLANDS)

Outside Brooklands Clubhouse, three Mini Coopers were ready to go. King Edward made sure logos on his overalls were visible to various smuggled-in representatives of the Martian media. Some of these badges represented the whimsy of long gone oil and car parts companies. Others denoted contemporary organisations with an interest in this enterprise. The orange globe of Mars Minerals, the red oval of STP Oil, and the collapsing rectangle of Firestone Tyres, all sat together on chest and upper arms.

The loading of a single small bag into each Mini's boot followed this chaotic photo call.

"Right come on, it's time," declared Montagu. "And I just want to say this..."

A hush descended on the mass of car enthusiasts straggling up onto Members Banking.

Montagu appeared to be grappling with an emotion that was too big for his bulky body and practical mind. When he opened his mouth, nothing came out. Edward saw what was happening and stepped forward. He was used to public speaking, and could see when a fellow on the rostrum had choked.

"As you all know, Lord Montagu is not a man for emotional goodbyes. His wife is glad to see the back of him. He has creditors who would stretch all the way around Brooklands if you lined them up. March and Devonshire have also bought a few cars they couldn't quite afford. Now as he probably won't be seeing any of you again for a while, Montagu will say that he'll miss you. He can indulge himself in such a sentimental outburst, because he knows none of you will be around to remind him about it. He will be over the hills and far away on Mars where they have motor racing, and where he will build a new Brooklands. Maybe one day you will come out and join us, and we will revive the Goodwood Revival. Until then, I say au revoir. We do not leave to find something new. We leave to find again what we have lost."

There was cheering and applause. As this storm of approval burst around them, Montagu turned to Edward.

"Thank you, Your Majesty."

Edward clapped Montagu on the shoulder, his hand slowing with hesitation just before impact. This intervention was just a favour to get a chap out of trouble. Now Montagu was calling him Majesty again. It just showed how things could get out of hand.

Montagu climbed into the red Mini. Edward had a last look at Brooklands, raising his hand in farewell.

"Cheerio, thank you and happy motoring."

With that he hunkered himself down beside Montagu. Twisting around to reach the seat belt, he could see Tarquin and other marooned members of the royal Martian entourage taking their places with March and Devonshire in the blue and white Minis. Slamming doors were double raps on a military snare drum.

There was unnecessary revving of engines before a tricolour triumvirate pulled away from the clubhouse. Montagu led a lap of honour, his Minis circulating in staggered formation, before high-speed choreography brought them into a line of red, white and blue. It was in this array that they raced through

Brooklands' gates, out into the world beyond. This world had no place for cars like these. Satellites worked out the most efficient way from A to B. Edward did not want to go to B. There had to be somewhere better than that. Wherever that place was, that's where he hoped the Minis were going.

CHAPTER 43 (THE THAMES)

The crew moved in unison under the watchful eye of Jerry Dramhaggle. This boat, sailing towards an unknown future, was also taking him home to Mars. The finish line was millions of miles away, west of Mortlake.

Jerry took refuge in meditative splash of blades and clunk of oarlocks. During the Boat Race, he had been aware of millions of people watching on his shoulder. Now it was just him and his crew. For a few quiet moments, he sat in peaceful solitude, enraptured by sublime rowing technique. Reality made a jolting return just before Westminster Bridge, when a police launch idling near the Old London Eye heaved round to give chase.

"Let's stay calm. Keep it nice and steady."

A disembodied loudspeaker voice blew across the river. Jerry pictured an angry, puffed-cheek cloud denoting an area of storms on an old chart.

"All nonessential traffic is to leave the river. Return to your point of embarkation immediately. Failure to follow our orders will result in the interception of your vessel."

"Ok, training run over. Give me thirty a minute and let's leave this joker behind."

Now Oxford opened up. Bacon's strokes became ragged, so Jerry tucked him down. Then in a familiar pattern, the crew dropped out in stages, leaving Northcote and McMercy to haul the boat to its limit.

As they ran through Westminster, small, dark figures were visible on the House of Commons Terrace, leaning over the river wall, split into groups by a series of black, Victorian lampposts. Perhaps Oxford's escape attempt had assistance from at least some of those powerful people looking out at them, hands shading eyes from morning sunshine. Jerry remembered images seen in history files, of people watching Apollo missions blazing towards a vault of blue sky.

A reeling sense of instability indicated that the boat was at top speed.

"That's it; tuck in three, two, one, tuck."

Northcote and McMercy pushed their oars into the gunwales and hunched down low. A glance behind revealed the police launch losing momentum, starting to wallow, giving up its fate to some internal computer conflict. Turning forward again, Jerry steered beneath Lambeth Bridge, and on towards Putney, where the Boat Race had started only a few weeks previously. It felt as though geographical ages had passed since that time.

Oxford now approached the Boat Race course. Putney Bridge swept overhead, plunging the river into sudden eclipse. Up ahead was the next challenge. The police, giving up any chance of winning a straight race, had changed tactics. A few hundred yards beyond Putney Bridge, a launch was ploughing back and forth, kicking up a disruptive wake. Oxford would have to go through that. The cox called for a burst of power, before tucking his crew down again to provide maximum stability. In tight lock-down, they leapt across London like an arrow from the bow of Sagittarius.

Jerry was shouting down his intercom to Matthew:

"Where are those friendly police boats you promised?"

Matthew's reply was broken into staccato phrases, punctuated by the shock of coming down hard in troughs between waves.

"Not all... friendly... Some... will help."

Water washed in from a vicious, cresting swell. Jerry flicked a switch, turning on a small pump.

By now, Oxford was into Fulham Reach. Two more police launches tried their swamping tactics.

"I need power now!" Jerry yelled at his crew, who straightened up into position. "Get ready for power thirty. Ready. Row."

Oxford started pulling through choppy water.

"You okay, Bacon?"

Hearing no reply, Jerry wondered why Bacon was putting himself through this. There was still a long way to go, and Bacon was already white with exhaustion. Something about Bacon's manner suggested that if he did die out here, then this would be a fitting end. Perhaps he just didn't fancy that retirement home just outside the gates of Sandringham.

CHAPTER 44
(SURREY AND
HAMPTON COURT)

Three Minis followed the Thames east towards Kew. From Brooklands, Edward, feeling thrillingly useful, shouted out cues for a route that led along a bike path following the route of a railway line that once ran into Waterloo. After speeding through a residential area called Ashley Park, the convoy dodged amidst neat rows of pods on Walton Bridge. The rows were precise but unmoving. Network problems appeared particularly bad today. Edward knew this was no accident.

From Walton, the route weaved around marina basins, bounced across rugby pitches, traversed a few suburban streets, and reached Kempton Park Racecourse, where Montagu knew people. The gates were open, and staff directed renegade Minis with firm hand signals. Montagu appeared thoughtful as white railing went spooling by. Perhaps he was remembering money lost in carefully considered bets.

From Kempton there was a short stretch through suburban Hampton, which opened out into Bushy Park. Here a grassy boulevard paraded between stands of chestnut towards a golden goddess Diana, standing on a marble column in the middle of an encircling pond. Back end out around Diana, a sharp right turn led across another neatly paralysed line of pods into Hampton Court Park. Gravel flew in front of the long façade of Hampton

Court Palace. Clods of grass scattered beside the Long Water, a perfect, formal, liquid mirror reflecting a blue sky.

The convoy had reached the Thames-side path before forces chasing them amounted to anything more than startled stares and excited pointing. While Montagu concentrated on his furious driving, Edward strained round to look at struggling police vehicles running like unusually fast trams behind three agile Minis.

"I think they've lost their power steering," chortled Edward.

"Where next, Your Majesty?" shouted Montagu. Edward glanced down at the paper map on his lap.

"Follow the river. Make for Kingston Bridge."

CHAPTER 45
(MORTLAKE)

Jerry Dramhaggle had to tell himself that he was not nearly home. Mortlake was approaching, but there was no finish line there anymore. A clumsy police boat made a lumbering lunge from a hiding place behind Barnes Bridge. A wall of police blue towered on Oxford's left, grinding against the hull, scattering and breaking two oars. For a few seconds, momentum carried the boat onwards. Then Jerry felt a cold chill beginning to rise around his legs.

A cox has to act quickly. In rough water, there are always split-second decisions to make, whether to continue rowing with the fastest current or to run for shelter. It was a time to run for shelter.

"We are holed and taking water. I am heading for Mortlake. If you have an oar left, pull it."

The crew hauled away, as though they were in a close finish with Cambridge. Speed was falling as water poured in.

"Come on! Pull through, pull through."

Oxford made a valiant effort, but sometimes even rigorous training and the spirit of an ancient, self-satisfied university aren't enough. Jerry was chest deep in Thames water before he stopped calling the stroke.

"Swim," he yelled, as though this was a command he gave regularly during training.

Only a short period of breaststroke was required to reach the slip at Mortlake. Everyone emerged like a bob of seals hauling out.

"How many times am I going to be washed up at this bloody club?" yelled Jerry. "Someone get me another boat."

Matthew led a rush up to the boat stands. Willing staff at Mortlake understood what was happening and gave what help they could. The crew reappeared carrying a snakeskin eight painted in a suspicious shade of light blue.

"Is that a Cambridge boat?" shouted Jerry in disbelief.

"Yes, it's Goldie, their number 2 boat. It's the best boat in there," answered Matthew. "Lucky for us they didn't have a chance to get it back to Cambridge."

"Lucky for us? Why haven't they taken it back to Cambridge? That's typical sloppy behaviour from the Tabs, leaving their boats lying about the place."

"There has been stuff going on," objected Northcote.

"If you think for one minute I'm going to cox you lot in that thing, you've got another thing coming."

"It was only a race, you idiot."

"Only a race, Nice? Is that all it meant to you?"

"Lads," shouted a flat-capped Mortlake staffer. "The police are at the gate. We are giving them some nonsense about members only, but we won't be able to hold them for long."

Jerry looked up at Matthew towering above him.

"I am still the club president. I say we use this boat. They will get in, and when they do, we will all be arrested. You as a Martian are in particular danger. So stop messing about."

Jerry took a breath and dropped his head. He glanced towards the river and saw a lumbering police launch, making its way towards them with a sideways, snakelike motion.

"Get that boat in the water right now," he yelled.

CHAPTER 46 (OLD DEER PARK)

Edward's introduction to rallying continued across parkland at Ham, through the grounds of Ham House, along Richmond riverside, and then out into Richmond's Old Deer Park. Bumping into Edward's eye line came a cream painted building of clean lines and classical aspect, topped by a dome gazing skywards, like a primeval, compound eye, seeing much and understanding little. March was on an open communications link talking about this odd building, which he called the King's Observatory. Apparently, George III observed the transit of Venus here in 1769.

"Here we are escaping to Mars, and he thinks he's on an open-top bus tour," grumbled Montagu.

Just beyond George III's observatory, a line of police cars tried to form themselves into a barrier. Montagu's Minis outmanoeuvred them with moves rehearsed at Brooklands, red and white feinting one way, while blue crossed their path in the opposite direction.

Montagu lost the back end on scrubby Old Deer Park grass. In recovering, he fell behind Devonshire and March.

"Not to worry," chirped Edward. "Old Deer Park can be a bit tricky. My ancestor, William of Orange, had a horse trip over a molehill here, you know. That was the end of him."

"Ah, the open-top bus tour continues."

The Mars House roof was now visible above a green mass of tree canopies, looking like a planet viewed over the horizon of a closely orbiting moon. Edward felt a flush of excitement, followed by a spasm of fear. While this motor tour had the appearance of an audacious escape attempt, he realised that his new masters were reeling him in. In the grip of Martian gravity, there was no way to stop his freefall.

Zig zagging through woods just west of Kew Gardens, they were about to face the most difficult part of the route. This led across what the media was now calling the 38th Parallel around Martian Kew. Edward wasn't worrying about it though. Whether his escape succeeded or not, his fate would follow him wherever he went. It didn't matter what happened. Successful escape or death by molehill, it made no difference. Edward relaxed. Perhaps floating in space was like this.

Soil splattered across the windscreen, swept aside by busy wipers. The newly cleared arch-shaped view revealed a Victorian factory; or was it a cathedral? A gate in a chain-link fence stood open, next to a sign announcing "Mars House Pumping Station. Thames Water, working with Martian Water Development Corporation."

"Can't even sort out a river of their own," growled Montagu. "They have to borrow the Thames."

Red, white and blue passed into the Mariner River supply tunnel. Here Edward lived through some of the greatest moments of his life, riding through a dark wormhole between worlds, array of headlights ablaze, flying in carefree sweeps left and right on walls as curved as Einstein's space-time.

Coming up into the Mars House, curtains of water winged out from a boisterous rally along a drained Mariner River. Edward rolled with the blows in his seat as Montagu skidded his way up a ramp leading onto the Martian plain. He saw a brief image of a chequered flag, like a game board thrown into the air as the game ends. Well-wishers pressed in on every side.

Van Cello's face appeared at the window, just as Montagu was explaining that you had to turn a little handle to make the window go down. After a few moments of instruction, Van Cello was able to lean in and shout:

"Welcome to Mars, Lord Montagu!"

CHAPTER 47 (THE THAMES)

A sharp, light blue bow, nodding in time with eight oar strokes, sliced through choppy water, up-river of Mortlake. On the far side of a long, slow left turn would be Kew Gardens, where Martian property with full diplomatic immunity reached to the riverside. Jerry Dramhaggle, in his privileged position looking forward could see police launches ahead. He showed no sign of anxiety, hiding his fears just as he did when watching a rival pulling away.

"Get ready for forty a minute. I need everything you have. That includes you, Bacon. Give me everything. Ready. Row."

Oxford speared onwards, the crew working to exhaustion before tucking down and trusting in their cox, who now had sole responsibility for getting them home. A few police vessels appeared to be trying to form a protective screen. It was hard to tell what was going on. If there were some friendly boats out there trying to help, they were not making their efforts too obvious. Potential allies might have been blocking aggressive moves of possible enemies, but the overall effect was to churn up a tempest. Going under Kew Bridge, disturbed water slapped between bridge supports, generating sets of waves coming in from both sides. Remembering lessons learned during both Ice Race and Boat Race, Jerry smoothed out his corrections and stayed teetering on a tightrope. It was at this point that he saw a blue shadow coalescing out of clouds of drenching uncertainty on his right hand side. Blue was the colour of heaven, of divinity, of authority.

"Blades in bow side."

Jerry saved the oars, but could not avoid a shuddering collision with a police launch, which then peeled away.

Jerry knew it was bad. He had no idea whether the collision was with a friendly boat making a mistake, or a hostile boat overcoming its steerage problems to land a blow. It didn't really matter, since they were going to sink. This impact had been worse than the collision at Barnes Bridge, which had sunk their last boat. Jerry could already feel cold water around his ankles. There would be no swimming for it this time. Kew Pier was too far away, and even a lumbering, computer compromised police boat would be able to catch someone struggling in the water.

"Bloody hell, Jerry," said Northcote stroking in front of him.

"Keep going, keep going, nearly there."

They weren't nearly there. Jerry knew that. He prepared for his seat to disappear beneath him. Water crept up his legs as he continued to call the stroke, expecting each one to be his last as an Oxford cox and a free man. At the end of twenty strokes, called with brisk, false confidence, they were still afloat. Something was not right. Jerry leant out and studied a section of hull damage. What was that strange laminate layer beneath low drag snakeskin? It looked like clear ice. A loose lump fell into the water and floated away. It floated away? Then in a moment of disgusted comprehension, it became clear that rumours were true - Cambridge had built a boat from material with a positive buoyancy responsive to changing conditions. The Tabs had built a boat that could not sink, allowing them to run in rough water.

"The cheating Tabs," yelled Jerry in the grey, terrified face of Northcote who no doubt was expecting sinking, drowning, arrest, and the bringing of shame to his university.

"We don't seem to be sinking," yelled Matthew from the bow,

his voice high pitched with stress and relief.

Kew Pier was drawing closer. There were turbulent eddies near the bank. Jerry jinked right so that the bow hit a wave head on, and then swerved back left again.

"Stop, stop! Check her down."

The crew squared their oars, producing eight flares as they forced their boat to a crawl close to the pier.

"Blades in stroke side."

Left side crew tucked in four light-blue blades, as their fellows on the right manoeuvered against Kew Pier. Willing hands helped everyone out of waterlogged seats. Matthew and Caroline lowered Bacon's limp body onto the quayside. Nanosuited Martian police officers demanded that Jerry accompany them to what they called a 'debrief'. Recognising the men who had made Wembury's life a misery at Mortlake, Jerry decided he was Oxford cox first and Martian second. He leant down beside his fallen comrade.

"You've done it, Bacon. You've rowed all the way to Mars. Not bad for an old boy."

Bacon nodded, but did not open his eyes.

"You alright, Bacon old fellow?" asked another familiar voice from behind Jerry.

This time Bacon did open his eyes, and seemed to stand to attention even as he lay on the ground.

"I'm very well, Your Majesty."

"Good," said Edward, kneeling down at Bacon's side.

CHAPTER 48
(WINDSOR CASTLE)

James was sitting in a room that belonged to royalty's analogue, clockwork routine. In smoky peripheral vision to his left, he saw a sofa, which was only comfortable with three scatter cushions stuffed behind your back. This stood next to a desk full of drawers and cubbyholes, ready to sort a quantity of long-lost Royal Mail. There was only one object on the polished desk surface - a box of watercolour paints, the lid standing open to reveal pristine squares of pigment, a periodic table of elements ready to make a new world in soothing, nostalgic washes.

To his right James could see the crossed oars of Oxford and Cambridge mounted on cream walls.

Drawing his eyes away from these modest signs of ownership, James looked towards a window, rendered mirror-like by the room's yellow light, reflecting the monarch's sitting room in Windsor Castle's Private Apartments. There was no sign of the night sky beyond, at which James had gazed earlier that evening, listening to Showertree describing auspicious planetary alignments, supposedly smiling down on the beginning of his reign. There were, admittedly, some less helpful placements, likened by Showertree to bracing beach walks on a winter's day.

James, moving his eyes only, glanced forward and contemplated the artist at work. This evening's engagement obliged him to sit for his first official monarch's portrait. He found that his position as the subject of an artist's concentration brought a similar kind of calm to that found in concentrating on a painting of his own. James considered the artist, painting him in his mind. Charles Quiller Woolner was perhaps not such a surprising choice for this commission. After spending most of his career as a self-promoting agent provocateur, Woolner had become something of an establishment figure in recent years. Here he was, wearing only a mildly androgynous trouser suit, standing like a fencer en-garde, with an easel as his opponent.

James wished he could be a painter. He couldn't of course, what with having to be King of the World. Nevertheless, it was intriguing to think about how he would paint his own portrait. He spent long minutes staring sideways at his bright reflection in dark windows. This careful self-observation resulted in a sense of fading away, like a dappled deer disappearing into sun-filled woods.

As James floated in an almost disembodied state, he seemed to meet his grandfather again. He saw an image of King John rowing at stroke in front of him. Beyond John, a line of monarchs pulled at their oars. This line stretched away, disappearing into distance so endless that figures seemed to go all around the universe and come back again behind him. At least James thought that these people were monarchs. It was difficult to tell. These images weren't official portraits. Henry VIII did not have infeasibly vast shoulders. The snowy face of Elizabeth I did not sit in a white ruff that might have doubled as a surgical support. James saw these people as ordinary men and women.

James felt ordinary, and yet he had an inevitable place in this company. As monarchs rowed him along, through nebulae water meadows on a river spangled with galaxies, James knew that when fate calls you to take your place in the boat, there is no escape, and there is no need to fear. You might not be one of the eight best, but everyone has a chance to be one of the best eight.

Printed in Great Britain
by Amazon